"Let's go for a swim," Gabe said as he kicked off his shoes and socks.

Nora choked on her breath. "Now?"

Gabe grabbed the bottom of his jersey and then pulled it over his head. Hard abs covered in a light patch of dark hair instantly came into view, and she would've choked again if she had been breathing.

She turned away and tried to focus on the tree. "You're not kidding are you?"

Half-naked Gabe came into view just as he grabbed the rope. "What do you think?"

Nora watched as he took a few steps backward, ran, and swung himself over the creek using the rope. She'd watched him do it tons of times when they were kids. That's why she knew instantly something went wrong.

It seemed to her that Gabe lost his grip or let go much sooner than he was supposed to. The grunt she heard scared her, as did the swear words that came out of his mouth as soon as he emerged.

Nora exhaled in some relief but she knew he was hurt. Without thinking, she took off her shoes and socks and jumped into the water. "What's wrong?" she yelled as she swam toward him.

"My shoulder," he said as he rolled it over and over again. "I couldn't hold on."

That's when she noticed the long, pink scar etched along the curve of his upper arm.

"Sometimes I forget, you know?"

Second Chance
—*at*—
Rancho Lindo

Sabrina Sol

FOREVER
New York Boston

Copyright © 2022 by Hachette Book Group

Cover art and design by Daniela Medina
Cover images © David Wagner Photography; Shutterstock
Cover copyright © 2022 by Hachette Book Group, Inc.

Hachette Book Group supports the right to free expression and the value of copyright. The purpose of copyright is to encourage writers and artists to produce the creative works that enrich our culture.

The scanning, uploading, and distribution of this book without permission is a theft of the author's intellectual property. If you would like permission to use material from the book (other than for review purposes), please contact permissions@hbgusa.com. Thank you for your support of the author's rights.

Forever
Hachette Book Group
1290 Avenue of the Americas, New York, NY 10104
read-forever.com
twitter.com/readforeverpub

First Edition: November 2022

Forever is an imprint of Grand Central Publishing. The Forever name and logo are trademarks of Hachette Book Group, Inc.

The publisher is not responsible for websites (or their content) that are not owned by the publisher.

The Hachette Speakers Bureau provides a wide range of authors for speaking events. To find out more, go to www.hachettespeakersbureau.com or call (866) 376-6591.

ISBN: 9781538722305 (mass market), 9781538722312 (ebook)

Printed in the United States of America

OPM

10 9 8 7 6 5 4 3 2 1

*This book is dedicated to my
#LatinxRom author friends—
your stories of love and hope
inspire me every day.*

Chapter One

Bam!

Gabe's eyes flew open. Every nerve and muscle tightened in defense. Familiar pumps of anxiety revved up his heart, making it thump faster and faster.

It took a few seconds for Gabe to translate his surroundings. There was no smoke or rubble. No blackened sky above him. No dirt beneath him either.

More importantly, there were no screams.

Relief and recognition set in. He wasn't in Baghdad anymore. He was home at his family's ranch in Esperanza, California. He was back at Rancho Lindo.

Gabe let go of the comforter he'd been clutching between both fists and exhaled long and hard. Pain shot from the fingers of his right hand all the way up to his shoulder. He sat up and shook out his arm a few times until the burning dulled. He waited another couple of minutes before he got off the bed and walked over to the room's largest window.

As he pulled the string on the blinds, light began to sneak into the room, chasing away the darkness in more ways than one. He squinted through the invading brightness and tried to focus on the ruckus happening below his second-story window.

Gabe watched as his older brother Cruz and two other men he didn't recognize loaded large metal bins onto the bed of a white pickup. He couldn't help but laugh at the ridiculousness of it all. An exploding IED hadn't woken him up. It had been trash cans filled with horse shit.

He was definitely back on the ranch.

Half an hour later, a showered and dressed Gabe was ready to finally start his day. He was about to walk out of his bedroom door when he noticed the large white box sitting on his dresser. It hadn't been there last night. He lifted the lid and found a brand-new black felt cowboy hat. He didn't have to inspect it to know it was a Larry Mahan Norte hat. It was the kind made popular by the iconic Mexican band Los Tigres del Norte. And it was the same one his dad always wore.

There was no card, no note. Yet the message was as clear as day.

His mother had obviously thought that if Gabe wore the same kind of hat that his father did, then they'd have something in common to chat about. Especially since talking wasn't really something they did. At least, not like they had before. Their relationship had always been strained since he'd left the ranch at eighteen. During his rare visits home, their superficial conversations usually revolved around the same three topics: the weather, whatever they were eating, and sports. But something had changed with his dad after Gabe's accident. He'd barely said anything to him the one time he'd come with his mom to see Gabe in the hospital. The phone calls during his time in the rehab center were mainly from his abuelita, brothers, and mom. Once in a while she'd hand the phone to his dad, who'd ask the same question, "How are you feeling?" To which Gabe always said, "Getting better." So his dad would say, "That's good," and then hand the phone back to his mom.

He hadn't even been around last night when Gabe had arrived from the airport. His mom said his dad was tired and had gone to bed early.

Gabe thought about wearing the hat, just so he wouldn't have to explain later why he wasn't. But the stubborn part of him wouldn't give in. Not yet. He put the lid back on the box and headed downstairs.

A tirade of squeaky yips and yelps welcomed him into the kitchen.

Princesa, his mom's white shih tzu, charged at him with the bravado of a raging bull. She attacked first by jumping up on her hind legs and scratching at his jeans just below his kneecap. Then she began nipping and tugging at the hem, growling like some cartoon version of a Tasmanian devil.

"Princesa! No!" Abuelita yelled from across the kitchen.

His mom had gotten the dog as a present to herself three years ago for her fifty-fifth birthday. Gabe had met Princesa during his last visit home and she was just as friendly as she was now. Abuelita had suggested that he keep dog treats in his pocket to try to bribe her into not attacking him. It never worked.

"I guess she still doesn't like me," he said when she wouldn't even let him pet the top of her head.

"She just doesn't know you," Abuelita explained,

and then pointed to the furry dog bed in the corner. "Princesa! Échate!"

Princesa gave him one last threatening growl for good measure and then obeyed. Apparently, she too was smart enough to listen to Abuelita.

He was about to ask where his mom was, since the tiny terror never left her side, when a familiar musky aroma hit him. "Please tell me I'm smelling what I think I'm smelling," he said as he walked toward Abuelita, who was standing next to the stove.

He put both hands on the back of her shoulders and leaned over her four-foot-ten-inch frame to inhale the wafts of simmering beef broth with onion and garlic. "Caldo de res," he confirmed out loud.

"Pues, it's your favorite, no?" his abuelita asked as if she didn't already know the answer. "Besides, you missed breakfast. I have to make sure you at least get a good lunch."

Gabe lowered his head and planted a big kiss on her left cheek. "Gracias, Abuelita."

Although he'd only come home a handful of times over the past twelve years, he could always count on Abuelita to pack each visit with as many of his favorite dishes as possible. So much so that he'd usually return to base a few pounds heavier. The hearty beef soup with assorted vegetables was always one of his requests.

Except this was no visit. Gabe was back at Rancho Lindo for the foreseeable future. Whether he wanted to be there or not. Although his right shoulder and arm were almost back to full mobility, it was his hand that was being stubborn. The surgeons at Walter Reed had told him it would never be as strong as it had been. And the army couldn't use an explosives technician with a shaky grip. So the Physical Evaluation Board had deemed him unfit and offered retirement. He hadn't accepted it at first. But after second and third opinions, Gabe had to face the fact that his military career was over. And until he figured out what to do with the rest of his life, he'd agreed to come home. What he hadn't agreed to was to make the move permanent. Gabe knew that's what his family wanted—expected even. Little did they know, he had no plans to work on the ranch forever. He'd had to have that conversation with them, eventually.

But not yet.

At least he could rely on Abuelita's cooking to get him through the next few weeks.

Abuelita moved from the stove to the large island in the center of the kitchen and began chopping carrots. Gabe poured himself a glass of orange juice and then sat down on one of the stools on the opposite side of the counter. He eyed a basket of assorted muffins and bagels along with a tray of Danishes and other pastries. Based on the spread of pastry items, he figured his mom had probably expected him to join them earlier. Gabe ignored the flutter of guilt and scanned the room, making note of what looked the same and what was different from his last visit two years ago. He and his youngest brother Daniel had arrived from the Santa Barbara airport after ten the night before and he'd been too tired to talk to anyone, let alone check out his childhood home. He'd known his mom had been disappointed. But he had been exhausted. And hurting. Not that he'd ever admit that. So he'd crashed and hadn't woken up until after eleven—missing breakfast and another opportunity to catch up with everyone.

He'd been home barely twelve hours and was already disappointing people.

Some things never changed.

He grabbed a banana from the nearby bowl overflowing with various fruits. Before taking a bite, he asked, "Where is everyone?"

"Tu papá, Cruz, and Tomás are working outside, of course. I think Nico went to go make some deliveries. Y tu mamá and Daniel went to town to pick up some things for the party."

"What party?"

Silence.

"Abuelita? What party?"

Instead of answering, Abuelita turned her attention back to the simmering pot on the stove.

Dammit. She was avoiding the question. That could only mean one thing. "I know how much you hate to keep secrets, Abuelita," he said. "Just tell me and then you can feel better." He hated manipulating her into spilling the beans, but he also knew how much it was killing her to keep quiet.

She let out a long sigh and then faced him again. "Aye, okay. They are making you a welcome home carne asada tomorrow night."

Gabe's muscles tensed, and he fought to control his irritation. He didn't want to take it out on Abuelita—it wasn't her fault. "I told Mom that I didn't want a party," he said carefully.

"I know, Mijo. But we haven't seen you in a long time, and we were all so worried when you got hurt. You should've seen your mamá, and your papá. It hurt them so much that they couldn't even visit you in the hospital that much. Let them do this for you."

Even after all these years, he still hadn't built up a resistance to the Abuelita guilt.

"Fine," he said after a long sigh. "But that's it. I don't want anyone to do anything special for me anymore, okay?"

She shrugged. "Pues, if that's what you want?"

"Yes, that's what I want."

Abuelita nodded and put down the knife she'd been using to cut the carrots. Then she turned around and shut off the stove burner.

"Wait," Gabe said. "What are you doing?"

Abuelita shrugged her shoulders. "You say you don't want anyone to do anything special for you, so I guess I won't finish making the caldo."

Gabe held out his hand. "Wait. No. That's not what I meant."

"No?" she asked. Her eyes were wide and innocent, but he knew better. He recognized that look—the one where she was pretending to not teach him a lesson.

"I'm sorry, Abuelita. I didn't mean that I didn't want the soup. Can you please still make it for me?"

She smiled and pinched his cheek. "That's better. Now go get me some calabacitas. Find Nora. She will help you."

A few minutes later, Gabe walked out the back door into the late August sun. Rancho Lindo was just over twelve thousand acres, and most of it was only accessible by truck, utility vehicle, or horseback.

Fortunately for Gabe, the ranch's garden was on the south side of the property, near the stables and main barn. It would take him less than ten minutes on foot. He followed the cobblestone path he'd walked probably a million times growing up. But on this particular day, it didn't lead him to the partially fenced-in patch of dirt that used to grow Abuelita's small collection of herbs and vegetables. Instead, Gabe was surprised to see rows and rows of green sprouting from the grounds of a large, plentiful garden.

He walked through the open gate of the garden's wooden picket fence and took in the view around him. That's when he noticed it. A greenhouse.

It sat on the other side of a group of tall cornstalks and just past a cluster of leafy greens labeled *Cucumbers*. He walked over to the arched structure covered in thick plastic and stared at it for a few minutes. It hadn't been there the last time he'd come home. In fact, none of the bigger vegetable or fruit patches had been there before. Abuelita had sent him to get squash from someone named Nora. Maybe she was the one responsible for this bigger garden and new greenhouse?

He was about to walk inside it when he spotted two huge wooden crates filled with tomatoes. But not just any tomatoes. These were the biggest and reddest tomatoes he'd ever seen.

Gabe picked up two of the plump fruits and marveled at how his curled fingers barely reached their midpoints. Did they taste as sweet as they looked? He had to know. Slowly, he brought one up to his mouth.

That's when someone behind him cleared their throat.

"Excuse me," he heard a woman say in a very annoyed tone. "Can you please stop fondling my tomatoes?"

He turned around with every intention to inform the garden's security guard that technically they were his family's tomatoes. But when he came face-to-face with the woman, Gabe decided for various reasons that it was best to keep his mouth shut.

First of all, her narrowed eyes and pinched lips let him know that she was every bit as annoyed as her voice sounded. Second of all, despite her small frame, he could tell she was as formidable as Abuelita—which meant she wasn't someone who would back down from an argument.

And third of all, she was damn beautiful. He needed a minute to take her all in.

Her dark hair was twisted into a single braid and covered with a white bandana headwrap which framed her tanned face and large dark eyes. She wore denim shorts and a white tank underneath an olive green, long-sleeved shirt. Even though the shirt was long and flowy, it didn't hide her ample cleavage, curvy hips, or smooth and toned thighs.

His eyes traveled back to her face and he couldn't help but notice her perfect pink lips. And for a second he wondered what she would taste like.

Was this Nora, the woman he'd been sent to find?

He still didn't say a word when she finally walked over to him and took the tomatoes from his hands.

"These are part of the batch I'm taking to the farmer's market tomorrow. If you bruise them, then no one will buy them," she explained as she put them back into the crate.

Gabe finally found his voice when the woman reached for the door to the greenhouse.

"I need squash," he yelled after her.

She stopped and looked back at him. "What kind?"

"Uh, the kind you eat?" He realized how stupid that sounded but she'd surprised him with the question.

"My abuelita sent me," he explained when she got closer again. "I'm Gabe Ortega."

The woman squinted up at him. "I know who you are. What kind of squash does Doña Alma need?"

I know who you are.

Why did it sound like an accusation? Her tone surprised him. So much so that he didn't notice that she was no longer standing in front of him.

Gabe's long legs helped him catch up to her as she walked quickly in the direction of the gate where he'd come in. He glanced sideways to look at her and a sense of familiarity washed over him. Was she working on the ranch the last time he'd been home? No, he definitely would've remembered meeting her, especially with that attitude.

"You must be Nora, right?" he said.

Instead of answering, the woman picked up her pace, turned left at a red wheelbarrow, and proceeded down a row lined with raised beds of dirt and greens. Gabe didn't bother to match her speed this time, and decided that following behind her wasn't the worst thing in the world. Until, she stopped suddenly and he nearly crashed into her back. Being so close to her revved up his attraction all over again. And he couldn't shake the feeling that he knew her from somewhere.

Calm down, Ortega. You don't even know this woman. Maybe she's not who you think she is?

"I am Nora, by the way," she said as if she'd read his mind. Then she crouched down to inspect one of the dirt beds.

"Nora," he repeated as if saying her name out loud would help him place her. It didn't.

"So what am I picking for Doña Alma? Zucchini? Yellow squash? Butternut?"

Gabe scanned the spread of green in front of him.

Not that he even knew what he was looking for. "Uh, I'm not sure, actually. She didn't specify."

"What is she cooking?"

"Oh. She's making me caldo de res."

"Of course she is," he heard her mutter. "Well then, I'll send you back with some zucchini and chayote."

As Nora picked the vegetables from a nearby section of the garden, Gabe wondered why she seemed so irritated with him. How could he have known that he wasn't supposed to touch her tomatoes? Though he got the sense that there was something else behind her prickly demeanor. It was almost as if she didn't like him even though she'd only known him for less than ten minutes. He was intrigued.

"So how long have you been working on the ranch?" he asked as he watched her inspect each vegetable she pulled from the ground.

"Just over a year," she answered without looking at him.

"And have you always been into gardening?"

This time she raised her eyes and met his. "I'm a horticulturist."

"Oh. Cool."

Really?

"Well, the garden looks amazing. Especially the greenhouse. You've really made the place, uh, grow." God. What the hell was he saying? Gabe knew he sounded lame. He was normally a pretty smooth talker, but something about her jumbled his brain and the words coming out of his mouth.

Nora the horticulturist finally stood up and handed him two large zucchinis and two smaller light green vegetables that he assumed were the chayotes.

"Tell Doña Alma that I'll bring her some more later to stock up her pantry. I usually try to check to see what she needs in the morning, but I forgot today."

Gabe nodded in response. He expected her to leave him then, but instead she said, "So. Are you home for good like they're saying?"

He knew the "they" without her having to explain. He'd bet good money that Cruz, his mom, hell, even the rest of his brothers, were telling everyone they knew that Gabe was going to help run the ranch. Maybe he should've just went along with it. But there was something about the way Nora asked the question. Like she knew it wasn't the truth and she was daring him to lie to her.

Something in his gut wanted to prove her wrong. He decided to go with the truth.

"We'll see," he said with a shrug. "I know that's what they expect, what they want. But I need time to figure things out first."

If he thought she'd be surprised, or even pleased, by his response, he'd be wrong. Instead, her straight expression fell a little, and for a second, he thought he saw disappointment in her eyes. He wanted to explain, but she got her words out first.

"Well, then," Nora said before walking away.

As he headed back to the main house, Gabe tried to figure out why it seemed like he'd become Nora's least favorite person on the ranch. It was such a shame though if that was the case. He would much prefer spending time with the pretty brunette than doing whatever work Cruz and their dad had in store for him over the next several weeks.

It's not as if Gabe didn't love a good challenge. It

was the reason he'd joined the army in the first place. His family, especially his father, had been dead set against it. So much so that they'd gotten into a huge fight about it and Gabe had enlisted at eighteen and left home to prove to himself that he could be more than just a rancher.

For some reason, he couldn't help but feel like he had something to prove to Nora too.

Still, it was probably better this way. He had to focus on his recovery and getting the strength in his hand as back to normal as possible. He also needed to find a job that didn't involve shoveling manure into trash cans.

Nora was a distraction he didn't need. Not if he wanted to leave Rancho Lindo again.

So as much as he wouldn't mind trying to figure her out, Gabe decided it would be better if he kept his distance from the garden and the pretty horticulturist who guarded its tomatoes.

After all, the property spanned thousands of acres. How hard could it be to stay away?

Chapter Two

So much for a small family party.

Nora scanned the backyard of Rancho Lindo's main house and counted at least sixty-two people. Most were those who worked on the ranch and their own families. She also spotted a few of the Ortegas' neighbors and some people she knew from town.

And they were all there to welcome Gabe back home.

She checked the time on her watch again. She'd told herself she was only going to stay an hour. Technically, it had only been forty-nine minutes, but Nora gave herself permission to get up and leave.

First, though, she had to plan her escape route. Because if she ran into any of the Ortegas on her way out, most of them would keep her chatting until midnight. She was going to have a long day tomorrow and needed to get to sleep as soon as possible.

From her folding chair nestled in the corner of the patio, Nora scanned the crowd and made note of each Ortega and their position.

Santiago Ortega, her boss and the family's patriarch, was stationed at the patio's large, built-in barbecue grill still tending to his carne asada. He was a towering man with a resting bear face—serious, a little scary, and full of hair. Although he could be intimidating to strangers, Nora knew he was a big, old, sentimental softie when it came to his family and Rancho Lindo. And he was as comfortable in front of a grill as he was wrangling cattle. He always selected the cuts of beef or chicken himself and marinated them with his secret seasonings the day before. Señor Ortega took pride in the fact that every cut of meat came from his ranch, and he believed only he could grill them the way they deserved.

He wouldn't be moving anytime soon.

Satisfied that she could leave easily as long as she stayed away from the grill and other side of the patio, Nora searched for the rest of the family. After another minute or so, she located Cruz, the oldest Ortega son and the ranch's second in charge. He was standing near the back entrance to the main house and looked to be in deep conversation with some of the ranch hands. He too wore his signature Stetson and usual non-working uniform of boots, jeans, and a henley. He was as big and as strong as his dad. Though Nora noted his presence seemed more commanding lately than Señor Ortega's. It was probably because he seemed to be taking more of a lead when it came to the ranch's lines of business. Although Cruz was always respectful and friendly, he was usually too busy to carry on a conversation with her unless it had to do with the garden. If he saw her leaving, he might wave. But she was confident he wouldn't go out of his way to stop her so they could chat.

Her eyes then fell on Tomás as he walked around the patio with his mom and Doña Alma. They would stop and hug different people they came upon and it surprised her that he was being so outgoing. Tomás once told her that horses were easier to talk to than most people. She almost confessed that she'd felt the same about her produce.

But where was Gabe?

Nora took another look around and couldn't find him right away. She wasn't surprised that he was missing from his own party. Typical.

She had recognized him as soon as she'd seen him standing in her garden the day before. Even from the back, she could tell it was him. Not only was he the tallest of the Ortega boys, he also had the broadest shoulders. When she'd finally seen his face, it was as if he were standing in front of her all those years ago. He was older, obviously. She spotted creases around his eyes that hadn't been there before. His dark brown hair had been longer and wavier when he was a teenager. The wild and carefree locks had fit his rebellious attitude perfectly back then. Now he wore it short and neat. She assumed that was a carryover from his active duty days. But the glint in his eyes and telltale smirk she saw yesterday told her that the army hadn't tamed everything about Gabe.

Familiar waves of want warmed her from the inside out and it took everything she had to not to show how much seeing him again had affected her.

Fortunately, Nora hadn't run into Gabe since she'd arrived for his welcome home barbecue. After their interaction the day before in the garden, she had hoped she'd have another few days before having to speak to Gabe again. The fact that he didn't remember her at all stung her pride more than she'd care to admit. Nora had tried to get out of coming to the barbecue altogether. She'd told Doña Alma that she was too tired after being at the farmer's market all day and just wanted to go to bed early. But the elderly woman had insisted. And guilted. After all, who would help her make the salsas and guacamole?

So Nora had gone home to quickly get ready. After taking a shower, she'd begrudgingly put on her favorite strawberry-print sundress, combed out her hair, applied mascara and lip gloss, and added her favorite necklace and earrings. Satisfied with the final result, Nora had headed back to the main house in the UTV she usually drove to get around the property.

Although she really had only gone to help Doña Alma, Nora had to admit she was just a little curious to see how the Ortegas' prodigal son would interact with everyone. She hadn't been working at the ranch the last time he'd been there for a visit. And from what she'd heard over the past few days, Gabe was known for keeping to himself and staying away from town.

Some things, and people, never changed.

That's why she'd asked him about whether he was staying for good. She wanted to hear him say it. Even if she already knew not to believe him. She'd learned that lesson a long time ago.

Nora would never understand why the second-oldest Ortega brother didn't like to stay at Rancho Lindo very long. This was his home. It could be his future too. But he'd never wanted it.

Like Gabe, she'd grown up on the ranch too. Although it was never technically her home. It was just a place to spend the summers with her tío and tía and where she learned how to ride a horse, milk a cow, and make things grow. In fact, helping Doña Alma in her garden is what made her want to become a horticulturist. But when her last job with the Department of Agriculture had her spending more time in a lab than outside in a garden, she had begun to doubt her career choices. The politics and bureaucracy had become too much. So when her boss wouldn't approve her time off to come to Esperanza for her tío's funeral because he wasn't considered her immediate family, Nora had had enough. She quit on the spot.

When she'd arrived in town all those months ago, she'd been lost. Not just because she was there to say goodbye to the only father figure she'd ever known. But because she didn't know what to do next. The offer to take over the garden and make it a new viable line of business for the ranch had come at exactly the right time. Yet another reason why she would always be grateful to the Ortegas.

Now she not only worked on the ranch, she lived on the property too—in the same little house where she spent her summers all those years ago.

"Do you need a refill?" a deep voice asked behind her.

Nora turned around to find Daniel, the youngest son, standing behind her holding two beer bottles. Nico was right next to him.

She smiled and shook her head. "No thanks. I'm just going to finish this one off and then head home."

"It's only seven, Nora," Nico said, and sat down next to her. "It's Friday night. Can't you at least stay out until eight or even nine?"

Nora laughed. "I could, but my sore back and swollen feet say otherwise. Besides, I'm headed to Santa Barbara at dawn for the farmer's market down there."

"That's right," Daniel said. "It's the second Saturday

of the month. That's too bad. I was hoping I'd get you and Nico to repeat your karaoke duet from our Fourth of July picnic."

The memory of the second-youngest Ortega trying to sing along to "Islands in the Stream" made them both laugh. Nico couldn't carry a tune to save his life. But what he lacked in talent, he totally made up for in showmanship and effort. He also had a way of convincing Nora to step out of her comfort zone. In fact, it was the brothers who had suggested to their parents that Nora take over the ranch's garden last year.

"Hold up. If we're going to be singing, I'm going to need at least two more beers," Nico told them.

Nora laughed. Daniel and Nico were her biggest cheerleaders—always had been. Although they were younger than her by a few years, she had always enjoyed tagging along with them on their daily adventures on the ranch. They were basically the brothers she'd never had.

In fact, she considered all of the Ortegas her extended family. Well, almost all of them.

Nora took the last swig of her beer, and that's when she finally spotted Gabe walking out of the house. Before she lost her nerve, she asked them what had been on her mind most of the day. "How has it been having him back?" she said, nodding her head in the direction of where Gabe was now talking to his mom on the other side of the patio.

"Good. But, then again, it's only been two days," Daniel said with a laugh.

Nico scoffed. "Two very long days."

Nora looked at Nico. "What do you mean?"

"Just that it's going to take some getting used to having him back here, that's all."

She couldn't shake the feeling that Nico was holding back, but she didn't press the issue. "And his arm and shoulder?" she asked instead.

Daniel shrugged. "He just tells my mom that he's fine. You know Gabe. Not exactly an open book."

Nora nodded. She definitely knew.

"Have you talked to him?" Daniel asked.

"Just a little. He came to the garden yesterday to get some vegetables for your abuelita." She paused before adding, "I don't think he remembered me."

Nico's eyes grew big. "Seriously? How could he not?"

"I guess I look different?" Or she had been invisible to him like she'd always thought.

"That's ridiculous. I'm going to fix this right now. Oye, Gabe!"

Panic made Nora leap from her chair. She blocked Nico, who had also stood up and was frantically waving his hands.

"Nico, no. Please. I don't—"

Before she could finish begging him to leave it alone, Gabe walked up to them.

"What's up?" he asked. Then he turned and noticed her standing next to him. "Hello," he told her with a curt nod.

Nora so wasn't ready for what was going to come next. Her short-lived anonymity when it came to Gabe might have been humbling, but at least it shrouded her from having to relive one of the most embarrassing and hurtful nights of her teenage life. Why couldn't she have at least another twenty-four hours before having to deal with the repercussions of Gabe knowing the truth of who she was? Her veil of protection from that memory was about to be pulled away and she braced for the impact.

"Gabe, I can't believe you don't remember Nora," Nico accused.

She refused to look at any of the brothers. That didn't mean she didn't feel the heat of Gabe's stare. Every nerve prickled with anticipation. And dread.

"What do you mean?" Gabe answered, obviously confused. "She's the horticulturist, right? We met yesterday."

Nico put his hands on his hips and shook his head. "God. You can be really oblivious sometimes."

"What are you talking about?"

In that moment, Nora prayed for the patio's talavera tiles beneath her feet to crack open and swallow her.

"Dude," Nico said incredulously and shook his head.

"This is Nora," Daniel chimed in. "You know? Chucho's niece? Remember?"

His eyes were on her again. She knew it without even seeing it. But she had to see it before it became painfully obvious just how embarrassed she was. Nora forced herself to turn her head and confront Gabe's recognition once and for all.

It took a few seconds for his puzzled expression to transform into surprise. And then everything between them changed.

"Honora?"

Her head jerked up to meet his eyes. Not many people called her that anymore. The sound of her full name on his lips surrounded her like a warm, familiar embrace and her traitorous body nearly swooned in his direction. It was as if she'd been transported back in time and all of sudden she was a shy and nerdy sixteen-year-old again. Fortunately, her brain wasn't as sentimental and she stopped herself from acting like a fool.

Instead, Nora offered him a small wave. "It's me."

"Holy shit!" he gasped, dragging a hand down his face as if to open his eyes even wider. "I knew you seemed familiar yesterday. Wow."

Whatever words she'd practiced for this moment went out the window. Gabe moved toward her, and before Nora could stop him, he tried to embrace her in an awkward hug. Awkward because she didn't hug him. In fact, her entire body went rigid at his touch. It was like a splash of cold water to her face, dumping her back into the present, where adult Nora knew better than to be charmed by Gabe Ortega simply saying her name.

So what if she'd once had a stupid crush on him? He'd made it clear back then and yesterday that neither Nora nor Honora were ever going to be anything more to him than a vague memory.

"Well, now that we're all clear about who I am, I'm going to take off," she said. "See you around."

Nora had meant for the last comment to be directed at all of the brothers, but she'd instinctively glanced in Gabe's direction. He was still staring at her, almost as if he couldn't quite believe who she was. And although the night air had felt cool against her skin seconds earlier, a new heat warmed her cheeks.

She pulled her eyes away from him and commanded her legs to move as quickly as possible through the crowd until she could be sure Gabe wasn't staring at her anymore. Nora stopped only to say good night to Doña Alma, and then she escaped out of the patio's back gate.

"Honora! Nora! Wait!"

Gabe was saying her name again. She knew she should stop. But first she needed to get control of all of the chaotic emotions currently having a dance party in her stomach.

In her mind, she counted down from ten.

Diez, nueve, ocho, siete…

Her breathing eased, and she slowed her pace.

Seis, cinco, cuatro, tres…

The warmth on her face and back of her neck began to cool.

Dos y uno.

At last, she was calm.

And that was the only reason why she stopped walking. She pivoted to face him.

"Hey," he said when he reached her. His tone was friendly. Nonchalant. She hated that. She hated that he didn't seem rattled like she was.

Nora forced her body to unwrangle itself from the bundle of nerves it had become. "Hey," she said as coolly as she could.

"Hi," he repeated before scratching his temple with his right index finger.

Wait. He was nervous.

"You kind of already said that," she reminded him.

He nodded. "I guess I did. Truth is, I'm still kind of in shock. I never expected to see you here after all this time."

Nora appreciated his honesty at least. She returned the frankness. "Same," she said with a shrug and a hesitant smile.

When neither of them said anything for what seemed like thousands of minutes, Nora took a step as if to leave.

"Wait," he said. "I wanted to tell you something."

Unsure of what on God's green planet he could say to her, she braced for all possibilities. It seemed to take forever before he said his next words.

"Uh, so I just wanted to apologize."

That was a possibility she hadn't expected. Had he really remembered everything? She wasn't sure if she wanted to have that conversation right then and there.

"For what?" she asked nervously.

"For not recognizing you yesterday."

Relief, coupled with disappointment, made her shift her feet. He hadn't remembered everything.

"It's fine. No big deal, okay? Good night," she said, and started walking again before he could see that it was a bigger deal than she dared to admit. Maybe her crush had been the very definition of unrequited, but she'd thought he'd have at least a vague memory of the girl she used to be. Why was she always being disappointed when it came to Gabe?

He moved in front of her and she stopped in her tracks.

"Wait. I also wanted to say how sorry I was to hear about your tío. I had tried to get a few days off so I could come to the funeral, but I couldn't swing it."

It was her turn to be surprised. "You wanted to come to the funeral?"

"Of course. Chucho was a good man. He was probably the only person on the ranch who let me do things my way. Even if it was wrong, he never came right out and said it. He'd just let me figure it out and if I couldn't, then he'd say, 'How about I teach you a different way?'"

A familiar pang of grief spread through her chest. Still, she smiled. "That sounds like him."

Her tío had been her mom's older brother and was more like a father to her than an uncle. Her parents had divorced when she was only seven years old. In the beginning, her dad would pick her up every Saturday to take her out for lunch and a movie or a trip to the park. Then his visits became more sporadic and unpredictable. Nora couldn't even count how many Saturdays she'd spent just sitting on the couch waiting for him to show up. On days that he didn't, she'd cry, tell her mom that she hated him and never wanted to see him again. On the days that he did, all was forgiven and she'd believe him when he'd tell her that he was going to be a better dad and promised to see her next week. But, by the time she was nine, her dad had disappeared from her life completely. Her mom had told her that he'd moved to another state and even had another family by then. That's when Tío Chucho and Tía Luz began inviting her to spend her summers with them on the ranch. Tío Chucho said it was to give her mom a little break, but Nora soon realized there were other reasons. They never had any kids of their own and they seemed to enjoy having her there as much as she enjoyed being with them.

When she went away to college and then eventually moved to another city for work, her visits to Rancho Lindo grew fewer and far between. Then a year ago, Tío Chucho passed away from liver cancer and Nora made what she thought would be her last trip back to the ranch for his funeral. But Daniel and Nico had other ideas.

"How's your tía?" Gabe asked after another moment.

Nora shrugged. "She's doing okay, I guess. She moved to Texas to be closer to her sister and the rest of their family. I try to call her every Sunday, and I'm hoping to go visit her in January."

"That's good," he said with a nod.

"Well, I gotta go," she said, and started to turn away.

"I can't believe you work here now."

Nora straightened. "Yeah. I live here too. Well, in my tío and tía's old cottage on the north side of ranch."

"Really? That's, uh, good too." Gabe's dark brows scrunched together as if he was still trying to make sense of what she'd just said. But why? Was it really that much of a stretch to believe that she was now officially part of the Rancho Lindo familia? She could've told him right then and there about how her summers at the ranch had inspired her to get a bachelor's degree in plant science and a master's in horticulture. Or about the years she worked as a researcher studying greenhouse management and the effects of light exposure on microgreens.

She didn't, though. Because she had nothing to prove to Gabe and she didn't need to justify her place on the ranch.

Nora cleared her throat to shake him free of whatever thoughts were battling it out inside his head. "Yeah. Um, you should probably get back to your party," she told him. She really was tired and didn't think she could take any more small talk.

But Gabe didn't leave. Instead, he stuffed his hands into the pockets of his jeans and kicked at a small pebble next to his left boot. "I should've known you'd come back."

Nora took a quick breath. "What do you mean?"

"You always loved being on the ranch. And you were always sad when summer was over."

"You remember that?" she asked.

He looked at her again. His gaze softened, and she couldn't help but notice the crinkles at the corners of his eyes when he gave her a small smile. "Of course I do. Why wouldn't I?"

She couldn't help but scoff. "It's not like we hung out a lot."

At least not until that last day.

"I may not have been around that much, but I remember Abuelita always making a big deal about how she wanted to make you feel better when the day came for you to go back home. She'd always make you a basket filled with peaches and strawberries and a batch of her biscochitos. I'd always try to steal a couple, and she'd always tell me they were for 'my Honora' and no one else."

Gabe laughed at the memory, but it only made Nora bristle. He hadn't really remembered her at all—only that Doña Alma had made her the same cookies he liked. Her pulse pounded hard and furious in her ears, beating away any urge to continue their conversation any longer.

"Okay, then. Good night," she said more tersely than she'd intended.

He picked up on her change in tone and raised his eyebrows in question. "What? Did I say something wrong?"

"No, you didn't. I'm just tired, and I really need to go home now," she said after a long sigh.

"Of course. Sorry for keeping you."

Nora nodded back and began to walk away. But she decided she had one more thing to say to Gabe.

"Just so you know," she said over her shoulder, "your parents and your brothers and your abuelita are very happy that you're home. So, once you make your decision about leaving, let them know right away. That way it doesn't come as a shock again."

She didn't wait to see or hear his response. Instead, she jumped into a UTV and took off as fast as the little motor could take her.

Gabe Ortega might be back at Rancho Lindo. But that didn't mean she needed to pretend she was interested in catching up or even being his friend. A long time ago, she'd made the mistake of believing the words that had come out of his mouth, and she'd been crushed as easily as an over-ripened tomato.

Besides, she'd bet good money that Gabe wasn't going to be around for the long haul.

It was only a matter of time before he became as forgettable to her as she had once been to him.

Chapter Three

The last of the guests left just after eleven p.m. and about two hours later than Gabe had hoped.

He should've expected that what was supposed to be just a small dinner for family had turned into the usual full-blown Ortega social event.

Even though he'd been annoyed, he'd been on his best behavior. He shook hands, kissed cheeks, and danced with every mom and abuelita who asked. But now he was tired. So very tired.

His parents and Abuelita had already said their goodnights, so Gabe figured it was safe to do the same.

"Well, I'm going to bed," he told his brothers. They'd gathered at the kitchen island and were finishing off the last of the tres leches cake their mom had made for the party. Another one of Gabe's favorites.

His youngest brothers, Nico and Daniel, weren't twins, but at only thirteen months apart, they might as well have been. Except Nico kept his black hair short and styled while Daniel preferred his a little longer and natural. Nico was lean, muscular, and always started his day with a run. Daniel was thicker and preferred beers to the green smoothies that his brother always drank. They never went anywhere without their matching brown Stetsons and big personalities. So, as usual, they were the life of any party.

Tomás was the third-oldest and definitely the more serious of all of the boys—even more so than Cruz. He was tall, lanky, and always seemed more comfortable in a stable than around people. It had been a surprise to see him mingling tonight. Maybe the other two were finally rubbing off on him.

That left Cruz. The oldest Ortega brother. The perfect son. The one who did everything and anything his dad asked. He lived for Rancho Lindo. So, of course, the two of them were always getting into it.

They were his brothers. His first friends and his first enemies. And now they were all back together again.

Tomás held up his fork. "Gabe, no way are you going to bed right now. Nope. Not yet. We haven't done it."

Gabe sighed. "We can do it tomorrow."

"That's what you said last night," Nico said.

"Come on, guys. I'm not feeling it."

Daniel walked over and slapped him on the back. "That's because we haven't done it. Then you'll feel it all."

Gabe was just about to argue again when Cruz walked back into the kitchen with a stack of shot glasses and their dad's most expensive tequila. The ranch's two black-and-white border collies, Oreo and Shadow, trailed happily behind him probably thinking they were getting some late night treats from the group. Unlike the miniature white menace, these two actually liked Gabe.

"No more excuses, hermano," Cruz said as he set everything down on the counter. "It's time for our shots."

Taking tequila shots with his brothers was one of the few traditions they'd held on to through the years. Every time one of them turned twenty-one, it called for a round of shots. Then, every party or holiday when they were together, a round of shots. Eventually, it was just whenever Gabe made it home, and it usually took place on his first night back. This time, though, he'd been putting it off. Like he'd told his brothers, he hadn't been feeling it. Maybe because a part of him didn't want to do it until he knew for sure he'd be leaving sooner rather than later.

Cruz poured the alcohol into the glasses and then passed them out to everyone. Gabe was the last to be served and all eyes were on him until he picked it up. Then the others did the same.

"To Rancho Lindo, may it always be our home," Cruz said.

"To friends and familia, may we never be alone," Tomás said next.

"To the loves we've lost and those we have yet to find," Nico added.

"To lessons learned and leaving mistakes behind," Daniel chimed in.

Gabe raised his glass. "And to forgetting the bad, so we can always remember the good."

"Salud," they all said in unison before downing their shots.

Three more rounds later and Gabe was definitely feeling something. He wasn't exactly buzzed, but he was a lot more relaxed. So much so that he didn't protest when Tomás started pouring round five.

"Hey," Nico said, "I just realized we forgot the limes and salt."

Cruz scoffed. "This tequila doesn't need limes and salt. It's that smooth."

Tomás nodded. "Very true. Besides, we're out of limes. I think Dad used them all for his marinade. But, hey, if you need them, Nico, I bet Nora has a stash in the back of the van."

The mention of Nora made Gabe sit up a little straighter. "I still can't believe she's Chucho's niece."

Daniel laughed. "Guys, you should've seen Gabe's face when we told him."

"Yeah, that wasn't your best moment, Gabe," Nico said. "Not that I was surprised. I'm sure you're going to be running into lots of people you forgot about. Who knows? There may even be a few who don't remember you."

Gabe didn't miss the underlying accusation behind his brother's words. It seemed like everything Nico had to say to him since he'd come back was loaded with a hint of hostility. It had surprised him. Gabe had been prepared to deal with old resentments from Cruz and his dad. But he and Nico had always gotten along. Something was definitely going on with him. He made a note to confront him about it later.

"You seriously didn't recognize her?" Tomás asked.

Gabe really hadn't.

Nora looked—and acted—nothing like the shy, quiet Honora he'd known all those summers ago. Sure, they'd been friendly, but they hadn't exactly been friends. When she wasn't with her uncle or aunt, she could usually be found tagging along with Nico and Daniel or helping Abuelita in the kitchen. A couple of times she'd shown up when he and his brothers would sneak away from their chores to swim in a nearby creek. Although he couldn't remember a time when she actually joined them in the water. Instead, she'd sit on a blanket under a big tree and read a book while they took turns jumping into the creek from their rope swing.

When they were all teenagers, Gabe saw less and less of Honora. Mainly because he had traded in afternoon creek swims for driving around town with his friends or movie dates with whichever girlfriend he had at the time.

Then he'd left Rancho Lindo for the army at eighteen, and that had been the last time he'd ever seen Honora.

Nora.

Gabe shook his head. "I really didn't recognize her," he admitted. "And I definitely don't remember that attitude."

Or that body.

A picture of her standing in front of him in that short sundress popped into his mind. Her hair was free of the braid and fell just below her shoulders. She wore small silver hoops in her ears and a simple silver necklace. It had taken everything he'd had not to stare at the charm that lay just above the dip of her cleavage.

"Attitude?" his brothers all said at the same time, chasing the sexy image away and bringing him back into the present.

"Yeah. Doesn't she seem a little standoffish to you?"

"Nora? Seriously?" Tomás just shook his head.

"I'm telling you she looks at me like I'm the devil." Maybe that was an exaggeration. But no one could convince him that Nora didn't like him for some reason.

"Nora doesn't have an attitude problem," Nico said. "Sounds to me like she has more of a Gabe problem. She's always been a smart one, that Nora."

Everyone except Gabe started laughing.

"What?" Gabe asked.

He thought about their conversation earlier that night. Gabe hadn't imagined the way she'd practically sprinted away from him. Yet she'd seemed pretty comfortable talking with his brothers only minutes beforehand. Could he really be the only Ortega that Nora didn't like? If so, why?

"I'm glad you all think it's funny that she hates me," he said.

"What did you expect?" Nico asked after downing another shot. "Just because you came back doesn't mean every person is going to fall on their knees in gratitude. Especially when you can't even bother to remember them in the first place."

Forget later. He definitely needed to figure out what the hell was Nico's problem. But before Gabe could respond, Daniel put his hand on Gabe's shoulder. "Don't worry, hermano," Daniel said. "Just give it time. Nora doesn't have a hateful bone in her body. It's against her nature to not like someone."

"Whatever. It's not like I'm ... " Gabe murmured and then cut himself off. He almost said it wasn't like he was going to be around that long. He cleared his throat and began again. "It's not like I'm going to have time to hang out with her or anyone for that matter. I'm sure Cruz and Dad have plans to keep me pretty busy."

"You got that right," his older brother answered. "Mom wanted me to leave you alone for a week. Does this mean you're ready to get to work?"

He wasn't ready. But suddenly talking about his ranch duties seemed lots easier than continuing to talk about Nora and her problem with him. Especially since he couldn't afford to spend the next few weeks trying to get her to like him. Even if it would be kind of fun.

No, he couldn't let himself be distracted by Nora.

"I'm ready," he told Cruz.

As usual, Cruz didn't waste any time listing all of the duties he'd planned for Gabe to take over. By the time he was done talking, they were the only ones left in the kitchen. The rest of his brothers had disappeared into their rooms upstairs. Even Oreo and Shadow had gone back to their beds in the family room.

"Damn, Cruz. There are only twenty-four hours in a day, you know," Gabe said.

"Hey. I've done everything I just told you, plus about a million things more before noon. I think you can manage."

Gabe tried not to groan in frustration. He believed Cruz because they were the same things he'd also done before noon when he was a teenager. But he had better motivation back then. Because the sooner he finished his work, the sooner he could do whatever he wanted—not what he was told to do. Even at a young age, Gabe always preferred anything else over the ranch and the responsibilities that came with it.

And Cruz was the exact opposite. He was just like their dad. They were both big, sturdy men who were more comfortable wrangling a bull than talking about their feelings. But when it came to Rancho Lindo, they were passionate, emotional, and its fiercest protectors.

Meanwhile, Gabe and his dad were alike in the worst possible way. They both had quick tempers.

Out of all of the brothers, Gabe was the one who seemed to butt heads with his dad over any little difference of opinion. As he got older, their arguments were always over the same one thing—what Gabe was going to do after he graduated from high school. His dad had wanted him to go to community college and eventually get a degree in agriculture and ranch management, like Cruz had. Gabe, on the other hand, had wanted to see the world, or at least any town other than Esperanza. He told his dad he'd be gone two years at the most and then come back and go to school just like he'd wanted. His dad wouldn't hear of it.

It all came to a head the summer he was eighteen. After one of their very big fights, Gabe ended up enlisting in the army without telling him or anyone else in his family. It might not have been the best way to handle everything. But it had been the smartest thing he'd ever done. Because he had found something he was good at. And he was able to travel to places he'd never even heard of before.

Freedom had come at a price, though. They'd still only exchanged fewer than a dozen or so words since he'd come back. Gabe knew his dad still hadn't forgiven him for the way he'd left. It was one of main reasons why he had stayed away for so long. His few visits home over the years had been only to appease his mom and abuelita.

Still, he'd lived his life on his terms. Could his brothers say the same?

"Can I ask you a question?" Gabe said.

"Sure," Cruz answered, and poured himself another shot.

"Don't you ever wonder if there's something else out there for you?"

He downed the tequila. "What do you mean?"

"I mean, is running Rancho Lindo really all you're going to do with your life?"

Cruz looked over at him incredulously. "Why are you making it sound like it's a bad thing? I'm an Ortega. Of course my life is this ranch. And now it's going to be yours too."

Maybe it was the tequila. Maybe it was the exhaustion of the entire day. Either way, Gabe didn't have the energy to dance around the assumption. "I'm not so sure."

"Classic Gabe. Stir up a tornado and then disappear before you can get hit by the flying debris. And, like always, the rest of us are left having to deal with the aftermath. I knew it."

"You knew what?"

"I told Daniel that you weren't planning on sticking around." His brother laughed, but the bitterness was evident. "He kept insisting things were different. That you were different. He really thought you were coming home for good."

"And what about Dad?"

Cruz straightened. "What about him?"

"What does Dad think?"

His brother's shoulders seemed to relax and Gabe wondered why. The question hadn't been a challenge or accusation. Why had Cruz reacted as if it was?

"Dad thinks what I think. I mean, can you blame him?"

Gabe shrugged. "Look, honestly, I don't know what I want. I just need to get my shoulder and hand back to how they were before the accident. Until then, I can't make any decisions about my future."

Cruz started collecting the shot glasses and put the cap back on the tequila. "So the rest of us are just supposed to wait for you to figure out your life?"

He didn't answer him. He didn't need this right now. Not tonight. Gabe closed his eyes and pinched the bridge of his nose. He willed the wave of anxiety he was feeling to crawl back inside. And then with one more exhale, he was back in control.

"Perfect." Cruz's remark made him open his eyes again.

"What do you want me to say?"

His brother put the shot glasses in the sink, except for one. Then he walked back to the counter and picked up the tequila bottle. "Nothing. But I'll just say one more thing, and then I'm going to head up to bed and finish this off. Ranch life doesn't wait for anyone, Gabe. That's not a luxury we have around here, especially now."

His eyes were full of heavy emotion—a rare thing to see from the usually stoic Cruz.

"What do you mean, 'especially now'?" Gabe had to ask.

Cruz cleared his throat and his disapproving glare was back. "I just mean that it's busy, that's all. So, while you're making up your mind, I still need your help. You start at six a.m. on Monday."

Chapter Four

The rod iron front entrance gate to Rancho Lindo was open when Nora returned from her errands in town.

That told her that there were visitors on the property.

Although Señor Ortega didn't like it, Cruz kept the gate open when he was expecting outsiders so he didn't have to deal with answering the intercom all day. The older man was worried more about animals getting out than strangers coming in. But they hadn't had an escapee in months, so it looked like Cruz was back to leaving it open.

Several minutes later, Nora drove the truck into the paved U-shaped driveway in front of the main house and parked. She grabbed the small white paper bag from the front seat and shut the door. The bag was for Doña Alma, and she needed to give it to her before she got back to her work.

But when Nora stepped inside the kitchen, it wasn't Doña Alma she saw. It was Cruz and his two faithful followers, Oreo and Shadow.

"Oh, hey, Cruz," she said as she hung the truck's

keys onto the hook next to the kitchen's back door. Instinctively, she gripped the small white paper bag.

"Hey, Nora. Did you get everything you needed?"

"Almost," she said, but didn't move from her spot. "I had to place an order for more pH test drops. Gene said I can pick them up on Friday."

Cruz nodded as he topped off the large pitcher he'd been filling from the refrigerator's water dispenser. Then he poured the water into the two silver bowls on the floor near the pantry entrance. The dogs ran to the bowls and began drinking.

Cruz walked over to the counter next to the fridge and leaned against it. "I'm sending Daniel on a supply run to Santa Barbara tomorrow," he told her. "He can get some for you if you need them sooner."

"That's okay. I'm not totally out yet. Thanks, though."

"Well, let me know if you change your mind."

There were a few seconds of silence between them before Nora finally worked up the courage to ask the question that had been on her mind all morning.

"So how is his first day back going?"

Cruz shrugged. "He showed up on time, so I guess that's something."

"That bad, huh?"

"Not bad. Just slow. It's almost like he forgot how to be..."

"A cowboy?"

"An Ortega."

The disappointment was etched all over Cruz's face. It didn't surprise her that Cruz and Señor Ortega would expect Gabe to be able to fall back into the routine of working the ranch so quickly. To them, there was nothing more important in this world than Rancho Lindo. It was in their blood. Taking care of the land and the animals was in their nature. Why wouldn't they think that Gabe should be exactly like them?

A sudden thought occurred to her. Was that why Gabe was so determined to be anything but a Rancho Lindo cowboy? She knew how hard it was to live up to other people's expectations of you. Sometimes the easier road was in the opposite direction. That way there would be no disappointed looks like the one Cruz had now.

"Just give it time," she told him. "I'm sure he'll get back into the swing of things soon."

Cruz shrugged. "Maybe. Or maybe he's already upstairs packing his suitcase."

Nora caught her breath. Could Gabe really sneak out on his family again so quickly? "What makes you say that?"

"I haven't seen him in over an hour. He was supposed to be helping Tomás intake our first stable boarder, and he says Gabe never showed. I was going to go check his bedroom, but honestly I think it would be safer for both of us if I didn't."

"Do you want me to?"

"No," he said, shaking his head. "Gabe is a grown-ass man. No one needs to be chasing after him."

She nodded. Cruz was right. Besides, what was she going to do if she found him? Scold him? Stop him? Like he would ever listen to her anyway. What Gabe Ortega did or didn't do was none of her business. She tried to change the topic.

"A new boarder, huh? That's good. I know Tomás has been working hard to get the word out."

"Well, we'll see. I'm still not impressed by the potential profit margin."

A small kernel of concern sprouted inside her. Obviously, Nora was not privy to all of Rancho Lindo's business dealings. She had no idea what the status of its finances were or weren't, for that matter. But having spent a good part of her life here over the years, she could tell things were different. Even in the past year, there were changes she couldn't ignore. The biggest one was that Cruz had definitely taken on more responsibility when it came to the overall management of the ranch. That meant he had his hand in every line of the business—including the garden. She met with him every month to update him on everything she had been working on. When she first took over the garden, he'd been more concerned about her plans to start selling the produce at the farmer's market and the building of the greenhouse. But the last few meetings had strictly focused on her expenses and profits. Fortunately, she was usually in the black.

Still, Nora knew there were rumors that the ranch was struggling. The latest one she'd heard was that Cruz had applied for a loan with a bigger bank out of town. She had no idea if it was true or not. She'd sensed that Cruz was carrying a huge weight on his shoulders and even debated whether she should bring it up to Nico or Daniel. In the end, she decided to broach the subject later. The return of Gabe was more than enough for the family to deal with for now.

Nora looked again at Cruz. "Well, I'm sure you guys will be getting more boarders soon. Tomás knows what he's doing."

He nodded. "Usually." Then he added, "Unlike some of my other brothers."

Nora didn't know what to say to that. Instead, she let Cruz know the gate was still open.

"Thanks for the reminder," he said, and walked to the back door. Then he whistled for Oreo and Shadow. As usual, they didn't hesitate and quickly ran over to him.

After Cruz and the dogs left, she stopped by Doña Alma's bedroom on the first floor of the main house. The elderly woman was in her favorite rocking chair and looked to be napping as a familiar Mexican ranchera song played from the small radio on the table next to her. Nora didn't want to wake her, so she tiptoed over to the bedside nightstand. Just as she was about to set the white bag down, she heard, "Is it time to cook dinner?"

Nora laughed when she saw Gabe's abuelita looking at her with half-open eyes. "No, Doña Alma. It's still the afternoon. I just came to leave you this," she said, and showed her the bag.

Her eyes opened all the way. "Qué bueno. Thank you, Mija. Yes, just leave it there."

Nora put the bag on the nightstand and then walked over to Doña Alma and sat on the edge of her bed. "Did you have a good nap?" she asked.

"Very good," Doña Alma answered with a big smile. "Pedro Infante was singing to me."

Nora looked over at the radio and smiled. "I'm sure he was."

She reached for Nora's hand. "How are you, Mija?" she asked. "You look tired."

Nora opened her eyes a little wider. "I'm good, Doña Alma. How about you? Are you feeling okay?"

"Más o menos," she answered with a smile. "I am almost eighty years old, so this is how I am every day now."

"What are you talking about? You have more energy than me."

That made her laugh. "Mentirosa," she said, teasing. "You are a bad liar."

"That reminds me. We have to start planning your birthday party. It's only two months away."

Doña Alma perked up immediately and clapped. "Yes, yes. I already made a list and gave it to Margarita."

Nora tapped her chin. "Let me guess. You want a Black Forest cake."

"Pues, naturalmente."

"And a mariachi trio?"

She wagged a wrinkled finger at her. "No trio. I want the full band. I deserve it, no?"

"Yes, you do," Nora said in between laughs. "Okay, what else do you want?"

"A margarita bar."

"Doña Alma! How do you even know what that is?"

"TV."

"Okay, but you can barely finish one margarita. Why do you want a whole bar?"

Doña Alma gave her a sly smile. "On my birthday, I plan to have two. Anyway, it's just for fun. I never had one before, so why not try it? When you're old like me you aren't as afraid of new things. You should learn from me, Mija."

"I'm always learning from you, Doña Alma," she told her.

"Then listen to me when I tell you that you should

go be with your friends more. Go out on dates. Drink margaritas. You have your whole life ahead of you. Try new things now before you're a vieja like me."

As usual, she was right. Nora knew she was missing out on certain things. This past year had been all about bringing the garden back to life and making some money for the ranch so the Ortegas wouldn't regret giving her a job. That meant working from dawn to dusk six days a week. Her idea of a good Saturday night usually involved Netflix, a bottle of wine, and falling asleep by ten p.m. A couple of the younger women from town had invited her out a few times, but she always had an excuse not to go. So then they'd stopped asking.

Nico and Daniel were probably her only real friends in all of Esperanza.

And Doña Alma, of course. She didn't want to ever disappoint any of them.

"Okay, okay," Nora told her. "I promise to not work so much."

"And have fun," she reminded.

"Yes, and have fun."

They chatted for a few more minutes before Nora went back outside. Before parking the truck at the house, she had dropped off the supplies she'd bought in town at the garden's gate and now she needed to put everything away.

First, Nora stacked the six sacks of soil onto her wheelbarrow and moved them to the side of the greenhouse with the others. Next, she hung her new hoe inside the storage shed and put away the packs of large growing trays next to the smaller ones she kept on a shelf. She looked around the shed and made a mental note to come back later to organize her supplies before her next trip to town. She hated buying things only to discover she already had them but they'd just been hidden by clutter. Nora could just imagine Tía Luz walking into her shed and clutching her chest at the sight of the contained chaos.

Finally, she walked into the greenhouse carrying the PVC tubes and replacement drips she'd purchased to fix the leaky section of the irrigation system. She made it halfway inside before spotting the intruder.

Gabe.

He was planted on the metal folding chair she sometimes used to sit on when she was filling new growing trays. His legs were crossed at the ankles, and his feet rested on a pile of mulch bags. A worn and faded gray baseball cap sat on his lap. That's when she noticed that his eyes were closed. Was he taking a nap?

Nora cleared her throat. He didn't even stir. She cleared it louder.

Nothing.

So she dropped the plastic tubes on the ground in front of her.

Gabe's eyes shot open at the commotion, but he didn't move. It was almost as if he was frozen. And if she didn't know better, she could've sworn he looked frightened.

Guilt washed over her. "Gabe!" Nora shouted. "Gabe!"

It took a few seconds before he seemed to realize she was standing over him.

"Nora? What are you doing here?" He put his legs down and sat upright.

She took a step back. "I should ask you the same question. Cruz is looking for you."

Gabe rubbed his eyes with the edges of his palms and rolled his shoulders. Nora noticed the small wince and the way he kept opening and closing his right hand.

"How long have I been here?"

"I'm not sure," she told him. "When I left for town an hour ago, you weren't here. Are you...hiding?" Nora couldn't help but laugh a little at the thought.

"I'm not hiding," Gabe answered, grabbing the baseball cap off his lap before standing up. He set it on the chair behind him and pulled his phone out of his front jeans pocket. "Shit. I've been here at least forty-five minutes. Cruz is probably pissed."

She didn't dare tell Gabe that Cruz was more disappointed in him than angry. "He was just wondering where you were."

Nora watched as he stretched out his fingers, tightened them into fists, and then stretched them out again. "Are you okay?" she finally asked.

He shook his hands out in front of him. "Yeah. I didn't get much sleep last night, that's all."

Nora had a feeling that it was much more than that. While she didn't know all of the details of his injuries, she did know he could've died in that accident. And she didn't have to be a doctor to see that he was still healing, in more ways than one. "You know, it's probably not a good idea to push your body so hard all at once. No one would blame you if you needed a few days to ease yourself into the work."

"Somehow I don't think that's really true, but that's mighty sweet of you to say," he said with a wry smile.

Nora met his eyes and something flashed behind

them. Something that was very different from sweet. She hated that she couldn't read him at all. That made her nervous.

Nora hesitated for a second. Was she imagining the flirtation in his tone?

Of course she was. "Well, either way, you should go find your brother," she finally said.

"I will. Eventually."

The playfulness in his voice was clear as day now. Yet she still couldn't quite admit to herself that he was teasing her. So much so that she didn't notice how much closer he was standing to her now. She willed herself to not be affected by the proximity of their bodies. "I . . . I really need to get back to work."

"I can help you," he drawled.

"I don't think so."

"Why not? Just tell me what you need."

Heat stung her cheeks. "Excuse me?"

Gabe laughed, and she knew he knew that she was flustered. "Whatever you need me to do, I'll do it, you know, for the garden."

It was clear now that he was just trying to get a rise out of her. She hated that she had fallen so easily into his trap.

He's just playing with you. You're just a distraction so he doesn't have to go back to work.

Whatever charms Gabe was trying to conjure up with that sexy smile of his wasn't going to work on Nora. She wasn't the pushover she used to be. She wasn't that naïve anymore to think that he would actually be interested in her that way. He just liked to tease. That's all this was. Well, she was too busy to fall for his games today. She bit back the urge to say something she'd regret.

"Like I said, I have work to do," she told him.

Instead of leaving, though, he sauntered closer and seemed to study her.

"Why do I get the impression that I make you nervous?" he asked, his tone playful and teasing.

"Annoyed is more like it," she blurted.

That made him smile even wider. "I can work with that."

His brashness startled her. What on earth was he doing? Wasn't this the same guy who once went a whole two weeks one summer without acknowledging her presence?

If she'd been in a bar or at a party and he was some random guy she didn't know, she might have been flattered. But she did know him. Warning bells sounded in her head.

She let out an exasperated breath before bending down to pick up the PVC tubes she'd dropped. "I don't have time to babysit you, Gabe. You want to hide from Cruz? You're going to have to find another spot to do it in." She heard a long sigh.

"I was just trying to lighten things up between us," he said. "I don't think we got off on the right foot the other day. My offer to help was serious."

Nora blew away the strands of her hair that had fallen in her face. "Thanks, but I don't need it."

"Suit yourself."

She watched his work boots as they headed toward the greenhouse's door. Then they stopped.

"Are you mad at me about something else?" he asked as he walked back toward her, still holding the baseball cap in his hand.

Why on earth was Gabe trying to start something

with her? Nora placed the tubes on a nearby work-
table and dusted her hands off before answering him.
"Nope."

"It just seems that, for some reason, I'm the only
Ortega that makes your eye twitch."

She froze. "My eye doesn't twitch."

"Yeah," he affirmed. "It kinda does."

Nora willed her eyes to stay still. "I don't know what
you're talking about."

He grinned. "You're trying very hard right now to
prove me wrong, aren't you?"

"What do you want from me, Gabe? I'm not mad at
you. I just don't have time right now to be your excuse."

That made him stop smiling. "Excuse for what?"

"To not be doing what everyone is expecting you to
be doing. And I'm not talking about helping Tomás
with his new boarder."

He straightened his back in obvious defense. "Now
it's my turn to say that I have no idea what you're
talking about."

She took a breath and debated saying anything else.
Again, what Gabe did or didn't do wasn't supposed to
be any of her business. But staying quiet might really
make more than her eye twitch.

"Look, we both know you've never been a real cowboy. Not like Cruz or the others."

He shifted his stance, and she noticed the clench of
his jaw. "So what?"

"So I don't think it's because you don't have it in
you. I think it's because you don't want to have it in
you. You're trying so hard to prove to them that they're
wrong about you. But maybe, just maybe, you're doing
all of this to prove to yourself that they aren't right."

If she thought he'd be angry at her, she was wrong. It was quite the opposite, in fact. His entire demeanor changed, and he just shrugged off her accusation.

And in a way, that was worse.

"Are you sure you're really a horticulturist?" he drawled. "Seems to me like you are pretty comfortable playing psychologist too."

Nora wasn't quite sure how to respond. She knew it wasn't her place to analyze Gabe's issues. Because, obviously, the man had issues. But she wasn't his family. Hell, she wasn't even his friend. Her opinion didn't matter to him, so why did she feel the need to share it now after all this time?

Her newfound bravado around him melted like a stick of butter on a hot skillet. "I've got a lot do, Gabe. Sounds like you do too, so..."

He nodded and put on his baseball cap. "Alrighty then. Have a good day, Miss Nora."

But instead of leaving, he took a step closer and seemed to study her for a second. "Why do you hate me?" he said, his eyes questioning.

Nora swallowed hard. He was waiting for her to respond, and she couldn't form the words thrashing about inside her head. Why would he say that?

"What? I don't hate you." It was the truth. *Hate* was a strong word, and she reserved it only for a few people in her life. Despite how she felt about Gabe, he was not on that list.

"Then why do I always get the feeling that I'm the last person you want to see or talk to around here?"

"That's not true." Her denial was rushed. Maybe too rushed.

He shook his head and looked at the ground. "Wow. You're a really bad liar. Remind me to play poker with you sometime."

Memories Nora had worked too hard to bury threatened to come roaring back to life. She wasn't ready to talk about the night he'd stood her up or the fact that he obviously didn't even remember doing it.

"It doesn't matter," she said with a shrug. "Just forget about it, okay?"

Judging by the expression on Gabe's face, she knew that wasn't going to happen. "It does matter, obviously," he told her. "Otherwise you wouldn't be looking at me the way you are now."

Nora bristled at his incessant questioning and observations. "Look, I don't hate you. I just...I just don't understand you."

His head shot back up in surprise. "What's that supposed to mean?" he asked, defensively drawing his shoulders back.

Why did Gabe always need to challenge everything she said? "It means that I don't know how to act around you because I don't know you."

He scoffed. "What are you talking about? You've known me since I was a kid."

"Maybe I've been around you that long, but that doesn't necessarily mean that I know you or you know me."

"We could fix that," he said, offering her a cheesy smile.

Nora hesitated. "Why?" she asked him.

He met her eyes with an intense gaze, as if he was trying to figure her out like a puzzle. "Why not?"

Because I don't trust you.

Because you've hurt me before.
Because I don't trust myself.

She wasn't about to admit any of those things to Gabe, of course. Nora averted her eyes so they couldn't spill her secrets.

"I need to get back to work," she told him instead.

This time she didn't wait for him to try to distract her. She turned on her heel and walked as fast as she could away from Gabe and his questions.

Later that night, even when she was safely tucked into her bed, Nora couldn't shake the feeling that she hadn't really escaped. Gabe had let her go. This time.

And next time, he was going to want answers.

Chapter Five

The smaller the town, the quicker the chisme spread.

Esperanza had fewer than two thousand residents. So that meant that the gossip mill was always working overtime. And what better topic than the return of Gabe Ortega?

Gabe knew this would be the case, and it was confirmed as he, Daniel, and their dad walked through Lina's Diner to their table. Sure, people waved and nodded in their direction. But he suspected those same people would be whispering and chatting about him as soon as he took a seat.

Gabe had been back for nearly a week, and it was starting to feel like he'd never left. As they'd walked down Center Street from their truck to the diner, he took stock of the fact that there were only a handful of new storefronts sprinkled in between businesses that had been there since he was a kid. This was the bustling hub of Esperanza. In the span of two blocks, you could buy your groceries, pick up your feed order, go the dentist, stop for a cocktail, and order your dinner to go.

When they were kids, Gabe and his brothers would

beg for a couple of dollars from their mom and then hitch a ride with one of the ranch hands headed to town. As a boy, Gabe could spend hours just walking from one end of Main Street to the other. Everything he ever needed could be found in the little stretch of road. And if it was a Saturday? There was a good chance he'd run into all of his friends there, doing exactly what he was doing.

Just hanging out.

It wasn't until he was old enough to drive that he and his brothers began visiting nearby towns. They would be amazed at some of the newer stores they had in those places, especially the big chain movie theater over in Buellton. It was big news when a mall opened up less than twenty miles away. That was when Gabe began to realize that there was more to the world than one main street. And he was determined to see and experience as much of it as he could.

Because much like the diner they were sitting in, everything and everyone in Esperanza stayed pretty much the same. No wonder he'd been itching to leave as soon as he graduated. Even now he couldn't help but wonder what he had seen in this small town in the first place.

"Place hasn't changed a bit," he observed out loud as he opened up the diner's menu.

"Sure it has," Daniel said. "They have chicken parmigiana now."

"Well, then. That *is* big news," Gabe said. His brother rolled his eyes, but his sarcasm was lost on his dad, of course.

When the waitress came over a few minutes later, he ordered his go-to: a cheeseburger, onion rings, and a regular Coke. Daniel ordered the same. His dad mixed things up a bit and asked for a turkey melt instead of his usual pastrami sandwich.

He still was trying to figure out how he'd been roped in by Daniel to join them for lunch. Gabe had gotten up at the crack of dawn, had breakfast, and began what had become his morning routine. First, he had to help feed the cows. That meant driving while Cruz pushed bales of hay from the bed of the truck onto the grazing field. Next, he and Daniel had taken a UTV out to the south perimeter fence to fix a few posts that were starting to lean. That took up most of his morning. So lunch in town meant lunch off the ranch and away from Cruz. It was obvious that it hadn't been his dad's idea based on the look of surprise on his dad's face when he got into the truck. Their conversations the past week had totaled up to probably only a dozen or so sentences. And they had all been about what Gabe needed to do, where Gabe needed to go, and what Gabe should do next time.

He had hoped that with Daniel there to be a buffer, lunch would be easy. Even enjoyable.

Of course, it was turning out to be as tense as always. Again, some things never changed.

Well, except for Nora.

She'd been an unexpected, and pleasant, surprise. He hadn't seen her again since that day in the greenhouse. Yesterday, he'd even stopped by to take a quick break from his to-do list. There was something so calm about the place. Maybe it was all of the oxygen in the air, but all Gabe had to do was take a few deep breaths and the cramps in his hand and shoulder muscles seemed to ease. He stayed for about fifteen minutes before Cruz had texted to meet him in the barn, and he'd left without seeing Nora. Only later did he let himself question why he'd felt a sense of disappointment. What the hell was happening?

Seeing Nora again all grown up had stirred up some strange new feelings in him. First, he chalked it up to a familiar fondness—after all, they'd basically grown up together. But he'd never been as close to her as the others. So that couldn't be it. What were the odds that he'd find her attractive after all these years?

It was very inconvenient to say the least.

Especially since it was obvious she didn't think very highly of him—or at all for that matter. Gabe had never been the type of guy to pursue a woman who didn't want to be pursued. Not that he had any intention of pursuing Nora at all. No, he was just curious. That was it.

It really was.

Satisfied with his own explanation, Gabe turned his attention back to Daniel and their dad, who was studying something on his phone.

"What are you reading?" Daniel asked before taking a drink of his Coke.

Their dad took off his glasses and put his phone on the table. "Just some emails," he answered, and rubbed his eyes.

That's when Gabe noticed how much older his dad looked. But it wasn't just the fact that his full beard was more silver than black now. His face, weathered by the California sun for decades, was thinner—more gaunt. His usually plump cheeks had been replaced by saggy wrinkles, almost like a deflated balloon. To Gabe, his dad had aged more in the last two years than he'd ever seen.

And he looked tired. Exhausted even.

A worm of guilt weaved its way through Gabe's gut as he wondered how much he was to blame for his dad's transformation. Not wanting to think about it any longer, he dismissed the troubling thoughts and tried to focus on other things.

"I still can't believe you have a smartphone," Gabe said pointing to the phone on the table. With no food to occupy his mouth, he figured he should at least try some small talk.

Their dad shrugged. "It's not that smart. If it was, that pinche phone would answer all those emails for me."

Gabe laughed at his dad's cursing. Not just because it was funny, but because it was almost comforting. Despite his outward appearance, his dad was still his dad.

Even if they couldn't really talk to each other anymore.

Their food came less than ten minutes later. But it wasn't the waitress who delivered it.

"Lina!" Gabe said, and stood up to hug the older woman after she set down their plates on the table. "It's so nice to see you."

She hugged him tight and then patted him on the cheek. "You too, Mijo. I heard you were here, so, of course I must come to see you myself."

"If you had come to the carne asada, you would have seen him already," Santiago said. "But I guess you were winning too much in Las Vegas, verdad?"

"Don't start with me, Viejo," Lina told his dad.

"Viejo? You're older than me, Mujer."

"Only by six months."

Gabe couldn't help but smile at the exchange between the two. Lina and her husband, Carlos, were two of his parents' oldest friends. And he'd grown up with their son and daughter.

"How are Omar and Mia?" he asked Lina.

Her face immediately brightened. "Wonderful. Omar and his wife visited last month and let us know they're going to have a baby!"

"Felicidades," he said, even though he couldn't quite believe that the guy who once passed out drunk in the middle of the high school's field was going to be a dad.

"And Mia is still living in New York. No husband yet, but she did get a new dog."

That made him smile again. Typical Mia. Sometimes he still couldn't believe she'd once been Tomás's girlfriend. Gabe always thought they were complete opposites, but somehow they had made it work. At least until Mia decided she wanted to go to college in New York. Both families were devastated. He wouldn't have been surprised if their parents had already been planning a wedding on their own.

"So, Gabe. How has it been being back at the ranch?"

He shrugged. "So far so good. I mean, Cruz hasn't fired me yet."

"And he hasn't quit," his dad said under his breath.

Irritation pricked the back of his neck. "Yet," Gabe said back.

"That's what you say now, but we all know you like to change your mind without telling anyone," his dad replied.

He opened his mouth to respond, but then Daniel laughed out loud—too loud. "No one is getting fired or quitting," he said, in an obvious attempt to defuse any tension.

Lina clapped. "Qué bueno! It makes me so happy to know that the Ortega boys are back together again and taking care of Rancho Lindo."

Gabe tightened his grip on his glass and forced himself to smile.

"Okay, well, I'll let you start eating before everything gets cold. I'm going to tell Carlos that we should stop by this weekend. If that's okay?"

His dad answered for them. "Sí, como no. You are always welcome. Just call Margarita to let her know when."

After Lina walked away, his dad started eating. But Gabe wasn't ready for his burger just yet.

"Why did you tell her that?" Gabe asked his dad in a low voice.

"Tell her what? They are always welcome to visit."

"No, not that. Why did you tell her that I change my mind without telling people?"

"Because it's true, no?"

Uneasiness spread through him. He wasn't ready to have this conversation. Not yet. Not here. "Are you really going to bring that up right now? I've only been back for a week, Dad."

"Y qué? It's going to be the same the week after that. I see that your heart isn't in it, Gabriel."

Daniel interrupted. "Dad, Gabe's shoulder and hand aren't even a hundred percent. He still needs time to heal. He can't make any decisions about staying permanently yet."

"It's true. Maybe I'll never be as strong as I used to be."

Their dad scoffed. "No manches."

"Dad..."

"You always have an excuse. Well, I don't need excuses. I need to know that I can rely on one of my sons to run Rancho Lindo."

"What are you talking about? Cruz is basically running the ranch already."

"No," his dad said firmly, shaking his head. "He works the ranch. There's a difference. Maybe if you paid attention once in a while, you'd know that."

"I really don't—" he started to say.

"It's time for you to decide if Rancho Lindo is going to be your home again," his dad interrupted. "You're not getting any younger. It's time to be a man and start the next chapter of your life."

"Oh yeah, and what's that?"

"Pues, finding a wife and having babies, of course. Your mother is ready to be an abuelita. She keeps putting pinche dresses and pyamas on Princesa, la probrecita."

Gabe was about to argue that not only was he not ready to settle down with a wife, but he still wasn't ready to commit to the ranch either. Then he noticed his dad's somber eyes and serious expression. And if he didn't know better, Gabe would've sworn that his chin was trembling.

Before he could analyze him any more, his dad abruptly stood up. He pulled a stack of cash from his pocket and tossed the bills next to Daniel's plate. "Tell Lina I'll take my food to go. I need stop at the general store. I'll meet you back at the truck."

When they were alone, Daniel shook his head. "Good one, Gabe."

"What the hell did I do? It's not my fault he's so stubborn."

His brother let out a bitter laugh. "Yeah, he's the stubborn one."

Gabe picked up a french fry and gnawed on it. "I don't get it. Why is all of this on me? Last I checked, we had three other brothers who could help Cruz."

Daniel swallowed the bite of his cheeseburger. "We each have an area of the ranch that we're good at. But, sure, we could be doing better. And obviously Dad thinks that by having you here, things will improve. You know why."

Gabe sank into the booth. For as long as he could remember, he was told stories about how four generations of Ortega brothers had owned and worked the land of Rancho Lindo. It was always expected that the fifth would carry on the tradition. Especially since his dad didn't have that with his own brother.

Tío Jesus had been his dad's younger and only brother. Gabe had few memories of the man since he'd died in a car accident when Gabe was only six. Yet, his dad made sure that his sons never forgot about him.

"It was my papá's dream for me and Jesus to run the ranch together," his dad would tell them. "And when that couldn't happen, then it was his dream for me and my sons to take over. Your abuelo would have been so happy and proud to see the five of you continue our family's legacy. It was meant to be."

Later that afternoon as he groomed the stable's horses, Gabe thought about his younger brothers and whether he could convince one of them to step up and take on more responsibility. The tricky part was going to be doing it in a way that made it seem like it was their idea and not his. That way some of the guilt he was feeling would go away.

He blamed Nora for this new conscious of sorts. Ever since the impromptu therapy session in the greenhouse, it was as if she was always in his ear now judging every thought he had about finding another job opportunity. Last night, he'd left a message for a buddy of his who had mentioned a few months ago that there might be a possible position opening up with his company in Seattle. But as soon as he'd hung up the phone, he'd immediately thought of her. That led to a sting of guilt for going through with his plans to leave.

Pleasant surprise or not, Gabe didn't need the distraction. Besides, the woman clearly didn't like him, so why should he care about her opinions?

Gabe had just finished stacking a few hay bales when the click-clacks of multiple hooves and paws approached the stable.

He watched as Nico and Daniel walked leisurely with their horses and figured they were done for the day. Oreo and Shadow, after spotting Gabe, charged full speed ahead, nearly knocking him over as usual. The dogs were expert cattle herders. But he sometimes wondered if they believed that humans also needed a nudge here and there.

"Good boys," he told them anyway, scratching the tops of their heads. "You did such a good job today."

"How would you know?" Nico asked as he entered the stable.

"Because they always do a good job," Gabe answered.

Daniel was already leading his horse into the stable too when he yelled over at Nico, "You can't argue with that logic, dude."

Nico walked over and squatted next to the dogs. "You guys did do a great job today." He was immediately rewarded with licks and heavy panting.

"Whatever," Gabe said, pretending to be annoyed.

"Don't worry, brother," Daniel said. "You can still be Princesa's favorite."

The mention of his minuscule tormenter made him scowl. "Yeah, that firulais loves me so much that she peed in my room the other day," he told them.

That made Daniel and Nico break out in laughter. "It's actually kind of impressive the amount of loathing she carries for you in that tiny body," Nico said.

"I think she's decided to tolerate me," he explained. "She still growls when I try to pick her up, but at least I don't think she'll bite my face off when I'm asleep anymore. At least, I hope she won't."

Daniel's attention turned to the dogs of the ranch that loved everyone and never held any grudges. "I'm going to take Oreo and Shadow up to the house to get them some water and their after-work treats. Nico, you want to take care of the horses this time?"

"No problem," Nico replied.

"I'll stay and help too," Gabe added. Without Daniel around, he could finally talk to Nico about the assistant ranch manager position. He needed to find out where everyone's head was at. If someone else wanted the job, then the pressure would be off him for good, and he could be free to do what he wanted. Whatever that was.

After Gabe and Nico removed the saddles and bridles from the horses, they checked each one for any sores or cuts. Then they led them outside into the corral and watched as they began to drink from the large water trough.

"So Cruz mentioned you guys are going to do the fall roundup next week," Gabe said, leaning against the rails.

Nico let out a long sigh. "Yeah. It's that time again."

Rancho Lindo usually held a few roundups a year, and they always involved a lot of planning and a lot of extra bodies. The group used horses and UTVs to move the herd from one grazing pasture to another one usually on the opposite side of the property. Nico and Daniel were the lead riders, and that meant they were going to be the ones calling the shots that day.

"I guess Dad wants me to help out," Gabe explained. "I think I was sixteen the last time I did one of those."

"I remember," Nico said. "We couldn't find you for hours because you couldn't figure out how to get that one calf to follow you."

Gabe nodded and sighed. "That's right. Then you came along and got her going as if it was nothing. You knew what you were doing even back then."

"Only because I'd already been doing it for years," Nico said. "But you knew that, so what are you really trying to get at, Gabe?"

He could always count on Nico to get straight to the point. "Okay, you're right. I'm just trying to figure out some stuff. And I thought I'd ask you your thoughts."

Nico straightened. "About you being number two?"

"Yeah. What do you think?"

Nico looked out into the distance. "Isn't that what Dad wants?" he asked Gabe. "What he's always wanted?"

"I guess. But I'm wondering why you're not throwing

your hat in the ring. Livestock is the bread and butter of the ranch, and that's your specialty. It doesn't make any sense why you wouldn't be taking on more responsibility and making some of the big decisions around here."

Nico shrugged. "Because I don't want to do any of that. In case you've forgotten, I'm not exactly an assistant kind of guy."

He hadn't forgotten. Although Nico and Daniel were basically two peas in a pod, Nico was the head-strong one. He liked doing things his own way and on his own terms. Like the time he decided at fifteen that he was going to enter a nearby town's bull riding con-test and broke two ribs in the process. Or when, a few years back, his mom told Gabe that Nico had brought home an extra steer from auction because he'd felt bad that no one else had bid on it.

Nico was the most impulsive of them all. Sometimes that kind of attitude paid off. And sometimes it landed you in the hospital.

Gabe was ready to try another angle to convince him, but apparently Nico wasn't done talking. "But," Nico added, "since you're asking, I think we're doing just fine without an assistant ranch manager. No need to fix anything if it ain't broke."

"I'm not so sure about that," Gabe said. "I know I've only been back a few weeks, but even I can see there are some problems."

"And you think you can run the ranch better than the rest of us?" Nico said, his expression hardening.

There was that attitude again. Nico was clearly bothered, and Gabe was tired of his digs. "All right, little brother," Gabe said, raising his hands. "Let it all out. It's clear you don't want the job, and you don't want me to have it either. But you've been giving me a hard time since I got back. You're obviously pissed about something, so stop acting like a moody middle schooler and just spit it out already."

Nico took off his hat and wiped his brow. Then he pointed the hat at Gabe. "Being a rancher isn't a hat that you can take off and on when you feel like it. I'm glad that you're back and getting a newfound appreciation for everything that goes on here. That still doesn't mean you know shit about what it takes to run Rancho Lindo."

Gabe held up his hands again. "Whoa. I'm not saying I do, Nico. But if no one else is going to step up, then maybe it needs to be me." Gabe surprised himself with that observation. He blamed his damn ego. Why was it that whenever someone told him he couldn't do something, then he automatically wanted to prove them wrong?

Nico put his hat back on and began pacing back and forth in front of Gabe. "It's just like you to think that you can do whatever you want, whenever you want. I'm sure you were one hell of a soldier over there. But you were kind of a bastard over here."

He grimaced. "What are you talking about, Nico?"

"I may have been only fourteen, but I understood perfectly just how much you loathed being around us. The minute you turned eighteen, your foot was out the door. And suddenly, none of us were good enough. Our home wasn't good enough. Our future lives were somehow less than what you wanted for yourself. How was that supposed to make us feel, Gabe? Sure, I was just a kid at the time. But even I know how bad you had disrespected Dad, Cruz, Chucho, and every single person who had been working their asses off to give you the opportunities they never had. And now you think you deserve to run this place? Wow."

Gabe stood speechless. Not because he was mad at Nico for saying all of that. But because every harsh word was true.

He'd been consumed with the idea that there was something better for him out in the world. When all he really had wanted was something different. He cringed thinking of all the times he'd told his dad as a teenager that the work his dad had done his entire life didn't mean anything.

Shame made him bow his head and stare at the dirt under his shoes. "I know I've made some mistakes, Nico. Doesn't mean I don't care about Rancho Lindo. Or this family."

"Yeah, well, sorry if it's going to take more than your words to convince me."

"You sound like Nora," Gabe scoffed.

"Really?" Nico asked as he walked over to the horses and collected their leads.

"Maybe I'm imagining it, but I don't think she likes me that much," Gabe admitted.

"You're not imagining it."

Nico's matter-of-fact affirmation took him by surprise. His brother obviously knew something he didn't. "Gee, thanks. So what should I do about it?"

"Nothing," Nico said with a shrug. "Nora doesn't need you inserting yourself into her work or her life. If I were you, I'd stay away from her."

"And why is that?" Gabe said defensively.

"Because we both know you have no plans to do anything except disappear on her. Just like you did before."

Chapter Six

Nora walked outside the main house's back door and was immediately greeted by a blaze of heat. It was as if Mother Nature had cranked up her thermostat to the highest setting in just the fifteen minutes or so she'd been inside. The arrival of September the day before may have signaled that fall was on its way. But the lingering summer temps hadn't received the memo.

With one hand, Nora adjusted her straw cowboy hat to make sure her face was as protected as possible from the sun's unforgivable rays. Then, with the other hand, Nora gripped the metal handle of the five-gallon bucket and began her short walk back to the garden.

As she got closer, she saw someone coming out of the greenhouse. It took her a few seconds to realize it was Gabe.

He spotted her almost at the same time and waved. For a moment, she considered pretending she hadn't seen him and changing direction. But with her luck, he'd probably follow her.

She sighed and headed toward him.

"Have a good nap?" she asked when she met him at the entrance to the greenhouse.

At first Gabe raised his eyebrows in confusion. Then he seemed to understand her question. "Uh, no. I mean I wasn't taking a nap. I stopped by to talk to you. Do you have a few minutes?"

Nora thought about the bucket she was holding full of vegetable and fruit scraps destined for the compost pile behind the greenhouse. She wanted to tell Gabe that she didn't have even one minute for him. Instead, she set the bucket on the ground. "Sure. What's up?"

He took a deep breath. His squared shoulders and pressed lips told her that whatever he was going to say was serious. Uneasiness washed through her. "Everything okay?" she said slowly.

"I think I know the reason why you're mad at me and I wanted to clear the air between us."

"I'm not mad—"

"Please let me finish," he said softly.

She nodded and closed her mouth.

"I replayed our conversation that first day and at the party in my mind over and over again and I thought maybe it was because I hadn't recognized you. But I couldn't shake the feeling that it went deeper than that. And I began to think that maybe it was because of something that had happened between us in the past. And that's when I realized. That's when I remembered what I had done. I know I owe you an apology, Nora."

Panic butterflies zoomed inside her stomach.

He knew.

He remembered.

And now he wanted to talk about it.

"Gabe..." she began.

"I'm sorry," he said, interrupting her, "I'm sorry I stood you up on the night of the Founder's Dance."

Memories of that weekend all those years ago came rushing back. It had been her last one on the ranch for the summer before her junior year in high school. That Friday had been pretty uneventful for the most part. Until she'd agreed to help Tía Luz and Doña Alma peel peaches for the pies they were making for the Founder's Day barbecue later that day. She'd already done a dozen or so when Nico and Daniel had come back from town and wanted to show their abuelita the new dress shirts and ties they'd bought for the upcoming dance. The Founder's Day dance was always held on the first Saturday night of August. It was held at the community center and most of the town's teens usually attended. She already knew that Nico and Daniel were planning to go with the Sampson twins. Tomás was taking his girlfriend Mia. Cruz was out of town with his dad at some cattle auction. She'd assumed Gabe was going to go with one of three girls he'd been hanging out with that summer. As usual, Nora had no plans to attend.

"Por qué," Doña Alma asked when Nora had told her exactly that.

"I don't dance," she'd replied. "Besides, nobody asked me."

Not that there were many options for dates at that time. Since Nora didn't go to school in Esperanza, her social circle was basically limited to the ranch. Nico and Daniel always invited her to hang out and sometimes Nora agreed. But she definitely didn't want to be a fifth wheel and tag along with them and their dates to the dance.

She thought the matter was dropped until Gabe walked into the kitchen a few minutes later. To her horror, Doña Alma asked him if he was going to the dance.

"I wasn't planning on it," he'd said in a bored tone before stealing one of the unpeeled peaches and chomping down.

Nora glanced at the older woman and could see the wheels turning. She kept shaking her head in hopes that Doña Alma wouldn't do what Nora thought she was going to do. But it didn't work. Because right then and there, Nora died.

"You should take Honora to the dance."

The words had hung in the air, cutting off the oxygen to Nora's lungs. At least that's what it had felt like. She'd had a crush on Gabe Ortega ever since the summer before when he'd casually asked one day what book she'd been reading and then told her that he had actually already read it. He'd spent a good ten minutes talking with her about it. Then he'd run upstairs to his bedroom and brought her back another book that he thought she would like. That had been the most he'd ever talked to her in the past couple of years, but it was enough for her to see him in a new light. An attractive light. An always-had-butterflies-in-her-stomach-when-she-saw-him kind of light. And now Doña Alma was telling him to take her out on a date.

It was almost too good to be true.

That's why she'd expected him to make up some excuse about why he couldn't. And a small part of her wanted him to say no. But to her shock, he looked over at her and then back at his abuelita and said, "Sure. Why not?"

After that, the rest of Friday and Saturday morning had felt like a dream. Her tía had taken her shopping for a pretty new dress and Mia, Tomás's girlfriend, had gone with her to the town's beauty salon so they could get their hair and nails done.

By six p.m. that Saturday night, Nora was primped and ready for her date with Gabe.

By six thirty p.m., she was still primped, but her nerves nearly made her bite her newly polished nails.

By seven p.m., her tía Luz was on the phone whispering about what to do with her.

Finally, at seven thirty p.m., there was a knock on the cottage's door. It wasn't him. It was Tomás and Mia with the news no one had expected.

Gabe was gone.

A few days later, she'd learned that he'd left to enlist in the army. And while she knew she was the last person who deserved a goodbye or an apology from him, it still would've been nice to get a phone call or letter. The fact he barely remembered her pretty much explained why she didn't receive either. Maybe Gabe had briefly been her friend when they were kids. But she was nothing to him now. It didn't matter that he was back at Rancho Lindo. Nothing had really changed.

"I do have to apologize because you didn't deserve that," she heard Gabe say.

If there was a feeling ten times worse than plain old embarrassment, then that's what Nora was experiencing. There was a time when she would've given anything to have Gabe say he was sorry for that night. All she ever wanted was to know that she had mattered to him. It was ridiculous to hope for that and she realized that now. She was an absolute fool to want what was happening between them in this moment. Because this was the worst.

Instead of melting into a puddle of mortification, though, Nora dug deep to keep her expression blank and unaffected. "I accept your apology. Now, if you'll excuse me, I have lots to do today," she said, picking up the bucket.

"Wait. Don't you want to hear why I never showed to pick you up for the dance?"

Nora sighed. "I do know. You ran away to the army that night."

He raised his eyebrows at her simplistic explanation. "Well, technically I enlisted the following Monday."

"Sure," she said with an uncontrollable roll of her eyes. "Okay. Is that all?"

"Can I at least explain what happened?"

If Nora was uncomfortable by the conversation before, now she was just irritated. Whatever explanation he wanted to give had nothing to do with trying to make her understand. He just wanted to assuage his old guilt.

Her current curiosity, however, wouldn't let her walk away just yet. She put down the bucket and folded her arms across her chest. "Fine. Go ahead."

Gabe pulled a bandana from the back pocket of his jeans and wiped off his forehead. It gave her a small sense of satisfaction to think he was sweating because of her and not because of the relentless heat.

"That Saturday I was basically on my own," he began. "Mom and Abuelita had left to go to a birthday party and Dad and Cruz were still on their trip up north. My brothers were at the Wilsons' property helping out with some sort of emergency—I don't remember exactly. So that left me to deal with everything else on the ranch that afternoon."

Even though she still didn't think it mattered anymore, Nora nodded for him to continue with the rest of his story.

Gabe did just that. "I had just come inside from wrangling a runaway heifer. I was covered in mud and manure and I was pretty pissed off. I was about to go clean up when my dad came storming down the stairs waving a brochure in the air. He and Cruz had come home early from their trip and he had brought me a new utility knife. My dad was putting it on top of my dresser when I guess he saw the brochure. It was for the army. I had gone with my buddy the day before to the recruitment office. Funny thing was, at that point, I hadn't really considered enlisting. I'd just taken the brochure to shut the recruiter up."

"Did you enlist just to shut him up too?" She couldn't help the sarcasm.

He ignored it and went on with his story. "Anyway, my dad was furious. I tried to explain to him that I wasn't really considering it but he wouldn't listen. And the more he yelled, the more I realized that maybe the army was exactly what I needed."

"How so?"

Gabe shrugged and kicked at the dirt in front of him. "Maybe it was a way to prove to Cruz and my dad that I could do something on my own, I guess. Anyway, I had never seen my dad so angry. He kept yelling in Spanish, and it was hard for me to understand what he was saying. So I just got more angry. But then he said in English, "How can you think that you can be a soldier when you can't even remember to clean up the stalls when I ask you to?"

"He just didn't want you to leave," Nora replied.

Gabe shrugged. "Except that's exactly what he told me to do next."

That made her wince as if she'd heard the words herself that day. The pain of reliving that memory was etched all over Gabe's face. "He was just hurt. I'm sure he didn't mean it," she said, trying to defend Señor Ortega.

"Either way, it didn't matter what he meant or didn't mean. Because in that moment I decided that I was never going to be who he wanted me to be. I ran upstairs, took a shower, and called my buddy to pick me up at the front gate. By the time I came back home a few days later, they couldn't do anything about it. I'd signed the contract. Then, after a few weeks, I left for basic training in South Carolina, and that was it."

"Fine," she said, not ready to let him off the hook just yet. "I get it. You left that night without a word because you were angry. But what about the next day? Or the next one after that?"

"I'm sorry I didn't realize how important the dance was to you."

"I didn't care about the stupid dance," she yelled, and met his eyes, not even trying anymore to hide the hurt. "You made me feel like a fool, Gabe. And it just would've been nice at some point for you to tell me that you didn't do it on purpose."

His eyes widened in shock. "What? I would never do something like that to you on purpose. And I guess I never called or wrote because I figured you wouldn't care if you ever heard from me again."

The rational side of her brain told her it was under-standable. After all, she wasn't the only one he didn't say goodbye to. And on the list of people who deserved one, she wasn't even in the top seven. Still, she couldn't shake the feeling of rejection that lingered after all these years. Gabe wasn't the first man who had left her waiting with only a broken promise to remember him by. Some people didn't deserve second chances and sometimes apologies were just words. They didn't mean or change anything. She'd learned that the hard way.

He walked closer to her and searched her eyes. "I know I hurt you back then and I know why I'm not your favorite person now. All I can say is that I'm sorry and that I hope you can forgive me one day."

Gabe seemed sincere. And if she was being fair, his explanation did make sense. She just wished he'd told her that night. She would've understood. Or she would've at least tried to. But he never gave her that chance.

Just like her dad.

It had been exhausting trying to stay mad at Gabe for something that happened so long ago. It didn't matter if he was staying or leaving; he was back for now and she needed to figure out a way to be around him. But as far as she was concerned, her opinion of Gabe Ortega was exactly the same as it was before.

"Well, like I said, I have a lot of stuff to do today," she told him, moving her hands to her hips.

"Why does it feel like you're still mad at me?"

"I'm not mad at you. Yes, I was hurt that night, but it was a long time ago. I already said I accepted your apology, didn't I? I don't know what else you want from me."

Gabe shrugged. "I guess I want us to be friends."

"You do?" she asked, and crossed her arms over her chest.

He laughed. "Why do you sound so shocked? I'm not some monster, Nora. I can be friendly when I want to."

"Of course you can," she said. "I just never thought you'd want to be friendly with me."

"Because?" he asked.

"Because you weren't before. Besides, why is it so important to you for us to be friends? You barely remembered who I was."

"That's not true. I just didn't recognize you, that's all."

"Same difference."

"It's not. It's been over twelve years since the last time I saw you, Nora. You were a teenager. Now you're a grown woman. A beautiful grown woman. And I never forgot about you. How could I?"

She shrugged. "Because it seems like you've forgotten lots of things, Gabe."

Nora was surprised when he seemed to agree. "Maybe. I'll be the first to admit that I've made lots of mistakes. Joining the army wasn't one of them. But how I went about it is definitely one of my biggest. I really am sorry I hurt you that night."

"I wasn't the only one you hurt." Nora took a deep breath and added, "The reason I'm struggling to believe you is because I'm worried you're going to hurt them again."

"Who?" Gabe asked.

"Your family."

He winced. Actually winced. "I'd never hurt my family."

She took a long breath and decided to tell him what he needed to hear. "I was here the day that they got the call about your accident. I've never seen your dad look so pale. Your mom and abuelita couldn't stop crying. All they wanted was to see you, to hop on a plane and be at your bedside. But they couldn't and that almost killed them."

His eyes flickered with pain. "That wasn't my fault."

"I know it wasn't, Gabe," she said softly. "And I know that eventually your mom and dad were able to visit you when you were back in the States. My point is that I was also here the day you called to let them know you were retiring from the army and coming home. It was night and day. I've never seen your mom so happy. All of them were."

"You really care about them, don't you?" he asked.

Nora nodded fervently. "I do."

Gabe finally seemed to understand. "I know I have a lot to make up for. And I'm going to do everything I can to make things right... with all of you."

She wanted to believe him, but her heart wouldn't let her. Old wounds and even older defenses made it near impossible to trust his words.

"You can't be something you're not, Gabe. No matter how much you want it to be true."

He met her eyes and probably saw her judgment and doubts. Instead of turning away, he took a step a closer as if to face them head-on.

"I'm going to prove you wrong. Just wait and see."

The intensity of his gaze made her inhale a sharp breath. And it wasn't until he was long gone that Nora remembered to let it go.

Chapter Seven

So are you going to get that dish for me today or do I have to wait until after I'm dead and buried?"

Gabe heard his mother's voice and remembered he was standing in the middle of the kitchen. Whatever thoughts that had been distracting him from what he'd been doing disappeared.

"Oh yeah, sorry about that," he said, and reached into the cupboard to bring down his mom's glass lasagna dish. "Here you go, Mom."

Princesa, who was lying under one of the counter's stools, snarled her annoyance as if she'd been the one waiting on Gabe. Although the teeny dictator still refused to allow him to pet her or even walk past her, she tolerated his presence when his mom was around. That meant the hems of his jeans were safe for now and Gabe took that as progress.

Margarita Ortega took the dish from her son's hands and shook her head. "What's gotten into you lately? It's like I'm talking to myself these days." She went to check on the ground turkey and marinara sauce mixture simmering on the stove.

"I guess I'm just a little tired. Cruz is a machine and expects everyone else to be just like him." That was the truth, but it wasn't the only reason why Gabe seemed off.

It had been two weeks since he had apologized to Nora. Since then, her attitude toward him hadn't really changed. And the more she seemed to not want to be around him, the more he wanted to be around her.

The other day he even asked if she wanted him to help her in the greenhouse for a few hours. She declined. Immediately.

His brothers, however, were a different story. They didn't think twice about giving him more stuff to do when he asked. Gabe knew he had a lot to make up for. And if his penance was shoveling manure every single day, then so be it.

That didn't mean he'd given up on looking for other opportunities. He had reached out to another friend a few days ago. But the position he had open needed certain certifications that Gabe didn't have. The well of contacts he'd been counting on was starting to run dry. He had a few more feelers out and hoped he could get at least an interview from one of them.

In the meantime, he would keep busy doing what he needed to around the ranch and also keep trying to figure out if one of the brothers wanted the assistant manager position instead.

His mom interrupted his thoughts and asked him to bring her the bowl of mozzarella she'd already grated. He did as she asked and then watched as his mom started assembling the cooked pasta strips inside the dish.

And just like always, his mom decided he was too

quiet. "How's your shoulder and your hand?" she asked after a few minutes. "I thought you were going to find a physical therapist in Santa Barbara?"

"I was. But it's not like I have a lot of free time."

"Your health is more important, Gabe. Your dad and Cruz will understand that. I'm going to call Doctor Allende in the morning and see if he can give us some names, okay?"

"Who's Doctor Allende? What happened to Doctor Griffin? Did he finally retire?" he asked.

His mom cleared her throat and went back to stir the meat and sauce. "No, Doctor Griffin is still around. Doctor Allende is your dad's doctor in Santa Barbara. Now that he's, that we're, both older, we just thought it would be a good idea to start seeing someone who was out there so we could do our lab work and regular tests all at the same time, instead of making extra trips. That's why I think he would know some good physical therapists over there."

"Okay. Thanks."

"How's it going with your dad?"

Gabe shrugged. "The same, I guess. He tells me to do something and then tells me I did it wrong."

She let out a long sigh. "You two need to get over your issues."

"Easier said than done, Mom. You know that."

"All I know is that both of you are burros."

Gabe arched his eyebrows in amused surprise. "Donkeys? Did you just call us jackasses?"

Her eyes grew wide. "No, I did not. I was saying you both are stubborn."

Gabe roared with laughter. "That's mules, Mom. Mules are stubborn. Donkeys are jackasses."

She slapped his arm. "Stop saying *asses*."

He couldn't stop laughing and made a note to tell the story to his brothers later. To his surprise, his mom cracked a smile herself. When he finally quieted down, she apologized for hitting him.

"Anyway," she continued. "Can you please make an effort to talk with your dad? It's hard for him to show his feelings, but I know he's happy that you're home."

"Are you sure about that?"

"Of course! You are his son. He loves you."

"Sure, he just doesn't like me that much."

"Cállate! Don't you ever say that again!"

Gabe flinched even though this time she didn't touch him. His mom hardly ever raised her voice. Why was she so angry? "Okay," he said, raising his hands in surrender. "Okay. I won't say that again. I'm sorry, Mom."

That's when he noticed the tears and her trembling lips. He enveloped her in his arms. "I'm sorry, Mom," Gabe repeated.

She didn't say anything right away. Instead, he heard only sniffles. That let him know that she was definitely crying. His heart sank. He hated when his mom was sad.

They stood there in the middle of the kitchen hugging for a few minutes. Finally, his mom pulled away. She didn't look at him and instead walked over to get a paper towel to dry her face and wipe her nose.

"Are you okay?" he finally asked.

She took a deep breath and nodded. "Yes. Thank you."

"I didn't mean to make you cry, Mom. I'm sorry."

His mom threw away the paper towel and went back

to sit down. "I know, Mijo. I don't know why I started crying. I just want everyone in my family to be happy. I don't like it when there are problems."

He grabbed her hand. "I'll try to talk to Dad. I promise."

Her face brightened and she finally smiled. "I appreciate that. He'll come around sooner or later. Don't give up on him. Por favor."

Her voice was still thick with emotion, so he didn't want to press her with more questions. "I won't. I promise. You know I will always do what you say, Mom. Because you're the boss," he said with a shrug.

"Only when Abuelita's not here."

Gabe laughed and began to wash his hands at the sink so he could help her fix the lasagna. When it was finally in the oven, they sat down together at the kitchen island to drink lemonade. Princesa, his own personal wet-nosed bully, had grown bored of telling him off and finally collapsed on top of her nearby bed. Her snores became white noise as his mom caught him up on the family gossip.

Although his relatives on his mom's side were now spread out across the country, most of them were born in the Mexican state of Jalisco. His grandfather— Raphael Sanchez—immigrated to the States as part of the Bracero Program back in 1959. The controversial program brought millions of Mexicans to the country to be temporary workers on fields and railroads. Eventually, his abuelo ended up as a farmworker in a town just an hour away from Esperanza. Soon after, Gabe's abuelita joined her husband in the United States. A year later Gabe's tío Eduardo was born and then Gabe's mom a year after that. Sadly, his abuelito died when Gabe's mom was still in high school.

Gabe's parents met by chance when his dad and his tío Jesus, on their way home from visiting relatives, decided to stop at a drug store for a soda. The way his mom tells the story, his dad fell in love with her at first sight. His dad insists it took at least ten minutes. She was nineteen. He was twenty-three. They had dated for three years while his mom finished college and then finally had a big wedding at Our Lady of Guadalupe and an even bigger reception at Rancho Lindo.

Gabe's family tree was rooted deep in the land beneath his feet. It was hard to ignore that kind of history. He'd always known where he'd come from— that was never the issue. The issue was figuring out where to go next.

Between the Ortega and Sanchez clans, there were lots of tíos, tías, cousins, and second cousins to get updates about. Sometimes Gabe couldn't keep all the families straight and often interrupted his mom to ask, "So who is she married to again?" or "Wait, didn't he die a few years ago?" The lasagna was ready before his mom had run out of stories.

As it cooled on the counter, she pulled up photos of her cousin Irene's fifth grandbaby. Gabe could sense the tiniest amount of jealousy despite her excitement and joy. And he couldn't help but feel a little guilty about it.

Of course he wanted to settle down one day and give her grandkids. He just needed to find the right woman. But that couldn't happen until he figured out his future. One of his brothers was going to have to step up in that department as well.

"Any of the guys have girlfriends right now?" he asked.

She sighed. "No. A few months ago, Nico was dating some girl, but we never met her. And I guess that ended. Daniel goes out every weekend, but it seems like he never stays with anyone for more than two dates. And, you know, Tomás hasn't dated anyone since Mia left."

"And Cruz?"

"Cruz only leaves the ranch to do something for the ranch. I think that boy is going to be a bachelor forever."

Sadly, he agreed. "He wouldn't know how to have a good time if it bit him in the as—butt."

His mother raised her eyebrow at his almost curse word. Thirty years old and he still had to watch what he said around her or else suffer la vergüenza. Abuelita and his mom really knew how to shame someone with just a look.

She poured him some more lemonade. "And what about you, Mijo? Any women I should know about?"

He shook his head. "Mamá, the only females I've met since I've been back home have four legs and kinda stink."

"What about Nora?"

The drink he'd just taken nearly came back up his nose. "What about her?"

"Tomás thinks you might have a little crush on her."

"Tomás needs to keep his big mouth shut," Gabe snapped.

"Gabriel..." his mother warned.

"Okay, first of all. I do not have a crush on Nora. In fact, I'm just trying to convince her not to hate me."

"Why does she hate you? Because of the dance?"

He shrugged. "That and some other things. But don't worry. I'm bending over backward to get her to be my friend."

Gabe couldn't believe he was talking to his mom about Nora.

"You know I'd do anything for you, right?" she asked after a few seconds.

"Yes."

"And you know that I will always be the first to defend you to anybody?"

"Of course. Although Abuelita might beat you to it," he said with a chuckle. But his amusement disappeared when he noticed his mom's frown and worried eyes. "What are you trying to say, Mom?"

She took a deep breath and covered his hands with hers. "Be careful with Nora."

"Okay?" He didn't really understand where this conversation was headed. He didn't like that one bit. Especially when his mom gave his fingers a squeeze.

"She has such a gentle and kind heart. I just want to make sure that you're careful with it."

Now he understood everything. "I'm not going to hurt, Nora. I swear. I'm just trying to show her that I'm not that same guy who stood her up all those years ago."

She nodded and let go. "Okay. Then I'm glad about that. You need a friend like her."

"What's that supposed to mean?"

"Just that Nora is smart and is the most giving person I know. Plus, she loves Rancho Lindo as much as we do. I think she can help you appreciate what we do here. It's good that you're spending time with her."

He couldn't argue with that. In the past two weeks, he'd seen the way she absolutely loved what she did. The woman clapped in excitement every time she harvested even just one vegetable or piece of fruit. Gabe actually enjoyed watching her in action. She knew her stuff and got a thrill whenever someone—not him, though—asked about it. There was something so interesting and impressive about her competence.

Hell, it was damn sexy.

Whoa. Where did that thought come from?

Gabe winced inwardly. No wonder his own mother thought of him as the Big Bad Wolf to Nora's Red Riding Hood.

"Can I ask you something, Mijo?"

When his mom asked permission to ask a question, he knew he probably wasn't going to want to answer. He nodded anyway.

"Why haven't you worn the new hat I bought you?"

Guilt slammed into his chest like a charging bull. He'd expected the question sooner or later. He just hadn't expected it now.

"I will. Eventually."

"Gabriel, that's not what I asked."

He rubbed the back of his head and shrugged. "I haven't worn a cowboy hat in years. I'm more of a baseball cap kind of guy now. But that doesn't mean that I don't like it or that I won't wear it."

"You know if you put it on, it won't magically handcuff you to us, right?"

"Mom, that's not what—"

She held up her hand to stop him. "I know that you're under a lot of pressure and your dad and Cruz aren't helping. But I need you to understand that you're still going to be my son whether or not you live or work on Rancho Lindo. Stay. Don't stay. Just don't leave us here." Then she tapped him on his chest just over his heart.

He shook his head vigorously. "I would never. I promise."

She offered him a small smile. "Good. That's all I want."

When she left him to go tell his dad and everyone else that dinner was ready, Gabe thought about everything she had said. How was it that his mom always knew what he was thinking or doing without him ever saying a word? This mother's intuition thing was a little scary. He thought about the hat sitting on his dresser still in the same box he'd opened weeks ago. He had meant to wear it one day just so he could avoid a conversation like the one he'd just had.

And maybe subconsciously he had seen putting on the hat as a symbol of him accepting the role he still wasn't sure that he wanted.

Madre de Dios. Who knew a cowboy hat could be its own Pandora's Box?

Chapter Eight

The after-Mass pancake breakfasts at the Esperanza Community Center were the place to be every first Sunday of the month.

And not just because Lina's buttermilk flapjacks were delicious.

It was the time to socialize with your neighbors, get caught up with town news, and, most importantly, get a good look at any new transplants and pass judgment on whether they belonged in Esperanza.

Since Nora had been a familiar face, her first pancake breakfast back had been relatively easy. So it seemed reasonable for Nora to assume that Gabe's would've been too.

It turned out that the congregation of Our Lady of Guadalupe had quite the fascination with the Ortegas' prodigal son. And, lucky Nora had a front row seat for the show.

She and the family had sat together at one of the round tables in the middle of the room, probably not the best spot if Gabe had wanted to remain inconspicuous like he had during Mass. But, no, here he was. Smack dab in the center of a tornado of inquiring minds.

"How's the shoulder?"

"Why haven't you come by to visit us yet?"

"Are you seeing anyone, because my granddaughter just broke up with her boyfriend and I think you two would hit off."

At first, Nora tried to pretend that she wasn't interested in his conversations. She tried to ignore them by commenting on the fluffiness of the pancakes to Nico. When that didn't work, she tried to engage Doña Alma by asking for an update on the latest episode of her favorite telenovela. But neither took the bait because both were as interested in the scene before them as much as Nora was. They just didn't care how obvious they looked.

She gave up and spent the next twenty minutes enjoying her breakfast and the sheer uncomfortableness written across Gabe's face.

Nora decided it was what he deserved.

Gabe still wasn't very enthusiastic about his ranch duties, according to a few workers on the ranch who had shared their observations with her. It was a disappointing rumor she had confirmed herself to be true after finding him napping in the greenhouse twice in the past week alone. Daniel had told her that Gabe and Cruz argued with each other almost every day. In fact, one argument had become so heated that Nico had to break it up before their dad heard them.

Nora had initially guessed that Gabe would be gone within six months. Now it seemed like he wouldn't even last until October.

So she wasn't about to be bothered if the townsfolk

of Esperanza interrogated him every single Sunday until he left.

After Mass, they all walked back to their respective vehicles. Nora had hitched a ride with Tomás and Nico, while everyone else had gathered inside Señor Ortega's Chevy Tahoe. But now that it was time to head back to the ranch, Gabe decided to ride with his brothers and joined Nora in the back seat.

"Did you enjoy your breakfast?" she couldn't help but ask him after he buckled his seat belt.

"I always enjoy eating pancakes, so yeah," he said as he looked out the window.

It wasn't exactly the response she'd expected. She pressed on. "You were quite the popular attraction. Guess everyone is happy to have you back in town."

"I guess so," he answered, again not even turning in her direction or giving her anything to respond back to.

She didn't know what else to say. It was no fun trying to tease someone who wasn't in the mood to be teased. It would've been her perfect opportunity to turn the tables on Gabe, who seemed to be an expert in getting her flustered and defensive. It frustrated her that he wasn't taking her bait.

Nora blew an errant hair in front of her right eye in exasperation. She leaned her head against the cool window and didn't say another word the rest of the trip.

When they pulled into the driveway, Gabe was the first one out of the car and quickly disappeared into the house before the rest of them could even open their doors.

"What's up with him?" Nico asked.

"I don't know," Tomás answered. "Maybe he's not

feeling good? He didn't really eat, and you know how much that guy loves to eat. He has to be sick or something for him not to have gobbled down a whole stack of Lina's pancakes."

That's when Nora realized that Tomás was right. Gabe had barely touched his food. Could he be sick?

She dismissed the small swell of concern in her chest.

Nora said her goodbyes to the rest of the family who had arrived only a couple of minutes later and then headed back to her cottage.

After changing into a T-shirt and a pair of leggings, Nora settled onto her couch and called her tía. Their weekly catch-up was her favorite thing about Sundays.

After Tío Chucho's death, the Ortegas had let Tía Luz know that she could continue living on Rancho Lindo even though she had stopped being their housekeeper once he had gotten sick. But Tía Luz had decided she wanted to move closer to her family. She'd even told Nora to come live with her after Nora had quit her job. And she might have if she hadn't been hired by the Ortegas instead.

Although she missed her tía terribly, Nora knew that it had all worked out for the best for the both of them. Especially when she heard about all of the things her tía was experiencing, thanks to her sisters and their large families.

"It sounds like you had a good time," Nora said after hearing about her recent trip to see other relatives in Arizona.

"I did," she said. "It was nice seeing everyone again, especially since some of them couldn't make it to the funeral."

Sadness pinched Nora's heart at the memory of her tío's services. She ignored it though. Her tía sounded happy and she didn't want to ruin that. "I'm glad you were able to go. Maybe next time I can go with you. Or we could go somewhere else."

"Like a vacation?"

"Yes, like a vacation. We should plan a trip together."

"Oh, I would love that, Honora," Tía Luz said.

Nora grinned into her phone. "Me too. Let's look up some places when I'm there in January. Maybe we can go somewhere in the spring."

"Ay, that's the busiest time of the year for the ranch. I don't want to take you away from your work. How about we plan something for the summer instead?"

Even now, her tía Luz remained loyal to Rancho Lindo. Nora couldn't help but smile.

"Sounds good to me. Although I wish we didn't have to wait a whole year for a vacation. I could use a few days away now."

"Why? What's wrong?"

"Nothing's wrong. I've just been busy."

"And Gabe? Comó es?"

Nora couldn't hide her surprise at the mention of his name. "Um, fine. I guess?"

"Doña Alma says he's been helping you."

She rolled her eyes. Of course Doña Alma would be gossiping with her tía. The two women had always been the president and vice president of their own little chisme club.

"He helps me as much as Nico and Daniel do," she said. If by *helping* she meant napping in her greenhouse.

"That's good. I was worried."

"Worried about what?"

"I was worried things would be hard between you two because of what happened...before."

Uneasiness settled into her chest. Nora really didn't want to talk about that particular subject with her tía. And no way was she going to tell her about Gabe's apology. It was best to veer the conversation into a different direction. "You don't have to worry, Tía," Nora tried to assure her. "Gabe and I are fine."

She heard a sigh of relief on the other end of the phone. "Qué bueno. That makes me happy. Everything else must be so hard for him."

"What do you mean?" Nora asked sharply.

"Well, he's been through so much with the accident, and Doña Alma says he's still not completely better. Then you and I both know how much Señor Ortega expects of those boys. I'm sure Gabe has so much pressure on him. It's hard to heal when you are under so much stress."

Nora thought about the pancake breakfast and the relentless questions that were thrown at Gabe. No wonder he hadn't been chatty in the car. A wave of guilt overcame her. She'd enjoyed watching him squirm, but only because she'd believed he'd forget about it soon after.

She realized now that it really must have affected him.

"I never thought about it that way," Nora admitted. She had been so worried about Gabe hurting his family that it never crossed her mind how everything might be hurting him.

Nora heard her tía sigh again. "We never know

what others are going through, Honora. That's why we shouldn't judge."

"I understand, Tía."

"Good. I hope you will make an effort to help him. I think that's what your tío would want."

She gulped down the taste of grief that soured her mouth. Her tía was right. If Tío Chucho were here, he would be going out of his way to make sure Gabe was doing okay. He would've already told Cruz to go easy on him. At least for now.

"I'll do what I can," Nora said.

"Good girl. Besides, Gabe was your first friend at Rancho Lindo. It's nice that you two can be friends again."

Nora nearly dropped her phone. "What are you talking about, Tía? Nico and Daniel were the first brothers to hang out with me."

"Not that first summer. They were at a camp in the beginning of June. Gabe was the one who stopped by the cottage the second day you were there to bring you some cookies from Doña Alma."

She vaguely remembered the cookies. They were biscochitos and still warm from the oven. But why had she always thought that Doña Alma had brought them over herself that first time?

"Maybe he brought the cookies. That doesn't mean he wanted to be my friend back then," Nora insisted.

"Well, he did come over more than that. Especially when he wanted to hide from Señor Ortega," Tía Luz said with a chuckle.

An image of her and Gabe climbing a tree began to materialize in her mind. And then the memory came rushing back to her.

"Was he with me when I fell from the tree behind our cottage?" she asked, even though she was now pretty sure of the answer.

"Yes, yes. Ay, pobrecito. He felt so bad and then Señor Ortega was so angry with him."

"But why?" Nora asked. "It wasn't his fault that I fell."

"I don't know," she said with a sigh. "Pues, maybe he thought Gabe shouldn't have let you climb the tree in the first place."

She still had the scar on her right knee from when she'd landed on a rock. Her ankle was also swollen and so Tía Luz had made her stay inside the cottage and off her feet. After a few days, more cookies were delivered. This time by Nico and Daniel.

And Gabe stayed away from her the rest of that summer.

New emotions mixed with the ones from the past took hold of Nora. For so long she thought she knew exactly who Gabe was. Could it be that she had misjudged him?

Or was Gabe exactly who she had remembered him to be?

"Honora, are you there?"

Tía Luz's voice broke through the deafening replay in her mind of every encounter she'd had with Gabe since his return.

"Sorry, Tía. Yes, I'm still here."

"Oh. Well, I was just saying that I hope Gabe decides to stay at Rancho Lindo," she said.

"Seems like everyone wants that. But I'm not sure yet if Gabe is convinced."

"Maybe you can help convince him?"

Nora laughed at the impossibility of the request. "I don't think so."

"All you have to do is show him why you love it there. That might help him remember that he used to love it too."

They talked for a few more minutes and then Nora promised to call her again next Sunday. After she hung up the phone, the thought that she of all people could get through to Gabe Ortega was still laughable.

The man was hard-headed and stubborn. And if his own family couldn't convince him to stay, then there was no way she could either.

Still, she promised her tía that she would make an effort to be more friendly. And she always kept her promises.

Unlike a certain tree climber she used to know.

Chapter Nine

Congrats, Daddy," Gabe announced, and gave Tomás a couple of pats on his back.

His brother pushed him away. "You're hilarious."

"What? You have a new baby, don't you? You definitely look like a proud papa."

"Yeah, whatever."

Gabe laughed and turned his attention to the new six-month-old foal Tomás had just brought home to Rancho Lindo. He'd left early, before the sun had even risen, in order to go pick her up from a breeder down in Orange County. Gabe had to give Tomás credit for that kind of dedication.

"She's beautiful, don't you think?" he said, his voice thick with pride.

"She is. You know who she reminds me of?" Gabe asked.

"Who?"

"Lady."

"Lady," Tomás said wistfully. "Yeah, you're right. She has the same temperament too. Maybe I should name her something similar to Lady?"

Gabe thought for a moment. "How about Dama?"

"I like that," Tomás said. "I think Lady would approve."

Lady had been a beautiful chestnut-colored American Quarter Horse they'd owned for years. Their dad had brought her to the ranch when she was only four and by the time Gabe was old enough to ride her, she was already ten. She was calm and docile but also had quite the personality. He and his brothers loved to take turns feeding her carrots and apple slices, and she loved to lick their faces in appreciation. Lady had to be put down when Gabe was a freshman in high school. The entire family stayed with her in the stall until she closed her eyes. It was the first time he had ever lost something he'd loved.

Although he could still feel that pang of loss, some of his best memories as a kid was when he learned to ride on Lady.

"Oye, can I ask you a favor?" Gabe said, turning to his brother.

Tomás pulled his eyes away from the foal and looked at him. "Sure."

"Do you think we could go riding sometime? It's been a while, and I've been putting off getting back in the saddle. I think it's time."

It wasn't like he had forgotten how to ride. But he was definitely out of practice and he didn't fully trust how his injuries would affect how he handled a horse. He trusted Tomás would know what he needed. Most importantly, he wouldn't judge.

"Yeah, of course. Just let me know when you're ready."

"Thanks."

They stayed quiet for a few minutes as they observed the new addition check out every corner of the corral. It always amazed him how quickly foals and young horses could adapt to new surroundings. Flexibility wasn't just about survival for them; it was embedded in their nature.

Could some things in life really be that easy?

"Let's go, baby bro," he said. "I heard Mom was making chile verde today."

His brother shook his head and laughed. "Why are you always so hungry?"

"Am I?"

The pair headed up the trail leading to the main house. Gabe decided it was a good time to talk to Tomás about stepping up to help run the ranch. First, though, he couldn't help but ask him something he'd been wondering about for a while. "So me, Daniel, and Dad had lunch at Lina's the other day."

His brother nodded in excitement. "Did you know they have chicken parm now?"

Gabe laughed. "Yeah, I heard. Anyway, Lina herself brought out our food, and we spent a few minutes catching up. She's still the same old Lina."

"She sure is. I bet she was happy to see you."

"Yeah. And she told me that Mia was still in New York. Did you know that?"

He nodded slowly. "I did."

"And?"

"And what?"

Gabe slapped his brother's shoulder. "What's the latest between you guys? Mom says you saw her when she came to visit last Christmas."

Tomás shook his finger at him. "I didn't see her.

Technically, I bumped into her coming out of the general store."

"Did you guys talk?"

"Not really. We said hi, asked each other how we were, and that was it. I don't know why everyone seems to think something is going to happen between us again. We've been over for years. And she's made it clear to me that's what she wants."

"But what do you want?" Gabe still couldn't quite believe that his brother was over Mia. You don't almost ask someone to marry you and then be okay with not talking to them ever again.

"I just want to move on with my life. Mia is thousands of miles away, and I'm not about to chase someone who doesn't want to be chased. My life is here. Hers is over there. There's nothing left to talk about."

Gabe was beginning to realize why he wasn't the only Ortega bachelor on the ranch. But he wasn't there to fix his brothers' love lives. He had more important business to discuss with them. He had to find out if there was someone else to take the spot under Cruz.

"So that was a really good idea to bring in boarders for the stables," he began.

"Thanks. I really hope it's going to make a difference," Tomás said.

"What do you mean?"

His brother didn't answer right away. Then he let out a long sigh. "Rancho Lindo is in trouble, Gabe. Financial trouble."

Gabe's heart sank at the confirmation of what he'd been suspecting. He might not have been involved in all of the day-to-day operations of the ranch, but he wasn't blind. There were at least half a dozen fewer ranch hands than the last time he had visited. Even the livestock had dwindled in numbers. He also knew the area was still in a severe drought, which affected the price of feed.

"How bad is it?" Gabe asked, not really prepared for the answer.

"Dad and Cruz are probably the only ones who really know the numbers. But it's been obvious for some time now. Then last month, Cruz asked me if I had any ideas on how to bring in more income. Boarding horses could be a good money-maker. That is, if Cruz gives it a chance."

"I'm sure he will. Besides, why let the space go to waste? Even if it only makes the ranch a few extra dollars, that's a few extra dollars we didn't have before. Cruz can't be mad about that."

Gabe had really meant what he'd said. Tomás's idea to board horses was a smart one. He was surprised they hadn't ever done it before. His brother always had a knack for figuring out problems. He was thoughtful, logical, and intelligent. Cruz needed a brain like his to develop and expand their sources for revenue. Especially if the ranch was struggling like Tomás said.

"You have lots of good ideas, Tomás. Why don't you ask Dad for more responsibilities around here?"

His brother looked over at him with raised eyebrows. "And why on earth would I want that?"

Gabe shrugged. "So you can do what you want without having to ask permission from Cruz or Dad. Think about it. You'd be able to implement some more of your ideas and they'd actually have to go along with them."

"I don't know. I'm kinda good with what I'm doing now."

"Yeah, but you'll never know what else you might be good at if you don't try."

Tomás stopped walking as they reached the garden's main gate and turned to face Gabe. "Are you trying to ask me what you already asked Nico?"

He shook his head. "What happened to keeping conversations between brothers private?"

"I'm Nico's brother too," he said with a shrug. "So technically we did keep it between brothers."

If Tomás knew, then he'd bet good money that Daniel knew. "Guess it's public information, then," Gabe said.

"Always has been," Tomás explained. "Ever since you agreed to come back, that's all Mom and everyone else has talked about. She was positive that you were ready to help Cruz run the ranch like he always wanted."

Gabe took a long breath. "And that's okay with you? With Nico? With Daniel?"

"There's nothing to be okay with. It's just what we've always known and expected."

"But why? I've been MIA for years."

"Because it's Rancho Lindo. It's your home. We just always knew you'd be back."

A ringing interrupted the conversation before Gabe could respond. Tomás pulled his cell phone out of his pocket and answered. He pointed to the house before walking away and talking to whoever was on the line.

Gabe didn't follow right away. He needed a minute to digest what his brother had just told him. He'd been so preoccupied with deciding if he should stay, he hadn't let himself even consider the possibility that there could come a day when there was no ranch to leave. His thoughts drifted to his dad. No wonder he looked so tired and stressed. The ranch was his legacy, his ancestors' legacy. Not to mention what Rancho Lindo meant to the entire town.

Back in the day, Rancho Lindo was the largest employer in Esperanza. If you didn't work on the ranch yourself, then someone in your family did. Plus, it was the town's main beef and pork supplier. It was why their neighbors—even the ones with ranches of their own—were so invested in its history and its future.

It was why he'd gotten the third degree a few days ago instead of a satisfying pancake breakfast.

At first, he'd been amused by the attention. Flattered even. But after the sixth or seventh question, he'd become annoyed. Especially when no one in his family bothered to rescue him from what had amounted to a full-blown interrogation. By the time they'd gotten back to the ranch, Gabe was furious. So furious that he'd changed and gone for a run without telling anyone where he was going. And when he returned two hours later, he immediately went upstairs, took a shower, and stayed in his room for the rest of the day and night.

He hadn't said anything about what had happened. He knew his brothers would only accuse him of throwing a tantrum, while his parents would have tried to convince him that it hadn't been as bad as he'd remembered. Gabe had decided it was better to just forget about it.

Besides, there were bigger things to worry about.

He needed to talk to Cruz and find out just how

bad things were financially. Then he was going to talk to Nico and Daniel. Since they had carved out a joint role raising all of Rancho Lindo's livestock, surely one of them could take on more responsibilities?

Rustling on the other side of the gate caught his attention. He was about to go investigate when he saw Nora emerge from behind a row of tall sunflowers.

"It's you," he announced.

"Sorry. I didn't mean to eavesdrop. I didn't even hear that much. I was just getting ready to load these crates of tomatoes onto the truck for the farmer's market tomorrow."

"Of course it would be tomatoes," he said with a laugh.

She didn't get the joke. He tried again.

"Next time, though, you might want to try hiding in the corn. They're taller."

Her eyes grew even bigger. "I wasn't hiding. I told you."

Even though she was adorable when she was flustered, Gabe decided to stop teasing her. "I'm joking, Miss Nora," he said, interrupting her denial. "Damn, you're almost as red as your precious tomatoes."

That made her cheeks turn even brighter. He decided right then and there that his new favorite pastime was making Nora blush. Only because it was so easy.

"Are you done now?" Her voice was tight and cut through his amusement immediately.

She'd figured out his game and looked more irritated than embarrassed. He knew it was time to stop messing around.

"I'm sorry for teasing," he said. "How about I help you pack up the truck?"

Part of him expected her to say no. He hadn't meant to piss her off. Even if she didn't want to be his friend, he shouldn't be trying extra hard to be her enemy either.

It must have started snowing in hell.

"Yes, that would be great," she said to his surprise. "I'm running a little behind today and would appreciate an extra set of hands."

It took them almost thirty minutes to load up all of the vegetables and fruits she'd prepared for the market the next day. Gabe hoisted the crates onto the truck's tailgate, while Nora stood on the bed and pulled them into place.

"This is kind of a lot of produce for a small-town farmer's market, isn't it?" he asked after counting over a dozen different types of vegetables and fruit.

Nora wiped her brow with the side of her right arm. "Maybe? But half of it is already earmarked for weekly orders. It's rare if I come home with more than one crate of leftovers."

Gabe couldn't help but be impressed. He knew for a fact there were some pretty big produce farms in the area. One of them was even the biggest supplier for a major grocery chain. "I would think with all the farms and ranches around here that you, we, must have a lot of competition—especially at the farmer's market. It's amazing what you've managed to do in such a short amount of time."

"Thank you, Gabe. That means a lot."

Nora's cheeks reddened even as she smiled. What a big difference compared to the scowl she normally seemed to have reserved just for him. He decided this was much better than teasing her. He let himself return the expression with a big grin of his own, and they went back to stocking the truck.

When they were finished, she jumped off the edge of the tailgate. He watched in horror as her ankle twisted on the landing and she nearly fell flat on her face. The only reason she didn't was because Gabe was there to catch her.

The scent of her shampoo or body wash tickled his nose. Flowery. Addicting. She always smelled too good. Too desirable. Gabe struggled to keep his emotions and urges in check. It would do neither of them any good if he let himself fall—literally and figuratively.

He straightened his back and retook control.

"I got you," Gabe told her.

Chapter Ten

Nora couldn't find her words. Or her breath.

Pain shot up her leg as she tried to regain her balance with Gabe's help.

"Whoa there," he said. "I don't think you should try to put any pressure on it yet. Let me take a look."

Gabe helped her sit on the edge of the tailgate and carefully removed her left boot and sock. She winced when she felt his fingers brush against the top of her foot. Her body's reaction had nothing to do with pain this time. The contact instantly heated her skin, and her whole body jerked in response.

Her eyebrows raised in question. "Sorry," he said, obviously believing he'd hurt her. "It looks like it might be swelling up a little. I think I better get you to the house so we can put some ice on it before it gets worse."

Nora nodded and tried to stand up. It was a lame attempt to prove that she wasn't some fragile doll that had broken into pieces. Except it did the opposite because she nearly fell a second time. Luckily, Gabe was there again to grab her. This time, he scooped her up.

"Put your boot and sock on your lap and then hold on to my neck," he told her.

"You don't have to carry me," she finally said.

"Well, I don't see any wheelchairs around here, so I think I do."

She was about to argue. But what was that saying about protesting too much? Nora told herself it wasn't a big deal that her arms were wrapped around Gabe's neck. Or that one set of his fingers were under her knee and the other set was only inches away from the side of her breasts.

Not. A. Big. Deal. At. All.

Sure, maybe teenage Honora might have died from a heart attack if teenage Gabe ever touched any part of her body. But grown-up Nora was mature enough to handle the current situation. That is until he stopped to readjust the way he was carrying her and one of his hands slid down the back of her thigh, nearly stroking the edge of one of her butt cheeks. Heat crept up the back of her neck and spread across her face, and instinctively she wanted to hide. She turned her head farther into the crook of his neck, accidentally brushing the bridge of her nose against it. His skin was scratchy and warm and she couldn't help but wonder what it would feel like to put her lips there. She inhaled instinctively to catch a breath and instead took in his scent. It was raw and natural. And did so much to her insides that she had to mentally restrain herself from burying her nose in his T-shirt.

An unexpected low groan made her look up at him. "Are you okay? Do you need to put me down?" she asked.

"I'm fine," he said, his voice deep and gruff.

When they finally reached the main house, it was empty. Gabe walked into the kitchen and started to set her down on one of the stools at the center island. Then he thought better of it and carried her all the way to the couch in the family room across the hallway.

After helping her get situated, he arranged a throw pillow under her foot. "How does that feel?"

She nodded back at him. "It's good. Thanks."

He seemed satisfied with her answer. "Okay, I'm going to get some ice," he told her, and placed his hands on his hips. "Try not to move too much. I'll be right back."

"I'll be right here," Nora said.

When Gabe disappeared into the hallway, she allowed her body to finally relax. She'd basically held her breath the entire time she was in Gabe's arms. They were strong and steady and she had tried so hard not to enjoy them being wrapped around her body. What was going on with her? She wasn't one to ever play the damsel-in-distress schtick when it came to men. She wished she would've walked on her own to the house. But there was a good chance she would've screamed in pain with every step.

Nora had never seen this side of Gabe before— thoughtful, considerate, and gentle. She chalked it up to being a soldier. She was hurt and he'd acted on instinct to get her to safety. That's all that was. She didn't need to read anything into his actions or intentions.

She heard the bathroom door open and watched as Tomás headed into the kitchen. He didn't see her on the couch.

"Hey, there you are," she heard him say. "You missed

lunch. I thought you were so excited about Mom's chile verde."

"Yeah, I got tied up doing something else," she heard Gabe tell Tomás. "I'll just eat later. Hey, do you know where she keeps those big freezer bags?"

Nora hadn't realized how long she'd kept Gabe. She wondered why he'd offered to help her in the first place. And he missed lunch because of it? And now he was staying with her even longer?

She was having a hard time decoding Gabe. She thought she'd had him all figured out. Now she wasn't quite sure what to think about him at all.

A few minutes later, he returned carrying a plastic bag filled with ice cubes and a dishtowel. Gingerly, he set both on top of her ankle.

She winced from the shock of the cold hitting her warm skin.

"Sorry," he said for the second time that day. "I know it hurts, but you should probably leave that on for about ten minutes. Then we can check to see how the swelling is."

We?

"Do want me to take you to see Dr. Griffin?" he said, and took a seat on the edge of the coffee table in front of her.

"No, I'm pretty sure I just twisted it. It doesn't feel broken or anything like that."

He nodded and studied the bag of ice for a few seconds. "Well, how about we hang out here for a little bit. If your ankle starts to turn blue or the swelling doesn't go down, then I think we go see the doc."

"Okay. But you really don't have to stay. I know you

probably have a lot to do. I've already taken up too much of your afternoon."

He shrugged. "I don't mind. Besides, I'd probably get in more trouble if I left you here all alone."

Nora smiled and nodded. A thought occurred to her and she opened her mouth to ask him something, but then closed it when she thought better of it.

Gabe still noticed. "What?"

"Nothing," she said, very unconvincingly.

He sighed. "Spit it out, Miss Nora. You're supposed to be relaxing, but you look like you're carrying the weight of a newborn calf on your shoulders. Just tell me whatever it is you want to tell me."

She took a deep breath and then rushed on. "Why are you trying to convince your brother to take the job your dad wants you to have?"

Instantly, Nora regretted opening her mouth. The man had been nothing but nice to her and she just threw it back into his face. She wouldn't blame Gabe for telling her to mind her own business. Because she absolutely should.

Then again, the future of Rancho Lindo *was* her business in a way.

She told herself that's why she was so invested in what Gabe's plans were. It had nothing to do with him personally. It was all about making sure the garden she'd worked so hard to build had the opportunity to survive and thrive for years to come. She didn't like to think about what would happen if for some reason Rancho Lindo ever had to close its doors. Mainly because she really had nowhere else to go. What would become of her or the twenty-plus people and their families who relied on the ranch for jobs and food?

Sure, she could probably find another government research job. Though she doubted that she could ever go back to being stuck in a lab. Like the plants and crops she tended to, she needed the sun.

She needed purpose.

Nora glanced at Gabe expecting to be scolded for sticking her nose where it didn't belong. But he didn't look angry. Or even annoyed.

"I guess it's time for my next session with Dr. Nora," he said with a laugh.

She hesitated before speaking again. "I'm not analyzing. I'm just asking."

He stood up and walked over to the room's large fireplace. He brushed his fingers along the edge of a brown frame that held a photo of the entire family. "Well, if you must know, I'm still not convinced it should be me."

"But why?"

Gabe stuck his hands in his pockets and shrugged. "Because I've never been good at this rancher stuff."

"How is that possible?" she asked incredulously. "You grew up here. I'm sure you were herding cattle before you were crawling."

That made him laugh again. "It's true. I have pictures of me wearing tiny cowboy boots when I was only two days old."

Nora smirked. "Oh, I know. I've seen them."

"Ay, I need to hide those from Abuelita again," he said as he walked back to the coffee table and sat down again.

"So what's the problem?" she asked.

He slapped his hands on top of his thighs. "Cowboy boots don't automatically make you a cowboy, Nora.

And having the last name of Ortega doesn't automatically mean you want to live and work on a ranch for the rest of your life. It's just one obligation after another. I don't want to turn into Cruz. The guy doesn't have any interests outside of this place. How on earth can he be happy?"

"I don't know," she said with a shrug. "He seems pretty happy to me."

"How is that?"

"Because he loves what he does, Gabe. And it isn't up to you or me to decide what's good enough."

"Fine. But that works both ways. I'm the only one who can decide what's best for me."

"Of course. All I'm saying is don't sell yourself short. If you don't want to be a rancher because it doesn't make you happy, then don't. But trying to convince yourself that you're not good at it? That's ridiculous."

"Not really. All of that stuff comes natural to Cruz and the others. It doesn't for me. Why do you think I joined the army?"

"It was more like you ran away to the army."

"Wow," he said with a laugh. "I don't remember you being this brutal, Nora."

She shrugged. "I think you don't remember lots of things." The dig at their past didn't seem lost on him. Nora bit her tongue before she said anything else.

Gabe told her, "I just need some time. That's all."

Nora let out a nervous breath. "Fair enough," she said, not wanting to press the issue any further. Mostly because she didn't want him to regret helping her. And partly because her ankle was frozen by now. She took the ice off and rotated her foot a few times.

"How does it feel?" he asked. She was touched by the concern in his voice.

"Better," she said with a sigh.

"Do you want to try standing on it?"

"Okay."

She turned her body and moved her leg off the couch and onto the floor. She was about to lift herself to a standing position when Gabe stood in front of her and offered his hands.

"Nice and slow," he told her.

Nora nodded and held on to him as he slowly lifted her off the couch until she was standing on both feet. A light stab of pain ran up her left leg and she buckled a little.

Gabe's fingers curled around hers, and he squeezed. "Just let me know if it's too much," he said softly.

The pain eventually dulled and Nora was able to stand straight. She looked up and saw Gabe's face contorted with worry. "I'm okay," she assured him. "You can let go now."

Nora wasn't sure if he'd heard her, because he didn't release her right away. She noticed though that the longer he held on to her, the concern in his eyes transformed into something else. Something deeper. Something that made her catch her breath.

And then Gabe blinked. "Are you sure you can put pressure on it now?" he asked.

When she nodded, he let go of her hands and took a step back.

"See, almost as good as new." She was sugarcoating it. Her ankle burned with pain, but she put on a brave face so Gabe wouldn't feel obligated to stay with her.

"You may be cute, but you're still a bad liar," he said.

Did he just call her cute? Not trusting she could keep her balance with the swell of emotions rocking back and forth inside her, Nora eased herself onto the couch. "It *is* better. But maybe I should rest it for a little longer."

"And ice it," he ordered.

"And ice it."

He was about to tell her something else when they both heard the chime of a text coming in on his phone. Gabe rolled his eyes. "Cruz," he said without even looking.

"I'm okay. You can go do what you need to do. I'm just going to stay here for a little bit. You really don't have to babysit me."

He hesitated but eventually agreed. "Fine. But don't you dare do any more work today. You should go home and rest. I can let Cruz know, and he can send Nico or Daniel to the farmer's market tomorrow."

"That's not necessary. I will be fine and perfectly able to go tomorrow."

"Okay, but one of the guys is going to go with you."

"No they aren't. I don't need the help."

"Nora..."

"Gabe?"

He dragged his hand over his face. "Madre de Dios. Why are you so stubborn?"

Nora pointed at him. "Pot." Then she pointed at herself. "Kettle."

"What in the world am I going to do with you?" he asked, shaking his head. His words were light and joking. Yet the way he looked her up and down made it seem like he wasn't talking about her ankle anymore. It sent a shiver through her.

She pretended like she wasn't affected and answered, "Nothing. Because you're going to go back to work before Cruz sends out a search party."

"Have it your way," he said with a shrug. "But if you change your mind, call me."

Why did it feel like they were talking about something very different now? Or was she just reading into things as usual?

"I won't," she said, leaning farther back into the couch.

Gabe tipped his head in acknowledgment and began to walk away.

"Thank you," she called out.

He turned and gave her a wink. "You're very welcome. See, I don't always run away."

Chapter Eleven

The sigh on the other end of the phone dashed the hopes Gabe had woken up with that morning.

"I'm sorry, man," his friend Alex said. "I found out that HR just implemented a hiring freeze. That position isn't available anymore."

The two had served together up until last year, and nowadays Alex was a headhunter specializing in placing retired veterans. He'd called Gabe when he'd heard about the accident and let him know that a position had opened up at his agency. He told Gabe to reach out when he was ready to work. Gabe didn't realize that he would be reaching out two months too late. Disappointment kicked him in the stomach. "Oh, wow. That's too bad."

"I know," Alex agreed. "I'm really sorry. I'm hoping the freeze is temporary, and things will get back to normal in a few months. Hey, why don't you give Jackson a call. I heard he was looking to fill some spots on his new sales team."

"Really? Okay, that sounds good. Can you text me his number?"

"Definitely. And if they open things back up here, I'll let you know."

"I appreciate that. I'll let you get back to work. Thanks, Alex."

Gabe closed his eyes after hanging up the phone. He tried not to let the frustration he was feeling get the better of him. He should've known it was too soon to get his expectations up. But after his conversation with Nora yesterday, it felt like he needed to do something.

"Everything okay?"

Gabe opened his eyes and saw Cruz standing in front of him. "Yeah. Just a little tired, I guess."

"It's only eleven. How can you be tired already?"

He didn't want to have this conversation with Cruz. "Did you need something?"

"Yeah. I want you to ride with me to the south gate."

"Ride? Why can't you take the truck?"

"Because Tomás and Nico took it to the cattle auction. Wait. When was the last time you rode a horse?"

"I still know how to ride. It's just been a while, all right? Anyway, I can't go with you."

"Why?"

"Abuelita asked me to take her into town. I'm just waiting for her to come outside."

"Liar. I think you just don't want to get back on a horse."

Gabe was about to argue when Abuelita walked up to them. "Okay, Mijo. I'm ready now."

He shrugged in Cruz's direction and also gave him a slight smile. It was always a bonus when he could prove his brother wrong.

The trip to town took less than ten minutes and

Gabe parked in the small parking lot behind Our Lady of Guadalupe Catholic Church. It was the only church in town, and it was basically his abuelita's second home. If there was something to plan, like a banquet or fundraiser, she was there. And if there was an opportunity to work, like picking up tablecloths to wash and iron, like today, she was there too.

They walked through the back door and looked for Father Marcos. As he walked through the church, Gabe took in the same two rows of wooden pews and same stained glass windows that stretched from the middle of the white stucco walls up to the rafters above. Sometimes during Mass, he would focus on one of those windows and try to count each colored section. He never counted them all. One of his brothers would usually try to get his attention because they were usually as bored as he was.

"Hola, Doña Alma." Father Marcos appeared from behind another door and walked over to them. He took Abuelita's hand and patted it.

Then he turned his attention to Gabe. "Gabriel, it's so good to see you."

Gabe stuck out his hand for a shake, but Father Marcos used it to pull him in for a hug. "It's good to see you too," Gabe said. "I think you got taller."

That made the older man laugh. It was the same thing he used to tell Gabe every Sunday. Father Marcos had been the only priest in the parish for as long as Gabe could remember. But his abuelita had already informed him on the drive over that a new, younger priest had arrived a few months ago. This Father Dominic would be taking over the parish by the end of the year.

"Did you know your abuelita lit a candle for you

every week while you were over there? And we dedicated a Mass to you every month," he said. "The whole town kept you in their prayers."

A knot tightened at the back of Gabe's throat. "Well, I guess they worked," he said after a few seconds. "I really appreciate it, Father."

Father Marcos smiled and patted him on the shoulder. "Que Dios te bendiga," he said.

He wasn't a churchgoing man like the rest of his brothers, but he appreciated the priest's blessing.

As the priest talked with Abuelita about the tablecloths needed for the upcoming spaghetti dinner fundraiser on Friday, Gabe wondered how much different things were going to be without Father Marcos. He was as much a part of Esperanza as the church building itself.

Maybe he was wrong about change being a good thing? At least when it came to the town.

After loading two trash bags full of green linens into the back of his mom's SUV, Gabe walked over to open the passenger door for Abuelita.

But she waved him off. "No, not yet. I want to go to the farmer's market."

He let Abuelita lead him down the only sidewalk of Esperanza's Center Street.

Besides the feed store and diner, Center Street was also home to Vera's Beauty Shop, the Santa Ynez Valley Bank, Bargain Thrift, the law office of Frank Hernandez, Valley Health Clinic, and Alfredo's Carnicería & Panadería. Meanwhile, Esperanza Road featured Kathy's General Store, Valley Barbers, Anderson Family Saddlery & Leather, the Graber Vineyard Tasting Room, Grand Burgers, and Oaktree Bar & Grill. Around the corner was Esperanza City Hall (slash community center), the firehouse, sheriff's station, post office, public library, and, of course, Our Lady of Guadalupe Catholic Church.

Two rows of pop-up tents were set up at the end of the road, which was closed off to traffic. As they got closer, Gabe could see vendors selling everything from jars of honey to homemade quilts.

He spotted Nora almost immediately. She was standing underneath a white canopy surrounded by crates of assorted fruits and vegetables sitting on folding tables. Gabe watched as she chatted with a woman who seemed to be buying two bags worth of items. She wore her hair in her usual side braid but this time it was covered by a black cowboy hat. Her plain black T-shirt fit her snugly. His eyes couldn't help but trace an outline over the curve of her breasts to the exposed skin just above the dip of the V-neck. A crate of corn blocked his view of the rest of her, but he'd bet good money that the jeans she probably had on accentuated everything else perfectly.

Gabe swallowed the sudden burst of attraction that came over him. It was as if his body remembered her all on its own. When he'd lifted Nora to carry her to the house yesterday, he hadn't expected how soft she would feel against his chest. She was a little thing, so he shouldn't have broken a sweat as he walked with her to the house, yet his pulse raced and he could sense beads of sweat forming on the back of his neck. The cobblestones beneath his feet might as well have been hot coals based on his reaction with every step.

He forced himself to stop staring and stayed back as Abuelita made her way to where Nora was. After her customer left, Nora greeted Abuelita and then pulled out a small white paper bag from underneath the table next to her. Gabe watched as Abuelita stuffed the bag into her large purse. Then she pointed at him and Nora's gaze locked with his.

Gabe waved. She didn't wave back.

This whole time he thought that something had changed between them yesterday. Could he really have gotten it that wrong?

Then Nora did wave and even gave him a little smile. He decided to ignore why on earth that might have made his entire day.

"So this is the famous Rancho Lindo produce booth," he said as soon as walked up to the tent. "Not too shabby."

"Why is it that your compliments never really sound like compliments?" Nora asked.

Gabe picked up an apple from the crate in front of him and took a bite. "I have absolutely no idea what you're talking about," he said with his mouth full. Yeah, things between them were definitely a little easier. "How's the ankle?"

She looked down at her foot and gave it a little wiggle. "Much better. It's still a little tender, but the swelling has gone down. I'll probably have to ice it when I get home, though."

Abuelita hadn't heard about Nora's almost tumble yesterday. After hearing about the incident, she was ready to send Nora home. But, of course, Nora insisted she was fine and could finish out the day.

"Pues, then I'm going to make you un remedio de hierbas. I'll have it ready for you when you get home."

"It's not the one that stinks, is it?" Gabe scrunched

up his nose thinking about the various ointments Abuelita had cooked up over the years. She'd soak elastic bandages in the concoctions and then wrap their legs or arms in them to soothe and heal pulled muscles.

She slapped his arm in response. "No stinks," she asserted. Then he watched her lean over to Nora and whisper, "Pero, tiene la tequila."

And she winked.

Gabe made a face over Abuelita's head that only Nora could see and she tried not to laugh. He was about to make another joke when she got called away by a man who had just walked up to the tent. He seemed to know her based on the goofy way he was smiling at her. Gabe turned to ask Abuelita who the man was, but she'd wandered off to the next tent.

"Can I pay for this with you?"

Gabe turned to see an older woman holding a dollar in one hand and two very large zucchinis in the other. "Uh, sure," he said, and took her dollar. He had no idea if the woman had just robbed Nora. Gabe figured it was time to go so he didn't do it again.

He walked over to where Nora was still talking to the dark-haired man and tapped her shoulder.

"Sorry to interrupt, but this woman just gave me a dollar for two zucchinis, and I figured I'm probably not the best person to take money from your customers, so here you go," he said, handing the dollar to Nora.

"Oh, thanks," she said. Gabe looked at the man and nodded. The man did the same. Then the three of them looked at one another in a few seconds of awkward silence.

Finally, Nora said, "Lucas, this is Gabe Ortega.

Gabe, this is Lucas Avery. He's the new assistant deputy for the town."

"Howdy," the man said. "It's so great to finally meet you."

Gabe nodded in acknowledgment. "Thanks. So how long have you been in Esperanza?"

"About six months. I'm originally from San Francisco."

"San Francisco? Wow, I bet it was quite the adjustment coming from there to here."

Lucas laughed. "It was. But I really like living in a town where you know everyone and everyone knows you."

"Really? Well, I guess you came to the right place."

Gabe didn't miss the glance that Lucas gave Nora. "I definitely did."

Irrational irritation tightened every muscle in his body. So much so that he caught himself flexing his hand to shake off the tension.

Nora handed the deputy a bag of items. "Here's your order, Lucas. I swear you must eat oregano on everything based on how much you order every week."

Gabe wouldn't be surprised if the guy hated oregano. He knew exactly why Lucas the deputy was Nora's best customer.

"What can I say? Your oregano is the best in Santa Barbara County—the best in the state even."

Gabe pretended to study a crate of apples so no one saw his big eye roll.

"You're sweet," Nora said. "That reminds me. I want you taste my raspberries."

That was about all Gabe could handle. He tried to get Abuelita's attention so they could head back to the ranch, but she was too busy chatting with a couple who were at the next booth. He made his way to the tables on the other side of the tent and began picking up small plastic trays and reading their labels. He recognized the trays of microgreens as the same kind he'd seen on shelving inside the greenhouse. Based on the amount of empty space left on the table, he assumed that Nora had already sold most of her supply and it wasn't even eleven in the morning yet.

Gabe turned around and scanned the rest of the tables. Most of the overflowing crates he'd helped load into the truck yesterday were down to a handful of items. That's when it hit him.

Rancho Lindo's produce booth was doing pretty fantastic. And he knew exactly who was responsible for it. A sense of pride swelled inside him.

Good for Nora.

"Okay, I'm ready to go home," Abuelita said, and hooked her arm through his.

Gabe looked over and saw that even though Nora was helping more customers, the deputy was lingering.

"Me too," he said.

As they pulled away from the town, Gabe's thoughts kept coming back to Lucas. Curiosity got the best of him.

"So I can't believe Sheriff Molina finally hired a new deputy," he said as he drove toward the ranch. "I thought for sure he'd never admit he needed some-one else."

"Oh, it wasn't his decision," Abuelita said. "Mayor Walker made some calls after some of the ranches had some vandalism last year."

Gabe had heard about that from Cruz. Fortunately,

Rancho Lindo was never hit. But the town council was up in arms. Until then, the biggest crime spree to ever hit Esperanza was when Old Man Becker woke up one morning and discovered all of his chickens gone. For an entire morning, everyone was on edge thinking that there was a chicken thief in town. But the chickens were later found on the back side of Becker's property and he realized that it was his German shepherd who had figured out how to open the gate on the chicken coop and must have herded them away.

Still, Gabe thought it was a good thing to increase the size of the sheriff's department.

"That's good that the town has another deputy," he told Abuelita. "Lucas seems like a good guy."

"Yes. He's very nice."

Gabe cleared his throat. "Looks like he thinks Nora is very nice too."

"Qué?"

"I think Lucas likes Nora, you know, like wants to ask her out on a date."

Abuelita laughed. "Pues, that's old news, Mijo. But he never does. Instead, he just buys bags and bags of oregano. His kitchen must smell like an Italian restaurant."

Gabe couldn't help but roar with laughter. He'd thought the same thing.

She sighed. "Too bad. I think he would be good for Nora. She works too much and needs someone to take her dancing or to the movies. Hopefully Deputy Lucas can be brave and finally ask her to go out."

"But, if she doesn't like him, then she shouldn't say yes."

"Who says she no like him?"

Gabe gripped the steering wheel as if his life depended upon it. "Wait. Does Nora have a crush on Deputy Lucas too?"

"Pues, no sé. But why not? He's handsome, he's sweet to her, and he likes her oregano."

He immediately decided that a mutual love of the herb wasn't exactly a good reason to start a relationship. "I don't know. I don't think Lucas is good enough for Nora."

"No?"

"No. He seems boring."

Abuelita laughed. "Ay, Gabriel. You no fool me. I think you don't like Lucas because maybe you want to be the one to date Nora."

"What? I think you've been in the sun too long, Abuelita. You're starting to talk nonsense."

"If you say so," she said with a shrug. Gabe recognized the tone behind her words, and he knew she didn't believe him. Not that it mattered. He honestly didn't have those kinds of feelings for Nora. In fact, if she wanted to date the deputy, then good for her. It was none of his business if she liked boring men with an obsession for herbs.

To prove it, he shared his opinion with Daniel later that night over dessert. His Abuelita had made buñuelos. But not just any buñuelos. These fried tortillas dusted with cinnamon and sugar had been topped with vanilla ice cream and a deliciously sweet raspberry sauce. They had been so good that he couldn't even talk until the last crumb on his plate was gone.

"So you really think Nora is into Deputy Lucas?" Daniel asked after he pushed his plate away. They were sitting outside on the back patio, while everyone else decided to finish their dessert in the family room so they could catch their favorite telenovela.

Gabe shrugged and sat back in his chair. "I don't know if she's into him, but he's definitely interested in her. How well do you know him?"

"We've talked a few times when I've run into him at the diner or at the feed store. He seems like a good enough guy. But what's up with the sudden interest in Nora's dating life?"

"I wouldn't call it an interest. I'm just sharing what I saw today at the farmer's market and wondered what you thought about them, you know, as a couple. You're pretty close with Nora, I figured you'd want to know."

"Well, sure. I don't want her going out with any jerks. But why am I getting the feeling that you're interested for other reasons?"

"What other reasons?"

"Like maybe you're thinking about asking her out?"

"What? Chale! No way."

Daniel's eyes narrowed. "Really?"

"Really."

He nodded. "Whatever you say, big brother. Whatever you say."

Chapter Twelve

Like a proud mama, Nora couldn't help but boast.

"Look at how big and red they are. And they smell sweet. I can't believe how great this first batch came out," she gushed.

Doña Alma and Señora Ortega each picked up a single raspberry from the basket and took a long, deep whiff. Slowly, each woman smiled before popping the fruit into their mouths.

"Delicioso," Doña Alma said.

"I can't believe how sweet it is," Señora Ortega added before picking up another one.

Nora had been worried when her first raspberry bushes hadn't ripened by last month. Doña Alma had told her to be patient and just continue to watch and wait. As usual, she'd been right.

Even after all these years, she was still learning from Doña Alma.

Nora was eleven when she'd made something grow for the first time. As the ranch's housekeeper, Tía Luz spent most of her time in the kitchen cleaning and helping to make meals for the staff. That meant Nora also spent a lot of time in there watching and taste testing. But it was Doña Alma who taught her the names of the different herbs she kept in small pots on the windowsill.

After she learned those, Doña Alma took her outside and showed her the garden and how to identify the different leaves and stems. Back then, the garden was only about a quarter of the size it was now. It was plentiful, though. Picking carrots, radishes, and zucchini became Nora's most favorite thing to do.

Eventually, Doña Alma showed her how to start a cilantro plant in a container that Nora then took home with her. Her excitement turned to heartbreak, though, when the plant never grew. The next summer, Doña Alma gave her another container to start over. By the time she left that year, little sprigs had already erupted from the dark soil. Determined not to let the sprouts die, Nora checked out every gardening book she could find in her city library and had her very first cilantro plant within a few months.

Summer after summer, Doña Alma shared her secrets on how to nurture and protect every variety of produce the ranch had. The most important lesson was to be patient. Not just because some plants took longer to ripen, but also because some didn't always grow the way they were supposed to in the beginning. The key was to gently tend to and guide them. Too much interference and the plants would shrivel up and die.

"You can't force nature," she'd tell Nora. "Even the most wayward plant can still find its way eventually. We just need to be patient."

As she looked at her beautiful raspberries, Nora

wondered if Doña Alma's advice also rang true for
wayward cowboys.

"Do you have more to pick or is this all of them?"

Doña Alma's question dashed away the thoughts
of Gabe, and Nora turned her attention back to the
women in front of her.

"Oh, there's more. I was just so excited to show you
that I just picked a few," she said.

The older woman clapped in delight. "Perfecto. I'll
need about four cups."

"What are you going to do with them?" Señora
Ortega asked.

"I'm going to make a jam," Doña Alma said.
"Gabriel loves raspberries, so I think he will like it."

"Ay, Mamá. You spoil that boy too much."

Doña Alma waved her finger in the air. "No cierto.
I spoil him as much as I spoil the other boys. But he's
been away for so long that I'm making up for it."

Señora Ortega sighed. "I'm so happy he's home. I
wake up every morning now and almost cry when I
remember that he's safe in his room just a few feet away
from me."

The elderly woman patted her daughter's hand, and
the two of them exchanged looks that tugged at Nora's
heart. It made her miss her own mother, who had
passed the same year Nora graduated from college.
They'd been as close as Doña Alma and Señora Ortega
were. It had devastated Nora to lose her. And now Tía
Luz was really the only close relative she had left.

Maybe that's why it bothered her so much to see
Gabe take what he had for granted. What she wouldn't
give to be part of a big and loving family like the
Ortegas. He didn't know how good he had it. He didn't

realize what he would be walking away from or who he was leaving behind.

Nora eyes stung with unshed tears. Why couldn't she erase Gabe from her thoughts? She didn't want the other women to see or else they'd start asking questions. She needed to escape.

"I'll go pick the rest of the raspberries right now. I'll be right back," Nora said.

She didn't give them a chance to say anything before running out the back. In her rush to leave, she stumbled over the door's threshold and crashed into a very sturdy chest. Her hand was only on the black T-shirt for a second, but there was no mistaking the ample solidness underneath the thin material.

"Whoa there," a voice said.

Strong hands braced both of her arms and Nora looked up to confirm what she'd already guessed. The shirt and the hands belonged to Gabe. "Sorry about that," she said when she looked up to meet his eyes. They were a rich, dark brown. Almost black, but not quite.

Stop staring at them.

Embarrassment immediately heated her cheeks. Then a different kind of warmth slowly spread over the rest of her body as it began to recognize—and enjoy—being held by him.

"Gabe," she said.

"Nora." His obvious amusement curved his lips into a wry smile. But as he stared into her eyes a little longer, his amusement transformed into concern. "Hey, is everything okay?"

Her heart rate quickened, and for a second, she wondered if he could feel it thump wildly against his chest.

She took a deep breath and blinked away whatever wetness still lingered in her eyes. "Yes, everything is fine. You can let me go now."

He considered this for a moment. "I could, but I don't want you to fall and hurt another ankle."

"I won't."

He opened his mouth as if to say something, but then closed it. His fingers squeezed her upper arms once before helping her straighten her posture. Then he let go.

"Thank you," she said, although she wasn't quite sure why.

"You're welcome." His voice was low and deep, sending shivers down her spine. "I'm just glad I was here to catch you. Again."

She moved to the left to get past him, but he moved in the same direction, and Nora nearly ran into him a second time. She laughed nervously and stepped to the right. And so did he.

"I swear I'm not doing this on purpose," he said with a laugh.

"I know." She wasn't sure why it was important for him to know that she wasn't annoyed.

He gave her a quick smile and then pointed to her ankle. "How is it?"

"Good," Nora answered. "Doña Alma's herbs and tequila really helped."

"I am one hundred percent sure they did. I'm glad you're better—well, that your ankle is better."

"Thanks. Okay, I better get back to work," she told him, and turned to walked down the back porch's steps.

"Me too. I'm helping Cruz build a new section

of the corral. I was just coming inside to get some water."

"That's great. I didn't realize Tomás wanted to make it bigger."

He hesitated before answering. "Well, it was kind of my idea. Now that he's trying to get more boarders, he's going to need to make some areas where he can separate the horses while they're in the corral. That way he doesn't have to worry about one escaping while he's opening the gate to put another one in the stable."

"Oh. Yeah, that makes sense." Nora couldn't help but be impressed.

"You're surprised, aren't you?"

"A little," she admitted.

"Look, I know you have your doubts about whether I'm invested in staying. And honestly, I haven't made up my mind. But that doesn't mean I'm not going to do what I can to keep this place running."

"Did you tell that to Cruz?"

Gabe scrunched his eyebrows together. "Cruz?"

"Does Cruz know that you want to do more for the ranch?"

"I have no idea." He shrugged. "I do what he tells me to do, so I'm assuming he does."

Nora sighed. Why did these brothers not talk to each other? "That's not the same. You need to let him know, Gabe. You said you wanted to prove me wrong, but what you should be doing is proving it to your family. What I think doesn't matter."

"But it does," he rushed to say.

She stilled at his words. "Why?"

"Because I don't want to ever be the guy who breaks promises again. And if you can forgive me, really forgive me, then maybe I'll believe that I deserve a second chance to fix things with my family too."

Nora didn't know what to say to that. She'd never heard him sound so genuine and so determined.

Maybe there was hope for Gabe Ortega yet.

Chapter Thirteen

Gabe was still thinking about his conversation with Nora when he pulled the truck in front of the main corral at Rancho Lindo. Cruz was already there waiting for him.

"Let's pile these up near the west gate," his brother said as Gabe began unloading the 4x4s he'd bought earlier that day.

Gabe only nodded and began grabbing as many pieces as he could carry. His shoulder was burning, and his hand was cramping again. Still, he gritted his teeth and pushed through. He was telling anyone who would listen that he was willing to do his part around the ranch. Now he had to show them.

With the two of them, it didn't take long to empty the bed of the truck. But on his final trip, Gabe couldn't support the weight of the wood anymore. The 4x4s he'd been carrying came crashing down a few feet away from the pile.

Gabe swore. He was in pain and beyond frustrated. His body continued to betray him.

"What happened?" Cruz asked after coming over to help pick up the lumber.

The last thing Gabe needed was Cruz saying something to their parents about the fact that he couldn't even carry a few pieces of wood. Or worse, Cruz might even think Gabe was exaggerating his pain in order to get out of working.

"Nothing. They just shifted, and I lost my grip on them."

Cruz seemed to accept Gabe's explanation and dropped the last of the boards onto the pile the way he wanted. "Okay. Have fun."

Gabe stilled. Was his brother really expecting him to fix the corral on his own? Even if his shoulder wasn't on fire, Gabe hadn't built anything in years.

"Wait," Gabe said. "I thought you were going to help me?"

"And I thought you could handle this on your own. Isn't that what you told me when you came to me with the idea?"

"I said I could handle picking up the wood by myself, not the actual construction. This is going to take me all day."

Cruz shrugged. "Nah. It's probably going to take you two."

"Come on, man."

His brother let out an exasperated sigh. "Fine. Let me go get my tools."

Half an hour later, the two of them had successfully removed the west gate of the corral. Cruz explained how they were going to build the new section. He made it sound like it was as easy as replacing a lightbulb. Gabe knew it wouldn't be for him, especially if it was going to be a struggle just for him to grip a hammer.

"Maybe we need a few more hands? That way we can finish it today."

"Everyone else is busy doing other things," Cruz said as he picked up a 4x4 and braced it against an existing board.

"What about hiring a couple of guys just for the day? Dad used to do that all the time when he had a big project to do."

"This isn't a big project. And we don't need to be spending money on something we can do ourselves."

"I doubt it would be that expensive."

Cruz slammed a nail into the wood with his hammer. "Ay cómo friegas," he said, clearly frustrated. "Stop trying to get out of this and get to work."

Why did his brother always twist the meaning behind his words? That was probably the main reason why he hadn't had a sit-down conversation with Cruz yet about helping to run the ranch. He knew he wouldn't listen or, worse, wouldn't believe him.

Gabe decided he would keep his mouth shut. At least for now.

They worked in silence for the next several minutes. He could tell Cruz was mad at him for bringing up the idea of hiring some guys to help. But he couldn't tell if it was because he didn't want the hassle or he didn't want to spend the money. Suspicion flared in his gut.

If the ranch was having money problems, it would've been nice to know how bad things were. Although he wouldn't be surprised if Cruz and their dad had decided to keep it between themselves. Just like always. Because if there was information that would be shared on a need-to-know basis, Gabe was usually one of the ones who never needed to know.

Irritated, Gabe yanked another 4x4 off the pile and an even sharper pain shot up his arm. His entire body tensed as he struggled to hold in his agony. He closed his eyes and took a long breath. Eventually, the pain became bearable again, and Gabe continued working on his section of the corral.

To his surprise, Cruz was the one who called for a break about an hour later.

"It's almost time for dinner. You can finish this tomorrow."

"Fine by me," Gabe responded. He finished installing the bracket he'd been working on, dropped the screwdriver on the ground, and took off his work gloves to look at his hand. Although it felt like it weighed one hundred pounds, it didn't look swollen.

"Does it hurt?"

Cruz's question hit him out of the blue. He looked over at his brother. "It's just sore. It's fine."

He nodded. "Maybe Tomás can help you finish it in the morning."

"Sure," Gabe answered. He expected Cruz to leave then, but he didn't.

"But you still need to help him," his brother said.

"I figured."

"I'm just saying…"

"I know what you're saying. I'm not going to make Tomás do it all by himself."

"Good."

"Anything else you need, boss?"

He watched Cruz's reaction closely. Except for a slight eye twitch, he was a statue.

"Actually, there are many things. But don't worry. I'll just take care of them like I take care of everything else," he replied.

"Meaning?"

"I mean that you seem to only want to do the bare minimum, Gabe. You put no effort, no pride into what we give you to take care of. I know the only reason you are even out here every day is because you don't want to hear Dad complain."

"That's not fair, Cruz. I've been busting my ass checking off every task you throw at me. I'm trying to prove to you and Dad and everyone else that you can count on me. But I'm not some hired hand to bark orders at."

Then a surprising thought occurred to him. Was this whole situation bothering him because he really wanted to know what was going on with the ranch? Or was he just bothered because Cruz refused to tell him?

"If I'm going to be running this place, then I need to know everything."

"Just because you shovel hay when you're asked doesn't mean you're ready—"

A woman's scream cut through the evening air, stopping Cruz mid-sentence. Without even looking at each other, they both ran toward the direction of where the scream had come from. It didn't take them long to find the source.

It was their mom.

She was kneeling on the floor of the backyard patio. Their dad lay next to her. His eyes were closed, and his dark skin looked pale and clammy. His brothers showed up just a second after him. Right away, Cruz yelled at Tomás to call 911.

"What happened?" Daniel asked as he knelt down to check to see if their dad was breathing.

"I don't know," his mom said through sobs. "He was carrying out the tray of ribs because he wanted us to eat dinner outside and then, all of sudden, he said he didn't feel good. He gave me the tray and started to walk into the house, and then he just collapsed."

Gabe met Daniel's worried eyes. "Is he...?" He didn't want to say the word.

"He's breathing, and he has a pulse," Daniel answered.

"The ambulance is on the way," Tomás announced.

Cruz bent down to loosen the buttons on their dad's shirt while their mom cradled his head in her lap. After a few seconds, his dad opened his eyes.

"Dad!" Nico yelled.

"Santiago," his mom cried out.

The paramedics arrived soon after that. They put an oxygen mask over his dad's mouth and checked all of his vitals. Whatever they saw on their monitors concerned them enough to tell his mom that they needed to take him to the hospital. She agreed and asked to ride with them.

"I'm coming too," Cruz said.

"Only one other person can ride in the back with us. You'll have to drive yourself," one of the paramedics said.

Their mom waved her hand at Cruz and the rest of them. "No, all of you boys stay here. I don't want Abuelita to be here by herself. You can't do anything there except wait. I'll call when I know what's happening."

They agreed and all walked behind the gurney as the

paramedics wheeled their dad to the ambulance. Gabe and the others watched it drive away carrying their dad and mom inside. He'd never felt so helpless.

After they left, Gabe and his brothers gathered around the backyard's fire pit. Abuelita had made them sandwiches, but no one was in the mood to eat. Part of him thought about calling Nora. She would want to know what was happening. But he decided to wait until he had more information. There was no use worrying her when he wasn't going to be able to answer her questions.

Nico passed around bottles of beer he'd already opened. They sat in silence, leaving only the sounds of the crackling wood and usual animal noises to fill the uneasy night air. Gabe knew they were all thinking of the same thing.

Daniel was the first to break the quiet. "He seemed off this morning, didn't he?" he asked no one in particular.

"He told me he was tired, that he didn't sleep good last night," Tomás added.

"Something is definitely wrong with him," Nico said. "He's always tired. He barely eats. The other day he couldn't even pick up one of the bales to put in the back of the truck."

Gabe sighed and leaned back into his Adirondack chair. "Maybe it's stress?" he said.

"He's always stressed. He's Dad," Daniel said.

"Yeah, but it's obvious he's been worried more than usual. Isn't that right, Cruz?"

His older brother took a swig of his beer. Gabe noticed the clench of his jaw. He knew something.

"Tell us what's going on, Cruz," Gabe pressed. "We deserve to know."

His brother cleared his throat. "We were waiting for the right time to tell you guys, but I figure there's never going to be a right time."

Gabe shook his head in frustration. "You could've been straight with us, with me. I could've helped you come up with ideas to fix it."

The confusion etched across Cruz's face morphed into something else he couldn't decipher. "You can't fix this, Gabe. No one can."

"Sure we can. Tomás is already lining up another boarder for the stable, and I know we can come up with some other things if we all put our heads together."

Cruz threw his hands up. "Gabe, what are you talking about?"

"I'm talking about saving Rancho Lindo! I know it's been struggling financially. But it's not like we're going out of business tomorrow. There's still time to fix this, and then Dad doesn't have to kill himself worrying about this place."

Cruz hung his head and shook it. "That's not why Dad collapsed."

"It's not?"

"Dad's sick," Cruz told them.

"Obviously," Nico said, the sarcasm dripping from the last syllable.

Cruz dragged his hand through his hair. "He has cancer."

Gabe stilled as dread invaded his insides. "Cancer?"

"He was diagnosed earlier this year. Just before..."

My accident. He knew that's what Cruz was going to say.

"How bad?" He had to ask. He didn't want to know the answer, of course. But he had to ask anyway.

The pain in Cruz's eyes was obvious. Gabe's heart dropped to his boots.

"Stage three. Well, it was stage three. I'm sure his doctors are going to want to run more tests after this."

Rage swelled in his chest, and he looked around for something to hit other than the cold air. "Is that why you two have been on my case? Because...because he might not be around for much longer?"

"Yes."

Gabe shot up from his chair. "Dammit, Cruz! You should've told me."

"You were recovering from the accident. Mom and Dad didn't want you to have to worry about him."

"And what about us?" Tomás said.

Cruz shook his head. "Dad was supposed to go see his oncologist next month and have another CT scan. Then they were going to tell all of you."

None of it made sense. Their dad was the toughest son of a bitch he'd ever met. And Gabe had served with some pretty hard men. Sure, he had noticed his energy was lower than before and he didn't eat as much as he used to. But Gabe had chalked it up to the usual stresses of running a business the size of Rancho Lindo. He'd seen it before, even as a kid. There were good times, and there had been lean times. And his dad had carried it all on his shoulders.

His dad was invincible.

"I can't believe this is happening," Daniel said, his voice cracking. Gabe willed himself to keep it together. He had to be strong for his brothers.

And for his mom.

"I'm sorry I had to tell you like this," Cruz said.

"Believe me, I wanted to tell you as soon as Gabe got here. But you know Dad."

He did know. It was the Ortega way. Keep everything to yourself. Don't show your emotions and especially never let anyone see your fear. His dad was one of the most stubborn men he'd ever known. And if Gabe didn't change, he was going to be exactly like him.

As his brothers bombarded Cruz with questions, Gabe just sat there in silence. He had questions too, but they were all pushed down by an overwhelming sense of regret. Why hadn't he tried to fix his relationship with his dad years ago? Why had he always dreaded his visits home, instead of being grateful he had a place to come home to? He'd taken his family for granted for so long. Part of him wanted to apologize to his brothers right then and there. But the words wouldn't come.

And then the anger arrived. He was pissed at himself for the way he'd acted when he first came back and he was pissed at Cruz for not saying anything that first night.

"Dammit, Cruz," Gabe finally said. "You can't keep shit like this from us. We're your brothers."

"Fine. You want me to be honest?" Cruz asked. "You're right. Rancho Lindo is struggling. Just like all the ranches in this area. We've cut as many ranch hands as we can afford to. That means I'm doing a lot more on my own just to keep up. So I can't focus on the ranch's future when I'm just trying to keep it going one day at a time."

"I'm here," he told Cruz. "I'm going to help you run Rancho Lindo."

"No, you're not."

Shock hit Gabe like a ton of bricks. "I don't understand. You need me here now more than ever."

"Maybe? But what I don't need is you doing it out of guilt or obligation. Isn't that why you left in the first place? Dad wanted to give you a chance to get used to the idea. He wanted to give you a chance to want to stay."

Stay. It was the word he'd been struggling with ever since he returned. It held such a deeper meaning. "I don't get you, man."

"And that's our main problem right there. You don't get me, you don't get us. Me, Dad, Tomás, Nico, and Daniel don't do this because we have to. We do it because it's in our blood and we can't imagine doing anything else. The dirt under our boots isn't something to clean off at the end of the day. It's part of our DNA. Forcing it to be a part of yours isn't the answer and isn't going to help anyone, especially not Dad."

"Just because I haven't always been here doesn't mean I don't care about Rancho Lindo. Why is it so hard to believe that? I'm not going to abandon Dad or you or this ranch when you need me the most."

Cruz shrugged and finished off his beer. "You say that now. But is that how you're going to feel six months from now? Or what about when . . . when he's gone."

Gabe's throat tightened at the crack in his brother's voice at the end of the sentence. He couldn't let himself think about his dad not being around. He wasn't ready to face that possibility. The only thing he could focus on at the moment was doing his part as an Ortega son. So what if that came from a sense of obligation rather than passion?

"I'm here now. Just tell me what to do."

Chapter Fourteen

When she woke up that morning, Nora was worried it might rain.

The forecast predicted a sunny day, yet Nora couldn't shake the feeling that the gray skies were a sign that the farmer's market could get canceled. Or worse, a sign of more bad things to come.

It had been a shock to hear about Señor Ortega's cancer. Besides being scared for him and the family, it had dredged up all sorts of painful memories about when her tío Chucho was diagnosed. Nora knew exactly what Gabe was going through. That's why she agreed when he offered to help her at the farmer's market. If this was what he needed to process the news about his dad, she was going to give it to him. It was the least she could do.

Even if spending more time with him only seemed to stir up some familiar emotions.

"How much we selling the blackberries for again?" The question came from behind her as she handed over a bag of pears to Mrs. Davila. She could feel his warm breath on her neck.

She thanked Mrs. Davila for her business and then tended to the crate of apples in front of her. It was that or turn around and have another part of her body accidentally brush against Gabe.

"Three dollars a basket or two baskets for five. And they can mix and match with the raspberries," she told him as she checked for imaginary bruises on the perfect peaches.

"That's right. Okay, thanks."

Gabe moved away, and Nora released the breath she'd been holding. Why was she so affected by his presence today? She blamed the fact that it was a little slow. And it was hot.

In between customers, they'd sit on upside-down crates and drink from their hydro flasks. And every once in a while, they'd spray themselves with the water bottle she used to clean off the fruit she'd cut up for samples. Gabe was wearing a white, sleeveless Sacramento Kings basketball jersey that showed off his muscular biceps. And it was hard to ignore the sprinkles of water glistening from those muscles. Old butterflies came alive again in her stomach, resuscitated by Gabe's genuine attempt to make up for what happened between them.

Don't you dare get a crush on him again.

She watched with amusement after noticing him examine some peaches way too closely.

"Don't tell me," she said after walking over to him. "You're going to make a peach pie."

Gabe set down the two fruits he'd been holding. "A peach salsa, actually."

Nora couldn't tell if he was joking. "Really?" she asked.

He shook his head and laughed. "Nope. Are you

kidding? I'm such a bad cook that I can't even make salsa—which requires no cooking at all."

"I doubt that," Nora told him. "I'm sure Doña Alma must have taught you a thing or two over the years."

"If she did, then I've forgotten it," he said, and bowed his head in exaggerated shame. "Years of eating on military bases will do that to you."

Nora couldn't help but laugh. It was good that he was joking around.

Gabe pulled out his phone, glanced at the screen, and then put it back in his pocket. "Any news?" she asked.

"No. I'll call my mom after lunchtime."

She nodded and went back to rearranging a crate of apples.

"Thanks again for letting me tag along today. I didn't feel like dealing with Cruz."

"Why? What happened?"

"Nothing. Everything."

Nora hated how much the two of them argued. Ever since they were all kids, they were like oil and water. She remembered them fighting more than she remembered them actually getting along or hanging out. One time, when they were both teenagers, they actually used their fists. Cruz had ended up with a busted lip and black eye. Gabe had scratches all over his face and neck. It took both her tío and Señor Ortega to finally pull them apart.

Nowadays, they just used their words. Very loud words.

Even still, it pained her to see them like that with each other. Especially since she'd seen how broken up Cruz had been after Gabe's accident.

"Have you talked to him since he told you guys about your dad?"

"Nope. I'm still mad he hid it from me, and he's still mad that he had to hide it from me. It's all very dysfunctional as always."

She knew that deep down they loved each other. She just wished they liked each other sometimes. And she wished she knew what to say. But before she could say anything, a loud screech drowned out the usual market crowd noises. And it was followed by, "Is that *the* Gabe Ortega?"

They both turned in the direction of the high-pitched female voice, and Nora cursed under her breath.

The unholy scream had come from Sandra Swift.

Of course. Nora rolled her eyes to the heavens.

Sandra Swift was Esperanza's most successful real estate agent. Mostly because she was the only one in town and also because her family owned a handful of properties in the Central Valley. Sandra was also a councilwoman—a title she thought gave her power over others, like Nora.

The leggy blonde sauntered over and collided with Gabe for an inappropriately long hug.

"Oh my gosh, Gabe," she squealed again after releasing him from her clutches. "It's so good to see you. I've been meaning to stop by the ranch to visit but just haven't had the chance. You don't hate me for that, do you?"

Nora doubted that would be a reason for Gabe to hate her. But there were at least one hundred other reasons that she could think as to why he needed to stay away from Sandra. She decided that she would share them with him as soon as she got the chance. High on the list would be the fact that, according to Daniel, Sandra had tried several times to meet with Señor Ortega and Cruz to convince them to sell Rancho Lindo.

Luckily, her request for meetings had always been ignored.

"Hey Sandra. It's nice to see you," he said.

Maybe he did hate her? It was never too late to hope.

As the two made small talk, Nora chided herself for being so catty. So what if she was only catty in her own mind. She knew she was better than that.

And then she immediately changed her mind when Sandra finally saw her standing there.

"Hello Nora," she said in the same syrupy voice she used in her TV commercials.

"Hi Sandra."

The woman picked up a peach and waved it around. "I always forget that you have a little booth here. I usually order all my produce online and have it delivered."

Nora was about to tell her she didn't need her business anyway when Gabe finally spoke up. "You should really try some of her fruits and vegetables. In fact, I'm sure Nora wouldn't mind if you took that peach, on the house, of course. Taste it and then you can come back tomorrow and buy a whole bag's worth, because I know you're going to love it that much."

She shot Gabe a look. Why was he giving away her peaches, especially to this woman?

But he wasn't paying attention, and she had no choice but to nod her head.

Sandra swatted Gabe's arm. "You're so sweet. We should've never broken up."

Nora's mouth fell open. "You two dated?" she asked.

"Kind of," Gabe said.

"For two months," Sandra said at the same time.

"It was high school," he added, as if that made some kind of difference.

Nora wasn't quite sure what to say about that. She'd had enough of being the sole witness to their little reunion.

As if reading her mind, Gabe said, "Well, we're getting some customers, so we better get back to it. It was nice seeing you, Sandra."

He smiled and walked away, leaving an obviously annoyed Sandra with a very irritated Nora.

"So you two work together at the ranch," she asked Nora.

"Um, kind of? I mean, Gabe does a lot of different things there. He doesn't have much to do with the garden, though."

"Do you know if he's seeing anyone?"

Nora tried her very best not to laugh. There was no way that Gabe would date Sandra. Or would he? She hated that she couldn't say for certain. Or that she even cared.

"I have no idea," Nora answered. "So do you need a bag for your peach?"

Sandra scrunched up her nose and handed the piece of fruit back to Nora. "It's too soft for me. I like my peaches hard and plump," she said, looking back at where Gabe was standing. Then she flashed a fake saccharine smile at Nora and headed over to the candle booth across the street.

A strange, wet feeling spread over her palm, and that was only reason why she stopped watching Sandra. She looked down and saw the imprints of her fingers around the peach. Nora didn't realize how hard she'd been gripping the poor fruit.

Nora turned around to throw the damaged peach into her discard box and tried not to care if Sandra ended up getting her claws into Gabe too.

It was about 1:30 p.m. when Gabe and Nora packed up the last of the empty crates. She'd insisted on driving to town that morning but asked if he wanted to drive back.

He shook his head. "I'm good. It seems like all I do is drive everyone around these days. I'm happy to be the one in the passenger side for once."

She was about to open the driver's-side door when he reached out and grabbed her wrist. "Unless you're tired. I don't mind driving if you want to close your eyes for a few minutes."

Nora looked down at where he was holding her. It wasn't the first time they'd touched. Her butt had been in his arms for several minutes, after all. Still, new sensations came to life inside her. Slowly, she looked up and met his eyes.

After a few seconds, she found her voice. "That's okay. I don't mind driving."

He offered her a quick smile and let her go.

Once they were in the car, Nora tried to make small talk. It wasn't going to be a long ride. That didn't mean she wanted to deal with any awkward silences, though.

"You're a pretty good salesman," she started. "I'm impressed by how you were answering everyone's questions."

"I didn't really do that much. They seem to sell themselves."

"They didn't at first," Nora admitted. "I can't believe how popular they are now."

When she took over the garden a year ago, building a greenhouse to grow microgreens had been the first project she'd wanted to accomplish. She'd already been growing a few trays at her apartment in Washington just for her own use and for friends and coworkers. So she knew she could start off with what she was comfortable growing already: radishes, broccoli, and arugula. After a few months, she began expanding and soon enough she had the best and most popular selection of microgreens at the farmer's market.

"Abuelita made me try the mustard once a few days ago, and I couldn't believe how much flavor was packed into such a little plant."

She laughed and nodded in agreement. "Right? You should try the radishes. Now, those are spicy."

"Oh, I already have. I tasted a sample from every tray when we were setting up."

"You did not."

"I did. I wanted to be prepared."

Nora's heart inflated at his endearing admission. She knew she was probably smiling like a goofball, but she didn't care.

"I'll give this town one thing—you can't beat the scenery."

Nora glanced over expecting to see Gabe looking out the window. Instead, he was staring directly at her. And he didn't turn away when she caught him.

Instead, she was the one to avert her eyes first and tried to focus on the road in front of her.

"Hey, is that Old Rio Road coming up?" Gabe asked.

"It sure is."

"Can you turn down it? I want to check something out."

Nora obeyed the request and made a left turn onto the unpaved road. There were only a few hundred undeveloped acres between the road and the west perimeter gate of Rancho Lindo. She knew that Señor Ortega had always wanted to purchase the land, but the owner had never wanted to sell. So the property remained open and untouched for as long as she could remember.

They drove less than a mile before reaching the end of the road. The Tres Aguas creek sat just a few feet away.

"Is this what you wanted to see?" she asked with a small laugh.

Gabe unbuckled his seat belt and was out the door before she even had a chance to turn off the ignition. She found him standing next to one of the bigger trees along the banks of the creek.

"I can't believe it's still here," Gabe said, and grabbed the knotted rope hanging from one of the lower limbs.

"Wow," she said, and moved closer. "I can't believe it's still here either. Guess Cruz did a good job tying it back then."

He eyed it up and down. "I wonder if the limb would break if I got on it now?"

She patted the thick trunk etched with grooves of history. "This oak tree is probably a hundred years old. At least. I think it's probably pretty sturdy."

"You're probably right."

Nora shielded her eyes with her hand and scanned the other trees and bushes surrounding them. One summer, she'd made it her mission to document every flower and plant in the area. Just for fun. Tía Luz had given her a special notebook just for her research, and Nora had filled it up in no time with her list and drawings. She didn't need to refer to the notebook now, as her expert eye identified the deep magenta pea-sized flowers of a Western Rosebud and the red, acidic berries of a toyon shrub growing just a few feet from where they stood.

"Hey, there's my reading tree over there," she said, pointing to a nearby coast live oak.

"You're right. Hey, that reminds me of a question I've been wanting to ask. Why didn't you ever get in the water with us?"

"What?"

"I distinctly remember you always sitting under that tree with a book while we goofed off in the creek."

"I didn't know how to swim," she admitted sheepishly.

His eyes grew wide and curious. "Really?"

"I didn't learn until I was in college. I asked a friend to teach me. I'm still not the best swimmer, but at least I won't drown."

"Good. Then you don't have an excuse this time. Let's go for a swim," he said as he kicked off his shoes and socks.

Nora choked on her breath. "Now?"

Gabe grabbed the bottom of his jersey and then pulled it over his head. Hard abs covered in a light patch of dark hair instantly came into view, and she would've choked again if she had been breathing.

She turned away and tried to focus on the tree. "You're not kidding, are you?"

Half-naked Gabe came into view just as he grabbed the rope. "What do you think?"

Nora watched as he took a few steps backward, ran, and swung himself over the creek using the rope. She'd watched him do it tons of times when they were kids. That's why she knew instantly something went wrong.

It seemed to her that Gabe lost his grip or let go much sooner than he was supposed to. He'd fallen dangerously close to the edge of the bank and she held her breath instinctively. The grunt she heard scared her, as did the swear words that came out of his mouth as soon as he emerged.

Nora exhaled in some relief. But she knew he was hurt. Without thinking, she took off her shoes and socks and jumped into the water.

"What's wrong?" she yelled as she swam toward him.

"My shoulder," he said as he rolled it over and over again. "I couldn't hold on."

Nora grabbed his wrist and held it so he'd stop moving. "Let me see."

He nodded and she slowly extended his arm toward her. Then she touched his bare shoulder and pressed gently. Gabe hissed at her touch.

"I'm sorry," she told him. That's when she noticed the long pink scar etched along the curve of his upper arm. "It doesn't look like you cut it or anything, so that's good."

"Sometimes I forget, you know?"

She nodded and then let go of his wrist. Together, they walked back to the bank of the creek. They picked up their stuff and headed to the truck. Since they were both dripping wet, Nora lowered the tailgate so they could sit for a while.

Neither spoke as they took turns drying themselves off with the one towel she happened to keep in the truck. The sun was still strong and hot, so it wouldn't be long before they were dry enough to head home.

"You know, we're only about five minutes away," she finally said. "We don't need to stay out here."

"I don't mind staying for a few minutes, do you?"

She shook her head and continued to bask in the warm rays. Honestly, she would have been perfectly content just sitting there with Gabe enjoying the peace and soothing sounds of the natural landscape surrounding them. When she closed her eyes, she could make out water softly lapping the rocks on the edge of the creek and a light breeze rustling through the leaves of the trees. Every once in a while, she got lost in the sweet cacophony of birds whistling to one another. So when she felt Gabe move beside her, it took her a minute to remember that she hadn't been sitting there alone.

"Cruz was telling me about your plans to try to get a contract with some nearby markets," he said out of the blue. "He really thinks the garden is going to be one of the more profitable lines of business for us. Rancho Lindo is really lucky that you came back."

Nora couldn't help but smile. "I hadn't planned on staying. But your brothers can be pretty charming and convincing when they want."

For the next several minutes, Nora told Gabe how she'd returned to the ranch for her tío's funeral but had no idea of what to do with her life when she went back home. Then, during the reception at the main house, she decided to visit Doña Alma's garden for the last time. Instead, she'd found nothing but empty plants and a few shriveled-up bushes. Nico and Daniel had found her there and explained that their dad hadn't wanted his suegra to be kneeling and bending so much.

All that remained of the garden was the few containers on the kitchen's windowsill.

"That's when Nico and Daniel decided that I needed to stay and grow back everything."

"Those two are always thinking up some crazy scheme," Gabe said with a chuckle.

She also laughed. "Always. Anyway, I didn't think they were serious. And before I could even think if I wanted to stay, they had convinced your dad that I should."

"Well, I'm glad you did," Gabe said.

A new lightness buoyed her, and she instinctively sat straighter. "Thanks."

But in classic Nora fashion, she couldn't *not* pick at low-hanging fruit. "You know, your family has done a lot for me. If your abuelita hadn't taught me about herbs and the differences in potting soils, I honestly don't know what I would have done with my life. I think that's why I've been giving you such a hard time about them. I see how much they love you. And now with my mom and tío gone, I guess it makes me miss having a real family. I would give anything to have what you have."

She let out a long nervous sigh after her raw admission. She hadn't said those things to make him feel guilty. She just felt like he should know where she was coming from.

"Me questioning whether to stay has nothing to do with wanting to get away from them. At least not anymore. But I don't want to stay because that's what everyone else wants. I need to make sure that I really have a place in the business. Not just because I'm an Ortega, but because I can make a difference."

In that moment, Nora finally understood Gabe. It

was the reason why she'd quit her job. It was the reason why she had agreed to take over the garden. At Rancho Lindo, she had the opportunity to literally help feed others. She also had a chance to leave her mark.

"The thing about family businesses is that sometimes doing things the way you've always done them isn't necessarily why they succeed. I think Rancho Lindo has lasted for generations because every person here has a purpose. I think you just need to find that purpose."

"And what if I can't? Or what if my real purpose is something else?"

Nora considered this for a second. But then she remembered something that Gabe had seemed to forget. As much as Señor Ortega wanted his sons to work with him, she knew deep down that he'd never risk his family's legacy on someone who could run it into the ground. Gabe's father obviously saw something in Gabe that he couldn't see in himself.

"For what it's worth, you did what you set out to do," she told him.

"Really? And what exactly would that be?"

Nora took a deep breath. "You proved me wrong. Not only are you still here, but you seem to really be getting more involved in the ranch."

"You might be the only one who sees that."

"I don't think that's true. Daniel and Tomás tell me all the time about the great ideas you have to bring in more business."

"That's the problem. They're ideas, not actual plans, because Cruz doesn't think I'll see any of them through."

"He just needs time. He'll come around."

"Maybe."

"Well, I'm not Cruz, and I can admit when I'm wrong."

Gabe smiled at her. "Does this mean you accept my apology for real this time?"

She nodded and lowered her eyes.

"Good. I'm glad." He grunted the last two words.

Nora looked back up and saw him wincing and rolling his shoulder. "You need to ice that when we get back to the ranch."

"I will. Just give me a minute, and we'll go."

She watched as Gabe continued to stretch his arm and shoulder. When he seemed to finally settle down, Nora waited quietly for him to tell her he was ready. Instead, Gabe sat there next to her just staring out into the field.

"Can I tell you something?" he asked eventually without glancing in her direction.

"Of course. Anything," she replied.

"Is it weird that I think it's weird that no one in my family has ever asked me about my accident?"

She shrugged and took a long breath. "I don't think it's weird that you think it's weird. But I also don't think it's weird that they haven't asked. They probably think it's painful for you to talk about."

He looked off into the distance. "I guess that makes sense. Or maybe it's too painful for them to hear? My family, well, mainly my dad and brothers, aren't the best at dealing with deep emotions. It's probably a good thing then that they aren't always asking about my injuries—for me at least. Sometimes my thoughts are best left unsaid."

Silence fell between them again.

"Why haven't you asked?" His question took her by surprise.

"I don't know. I guess I didn't feel like it was my place."

"That didn't stop you before," he said with a chuckle.

She laughed too. "True. But this is different. I may not know the details, but I know that you went through something very traumatic. It's obvious you're still dealing with the repercussions and it's not my place to push you to talk about something like that before you're ready."

"My unit had just finished our usual patrol and were heading back to camp," he began.

Her body tensed. "You don't have to—"

"I know."

"Okay."

Gabe continued looking everywhere but at her. "Our driver saw the IED in the road at the last minute and swerved to avoid it. But something still hit one of the tires and the Humvee flipped in the air and then rolled over one more time. Luckily, we were all wearing seat belts."

Instinctively, she reached out and grabbed the hand that he rested on his thigh. "I can't even imagine how awful that must have been for you."

"I fractured my shoulder, broke my collarbone, my arm, and my wrist," he said without even looking at her. "I've had a couple of surgeries, and there are so many pins and screws in me that I'll set off metal directors for the rest of my life."

Nora winced involuntarily. "I had no idea, Gabe."

"I was going to physical therapy over in Maryland. But I haven't done anything since I've been home. I guess I thought everything would heal on its own. Now I know I was just kidding myself. I'll probably never get back to how I was before."

She squeezed his hand. "Gabe, you were in a major accident. You could have died. It's going to take some time for your body to heal. You can't rush something like that."

He finally turned his head, and his dark eyes locked with hers. The pain she saw reflected in them was like a knife to her heart. And all she wanted in that moment was to take it all away.

"I was the best at what I did. For once in my life, I knew exactly who I was. I knew exactly where my life was headed. Now I'm not so sure."

Tears welled up in her eyes. She finally understood why he couldn't trust himself to be who his family expected him to be. Gabe was lost like she had been once.

Nora let go of his hand to touch his cheek. His eyes held on to hers for what seemed like forever. The birds, the breeze, and the water quieted until she couldn't hear anything but the blood rushing through her veins and her own stuttered breaths.

Slowly, Gabe's head moved closer to hers. He covered the hand on his cheek with his own and lowered it gently onto his knee. He reached back up to touch her face. "Nora," he whispered, moving an errant strand from her braid behind her ear. "Honora."

Anticipation swelled in her chest. Was this really happening? After all these years? Over the past few weeks, Gabe had chipped away at the stone of resentment and hurt she'd been carrying since she was a teenager. He had shown her that he wasn't the oblivious and shallow boy who hadn't given her a second thought back then. This man was layered, sensitive, and torn between doing the right thing and doing what was necessary. They were more alike than she could have ever imagined.

Whatever crush she'd had on Gabe when she was six-teen was gone. New, unexpected feelings had shattered that without her even realizing it until this morning.

It scared her.

Nora cleared her throat and pulled back from him. "We should probably get going. I promised your abuelita I'd pick some cabbage and carrots for her before she started dinner."

Gabe dropped his hand and nodded. "Of course. Let's go home."

She hopped off the tailgate, and he did the same. Soon enough they were back on the ranch and pulling in front of the garden gate. They worked in silence to move everything from the truck and stack the crates just outside the greenhouse. When they were done and Gabe made sure she didn't need anything else, he told her to have a good night.

"You too," she said. "And thank you. You really helped a lot today."

He smiled. "Thanks. I actually didn't mind it at all. I even learned a thing or two."

"Oh yeah? Like what?"

"Like the difference between tangelos and tanger-ines. And I also learned that pear trees can take up to six years to bear their fruit. It makes sense, though. Good things like that shouldn't be rushed. I know that now."

Nora couldn't quite read his expression. All she knew was that her pulse quickened at the way he looked at her. But before she could question or analyze, he waved and headed toward his house, leaving her in the middle of her garden wondering why she couldn't stop smiling.

Chapter Fifteen

Hey Nora," Tomás yelled out. "Need help?"

Gabe stilled. He hadn't seen Nora since the day of the farmer's market. He'd spent the last few days not really avoiding her, but also not really trying to find her.

His dad was home from the hospital and Gabe had been preoccupied to say the least. Doctors had said he'd been dehydrated and his body had been fighting off some sort of virus. An appointment with his oncologist later that month would hopefully provide some answers to the questions all of them now had.

Of course, his dad had ordered that everything—and everyone—remain business as usual. And that people needed to stop asking how he was feeling.

For Gabe, his dad's illness was a wake-up call. Cruz had said he didn't want him to take on more responsibilities out of obligation. That didn't mean Gabe was going to listen. If anything, he was determined to find ways to bring in new revenue for the ranch.

He already had come up with one possibility. But it involved Nora, which meant he had to talk to her. It wasn't lost on him that she hadn't been going out of her way to talk to him either.

It was obvious that they both knew what had almost happened there at the creek. He had wanted to kiss Nora. And she'd made it clear she didn't want to kiss him.

Maybe he'd imagined the mutual attraction?

That meant that Gabe had to make things okay between them. He didn't want to scare her off, or worse, give her a new reason to dislike him. He couldn't hide from her anymore.

Gabe took a deep breath and turned to see Nora walking toward them. He and Tomás were just about to head into the stable so they could get a stall ready for a new boarder. His breath caught in his throat at seeing her again. Flashes of images from that afternoon rushed into his mind. The way she'd jumped into the creek fully clothed to save him even though he hadn't needed saving. The way she'd grabbed his hand as he told her about the accident, somehow knowing he'd needed something to hold on to to get him through the memory. The way she looked at him with those big brown eyes of hers and how he couldn't help but get lost in them.

"Hey, Gabe," she said softly, giving him a hesitant smile.

"Hi Nora," he replied.

"Cruz said you were delivering the pumpkins today," Tomás said. "I can go with you if you want?"

"I can go," Gabe offered. He needed to get Nora alone so they could talk.

"That's okay," she rushed to say. "I can handle it."

"I'm sure you can. But Tomás here was about to make me clean stalls. Please let me go help you instead."

He ignored the questioning looks from his brother, who could obviously tell something else was going on. Luckily for him, Tomás knew when to keep his mouth shut.

"Fine," Nora said. "Let's go."

It wasn't until they were both in the truck that Nora explained she was taking about four dozen pumpkins to the town square for the upcoming fall festival.

"So you harvested this batch last week but you're only taking them to town now?" he asked.

"They had to sit in the sun after I cut them for about a week and a half so their shells could harden and the stems could heal up," she explained. "I want to make sure that the batch we give the festival are our best."

"I had no idea you were so passionate about pumpkins," he teased.

Nora rolled her eyes at him. "Pumpkins are probably one of the easiest things to grow. They don't need much. But ours are some of the biggest in town."

"Are they, now?" Gabe asked.

"Yep," she answered with a big proud smile. "That's why the festival committee likes using ours more for decorations than for the carving or throwing contests. They'll stack them with some haystacks outside the community center and around the town square. And they'll keep them there for a few weeks."

"That's cool. I guess."

Again she ignored his attempt to rile her up. "It *is* cool. Plus it's good PR for our stand at the farmer's market. We usually sell out every Saturday in October—and not just the pumpkins. The increase in traffic helps with overall sales, especially because I only pick the best of the best."

Gabe raised his eyebrows at her. "I had no idea you were such a perfectionist. Did I just find your only flaw?"

"Why is it a flaw if I only want to give the town the best pumpkins for the festival?"

"Because they're pumpkins. They can't be perfect."

"Well, of course I know that. But what's wrong with wanting as close to perfection as possible?"

"Because that kind of thinking only leads to disappointment. Trust me. I know."

Gabe wondered if Nora realized he wasn't just talking about pumpkins anymore.

"I don't think that setting high expectations is a bad thing," she told him. "No one should settle for something less than they want or deserve."

Gabe nodded in appreciation. "Well, I guess if everyone loves your perfect pumpkins, then good for you."

"Good for Rancho Lindo," she corrected.

"Right," he said. "Well, when you put it that way, how can I not be proud of these pumpkins too?"

Then out of nowhere, Nora said, "You should save one for Sandra."

Gabe scoffed. "Why on earth would I give a pumpkin to her?"

"I don't know. You were going to give her a peach. A pumpkin seems like the next logical step."

He didn't miss the sarcasm in her tone, and it made him laugh. "Wait. Were you mad that I offered to let her take that peach?"

"I wasn't mad. I was just surprised, that's all."

"Honestly, I was just trying to make her leave faster."

Nora's eyes widened. "You were? I thought you liked her. You dated her, didn't you?"

"Uh, yeah, and I also broke up with her," he said with a wave of his arms. "Plus, I was like fifteen. My taste in women hadn't fully developed yet. I'm very picky now."

A wave of laughter escaped from her. "Good to know that you agree that Sandra Swift is not pumpkin-worthy," she said after catching her breath.

"She's not even peach-worthy," Gabe said with a shrug. "I get it now. Sorry about that."

Nora smiled at his apology. "It's fine. I just don't like that woman."

"I thought you loved everyone in Esperanza."

"I do. Except for her."

"Fair enough. I should probably warn you though that she is going to stop by next week."

"Why?"

"I'm not sure. Cruz just told me that she's coming to meet with him and Dad. He only mentioned it because apparently she'd asked if I was going to be there and he had told her that I wasn't."

"Maybe you should tell Cruz that you want to be in the meeting."

"But I don't." He didn't tell Nora that he didn't think Cruz would agree to it anyway.

"I get that. Still, aren't you curious as to why she's coming?"

"A little," Gabe said with a shrug. "But not enough to spend an hour with her, my dad, and Cruz."

They arrived at the town square a few minutes later. Gabe exited the truck, put on his work gloves, and helped Nora start transferring the pumpkins from the back to the square's center gazebo.

"Send me some pics from the festival," he said after

they were all done. "I would love to see the literal fruits of my hard labor."

"You're not going to the festival?" Nora asked abruptly.

"Maybe, maybe not," Gabe said, and shrugged his shoulders. "I don't know if I've fully recovered from my last public event. I'm not sure if I'm ready for another town interrogation."

The thought of that pancake breakfast made him shudder.

"I'm sorry," she said softly.

"For what?"

Nora shrugged. "For not realizing how hard it's been for you coming back to all this after so many years. There are so many people watching you and expecting things from you. It's probably not the best way to heal, is it?"

"Maybe not. But things have gotten better," he said.

Her cheeks blushed, and he knew it wasn't because of the rising afternoon heat. That's when Gabe knew he hadn't imagined anything. Nora was attracted to him.

He waited a few seconds before opening his mouth again. "So are we okay?"

"You tell me."

Gabe stopped walking and she did the same. "I want us to be. That's why I wanted to talk to you. I wanted to apologize if I did anything that made you uncomfortable that day."

She looked down. "You didn't do anything, Gabe."

He dragged his palm over his face and exhaled a long, deep breath. "Technically, sure. But..."

"But nothing. You shared something very personal with me, and it affected both of us. That's all."

Gabe still felt like he needed to explain himself. He stepped closer and studied her face. "Talking about the accident stirred up all these emotions and you were being so sweet and comforting. I guess I wasn't thinking. It was a mistake, I know that."

Nora met his gaze head-on. "It's fine. We are good."

Instinct told him that she wasn't being completely truthful. He couldn't get a read on what was going on behind those eyes of hers. But if she didn't want to tell him, then he wasn't going to push.

Before they headed home, Gabe convinced Nora that they should stop at Lina's for a piece of pie. He ordered a slice of chocolate cream and she got the peach. When the waitress left, they had both burst into laughter at the inside joke.

"Is Tomás going to be mad that you're not back yet?"

Gabe shrugged. "Probably. I'll take him a piece, and he'll forgive me. What's his favorite?"

"Blueberry. He says Lina's blueberry pies are the best in the country."

"That's right. When he and Mia were together, he'd bring home a pie every time they went out on a date. Maybe if we get him to try something new, then he'll start dating someone new too."

"Just between you and me, I think the new vet has a little crush on Tomás," Nora told him. "But, of course, he hasn't done anything about it."

Gabe enjoyed hearing this little tidbit of gossip. Especially because he was going to put it in his pocket and use it to tease his brother at a later date. "My brother is completely oblivious when it comes to women. Personally, I think it's because he's still hung up on Mia."

"Really? After all this time?"

"He hasn't dated anyone since, right? What else could it be?"

Their pies arrived and Gabe wasted no time digging in.

"Maybe he just needs help finding someone?" Nora continued after her first bite. "You and the guys should set him up."

Gabe shook his head. "Not me. I am not in the matchmaking business nor do I ever want to be. You should ask Abuelita, though. She would be all over it."

Nora laughed. "I couldn't do that to Tomás."

"Actually, I think she actually has an eye on someone for you."

Her eyes grew big. "Me? Who?"

"A certain deputy who seems to have a deep, deep love for oregano."

"Lucas? Are you serious?"

"Yep. I saw it myself that first day at the farmer's market. He's got a thing for you, Miss Nora. You really don't see it?"

She shrugged and threw her hands up. "I mean, I knew he liked me. But I thought it was because he was new and trying very hard to make friends. He's never said anything, or done anything, to make me think he has those kinds of feelings for me."

Maybe it was his imagination, but he could've sworn that the air around them thinned. Gabe wasn't sure why, but he couldn't help but get the impression that there was something behind her words. He wasn't good at guessing games. He never had the patience. He itched with frustration. Talking about Tomás and Lucas and their hopeless prospects for romance hadn't been the best idea he'd ever had. Not when things between them were still so raw. So much in flux.

Still, part of him needed to know.

"Maybe I'm wrong. But what if I'm not? What would you say if he asked you out?"

Nora studied him, and it took everything he had not to be an open book. He didn't want her to know that he'd gone from insisting they couldn't be a thing to at least wanting to know if there was a chance in a matter of seconds.

"I guess I'd tell him that while I definitely wanted to be friends, I didn't think it would be a good idea. He just got to town. What if six months down the road, he decided Esperanza wasn't for him and he left? I need someone with deeper ties because I'm not planning on going anywhere."

"I'm not talking about marriage, Nora. What's the harm in a few dates?"

Wait, why did he find himself trying to make a case for Deputy Lucas? He just met the guy. Why did it matter that Deputy Lucas was getting shot down before he even had a chance to pull the trigger?

"In case you hadn't noticed, I'm not looking for temporary."

A cold realization came over him. Nora might be attracted to him, but it didn't mean anything. Nothing would ever happen between them because he couldn't give her what she wanted—forever.

"Understood," he said with a nod. "Poor Deputy Lucas. I almost feel sorry for the guy."

He'd meant that last part as a joke, but it wasn't in him to even give her a half-hearted smile.

Chapter Sixteen

It's good to be home, Nora thought as soon as she walked through the front door.

The cottage on the edge of the ranch's property hadn't changed much since when her tío and tía lived there. But after a year, she'd been able to add her own personal touches to make it feel like it was really hers. She'd replaced the 1970s orange drapes with sheer white curtains in the living room and light gray ones in her bedroom. It hurt her to do it, but she got rid of her tío's old recliner and bought a blue-and-white-striped cozy armchair to put in its place. She'd kept the dishes and knickknacks that her tía didn't want to take with her. But perhaps the most favorite thing of her tía's that Nora was able to keep was her sewing machine table. Nora had never been much of a seamstress until she swore she wouldn't let the table collect dust in the corner. So, for the past year, she'd been taking lessons from Doña Alma and had already made a few covers for her throw pillows and two placemats for her small kitchen island/breakfast table.

Nora walked into her bedroom, kicked off her tennis

shoes, and fell backward onto her bed. Her ankle was sore, but it was bearable. She stared at her ceiling fan and willed it to go faster. She didn't have the energy to get up and pull the chain. And on this 90-degree late September afternoon, Nora needed the fan to go faster.

Still lying on the bed, she wiggled out of her tan capri pants and slid off her white linen top to let the breeze from the fan cool her legs and arms. After a while, Nora's eyelids grew heavy and she fought to keep them open. If she fell asleep now, then she'd be out for the night, and it was way too early for bed.

It was just after two in the afternoon when she'd finally packed up and left the farmer's market. It had been an especially busy day. Gabe hadn't gone with her this time. She was still surprised by the fact that he genuinely seemed impressed with the products she was selling, especially the microgreens. To her pleasant surprise, Gabe was acting like he was actually interested in the business side of things.

After her long, relaxing bath, Nora took out her contacts, put on her glasses, and changed into a T-shirt and leggings. Next, she made herself a big salad and grilled a piece of salmon for an early dinner. The sun was setting when she decided to take her glass of wine and book outside to her porch. The evening air was still warm, but every once in a while, a light breeze would cool her before it became too uncomfortable.

It was a perfect Friday night.

Nora opened her book and was just about to start a new chapter when the rumble of a truck engine broke through the silence of her perfect Friday evening. She watched as the truck pulled up next to the cottage. It was Gabe.

He waved and then turned off the ignition. Nora wondered why on earth he would be at her home on a Friday evening. But her question died in her throat as soon as he got out of the truck. He wore dark jeans and a charcoal-gray T-shirt that fit his body perfectly. He looked so good that her knees and resolve to play it cool began to waver.

Gabe took the steps of her porch with one long stride and extended a mason jar in her direction. "Raspberry jam from Abuelita."

Nora couldn't help but smile and gladly took the container from him. "How did the jam come out?"

"Delicious. Amazing. The best thing I've eaten in a long time."

"Wow, that's a pretty bold review."

"Abuelita is a master chef, but something tells me your raspberries have a lot to do with it," he said earnestly.

And just like that, Nora's heart melted. "Thanks."

He stared at her for a few seconds and she couldn't help but feel self-conscious.

"Is there something on my face?" she asked, touching her cheek.

"You're wearing glasses," he stated.

Nora pushed them back farther on her nose. "Oh. Yeah. I need them to read," she explained, and lifted up her book as if to prove it.

Gabe still seemed to be trying to figure out something.

"Um, is everything okay?"

He laughed and shook his head. "Sorry. It's just you look more like you now, I guess."

"Come again?"

"You look more like you from, you know, before. It's like I'm seeing you for the first time again."

She wasn't sure how to respond to that. Before she thought better of it, Nora simply said, "I just opened a bottle of wine. Would you like a glass? Or I also have some beer."

Gabe smiled. "I'll take a beer, please."

Nora put the jar of jam in the fridge. Then she pulled out one of three bottles of the pale ale she'd bought just the other day. But she stopped in the middle of her kitchen once the realization hit that she had just willingly invited Gabe Ortega to sit on her porch and have a drink with her.

He wants to be friends, right? This is what friends do.

She couldn't believe how much had changed between them in the past few weeks.

At first, Nora had been hurt by his reaction to what had almost happened that day at the creek. Why had he been stumbling all over himself to apologize for something he didn't even do? She dared not imagine how he would've acted if they had actually kissed. It was clear he saw it as a mistake. A slip-up caused by him feeling raw and exposed about his accident. It had had nothing to do with her. He'd just needed someone to listen to him. He had been searching for solace in a pair of lips and hers just happened to be nearby.

To make matters worse, it seemed like he was trying to get her to go out with Deputy Lucas! So not only did the man *not* want to kiss her, he wanted to make sure she had someone else to kiss instead. It was beyond mortifying.

Still, she'd lied and told him everything was okay.

What else could she say? Admit that she found him attractive and it sucked that he didn't feel the same?

That was absolutely not an option.

After nursing her hurt ego for a few days, Nora convinced herself it was better to forget about what had happened. She shuddered at how things might be between them now if she'd given in to her momentary lapse of desire.

Any feelings for Gabe, other than friendship, would be an inconvenience to say the least. Not only would it be a bad idea for her to have romantic feelings for an Ortega brother, this one in particular might not be in it for the long term. And she certainly wasn't going to do anything to risk her business—or her heart—on a guy who had one foot out of the barn.

Warmth rushed to her face at the possibility.

Stop it. He's just another friend. That's all.

Straightening her shoulders, Nora went back outside.

It honestly surprised her to see him still sitting on her porch. She handed him the beer and took the seat next to him.

"If you don't like it, you won't hurt my feelings if you don't drink it. I can get you some water or lemonade instead."

Or you can leave and pretend I'm not trying to make you stay with offers of assorted beverages.

"No, it's good," Gabe said after taking a swig. "Thank you."

"You're welcome," she replied.

He cleared his throat and Nora noticed the beads of sweat dotting his hairline. Was he nervous?

She was about to ask if everything was okay with his

dad, when he said, "The jam isn't the only reason why I came over tonight."

"Oh. Okay. What's up?"

"I really think we should look into getting the microgreens into some grocery stores," he rushed to say.

She nodded. "That's the goal."

"Right. I know you wanted to wait at least another year so you can increase your production. But I think we should really start having those conversations now. You have product samples, you already have an established customer base, and, well, you have me."

She couldn't help but laugh. "I didn't realize."

"I have connections, Nora. I'm giving you permission to use me."

And just like that, the air crinkled with tension as the innuendo hung between them like an unspoken dare. It challenged them to confront the lingering looks and accidental touches they'd danced around for weeks. An electric energy buzzed just below the surface of her skin and it took everything she had to try to dull the charge she now felt whenever she was around him.

Yes, she was attracted to him. Yes, she'd spent more nights than she cared to admit dreaming about what would have happened if she'd allowed herself to get swept up in that moment. So what if he wore jeans as comfortably as other men wore sweatpants? And so what if his jawline looked like it could sharpen a steak knife with just a few strokes? That didn't mean she should risk their tenuous friendship for something that couldn't last. But business was an entirely different matter.

Gabe cleared his throat and continued. "And I want you to know that this would be a partnership—it's not going to be only a Rancho Lindo product. You deserve the credit and the money. I'll make sure you get them both."

She was surprised at Gabe's faith in her. Delighted even. He really believed that this could work. How could she not say yes?

Nora took a breath and met his eyes again. "Well then. I guess I better get you another beer."

An hour later, they were still on her porch brainstorming ways to amp up her microgreens production. "I've been wanting to expand the varieties," she shared. "I think I'm going to try to grow flax next."

"Really? Why flax?"

"Last month, I was down in Santa Barbara for their farmer's market. A handful of people asked me if I had flax microgreens. One woman told me she didn't like the quality of the ones sold at a nearby health food store. I did some research, and they are getting pretty popular. I think I could sell a lot."

Gabe took a step closer. The sun was behind him and she had to squint her eyes in order to study his expression. There was brightness there that had nothing to do with UV rays.

"Can I ask a favor?"

She was sure he didn't mean for the question to sound dangerous, but it did. At least to her. What would she be agreeing to? Her curiosity though would only let her give him one answer.

"Sure," she replied.

"Can I help you with the flax microgreens? I'm talking beginning to end. I want to learn it all."

"Oh," Nora answered in surprise. "Yeah, of course."

"I'm being serious."

"So am I."

If she'd taken a few more seconds to think about it, Nora might have answered differently. She thought Gabe's enthusiasm was adorable. Hell, it was damn attractive. A new restless energy stirred within her, making her pulse quicken and her senses sharpen.

After agreeing to next steps, their talk turned to Gabe sharing stories about the places he'd seen during his service. He had just finished telling her about the time his abuelita tried unsuccessfully to re-create a rice dish he'd written to her about while he was in Kabul, when a thought seemed to suddenly occur to him.

"Speaking of Abuelita, what was in that bag you gave her at the farmer's market that one day?"

The question made her smile, but she wasn't ready to divulge. "She needed something from Kathy's store, so I picked it up for her."

Kathy and her husband owned the town's general store. They carried everything from socks to gallons of milk. It was basically the Target of Esperanza.

Gabe narrowed his eyes. "Something? Like...?"

"She didn't tell you?"

"I didn't ask."

"Well, if you want to know, then you'll have to ask her."

"Why do I get the feeling that you and Abuelita are best buddies?"

She never thought of their relationship that way. But in a way it was true. "Maybe we are."

He finished off his beer and set the bottle on the ground next to his foot. "You know she thinks of you as a granddaughter, don't you?"

Warmth hugged her heart. "She does?"

"Of course. She used to say you were *her* Honora. And now you're *her* Nora."

She never knew her mother's parents. Apparently, they had been older when her mom was born and they'd passed away when Nora was just a baby. And since she never had a relationship with her father, she never knew any relatives on his side. She'd be lying if she didn't admit that she did consider Doña Alma a grandmother figure. In fact, when Nora was ten or eleven she even asked her tía Luz if she could call her Abuelita like the boys did. Tía Luz gently told her that it was more respectful to call her Doña and Nora never asked again.

"Sometimes she scolds me like I'm one of her grandchildren," Nora said with a laugh. "She's always telling me that I work too much and that I'll never find a husband if all I do is hang out with vegetables."

Gabe roared with laughter and slapped his knee. "Oh yeah, if she's pestering you about your love life, then you are definitely part of the family."

Maybe it was the wine or the fact that Gabe had just given her the biggest compliment. Either way, Nora rushed out, "This is nice."

He nodded. "It is," Gabe said. "I'm glad things are better between us."

Nora met his eyes and the sincerity reflected in them took her breath away. All she could do was nod in agreement and give him a quick smile.

"I wanted to let you know that having Dad back home from the hospital has me thinking a lot about things, and you're right," Gabe said. "I owe it to my family to be up-front about my plans. That is, once I know what my plans are."

Her heart dropped a little. "So you still haven't decided that you're staying?"

"Long-term, no. But I'm going to do whatever it is my family needs me to do right now. Although, I'm not dead set against staying anymore like I was when I first got here."

It wasn't exactly what she had hoped to hear, but she would take it. "Good," she told him.

"Good," he said back.

They looked at each other. Probably each waiting for the other to say something else. Familiar waves of desire made Nora shift in her seat. He wasn't Nico or Daniel. Or even Tomás. She was so unsure of how to be around him, especially now that they were friends and possibly going to be business partners.

Gabe made her feel things she hadn't in a very long time.

But she hadn't decided yet if that was a bad or good thing.

Chapter Seventeen

Gabe studied the female standing in front of him and tried to read her mind.

Did she like him?

Did she hate him?

Did she want to trample his face into the dirt?

But Juno, the eleven-year-old American paint horse, didn't give him any clues as to what kind of thoughts were going on behind those huge dark eyes of hers.

"She can tell you're nervous," he heard Tomás say from behind him.

He turned away from Juno and focused on his brother. "How do you know?"

"Her tail."

Gabe's eyes moved to Juno's tail and noticed it was swishing back and forth. "Is she about to attack me or what?"

Tomás laughed. "No. She's just uneasy. Just don't do anything to startle her and you'll be fine."

He tucked that important instruction into his mind and then proceeded to get Juno ready for their first ride together. "Be gentle with me, girl," he said out loud as they began their journey to the north end of the property. Tomás and his horse, Peanut, trailed behind them.

Juno's gait was smooth and that helped Gabe relax. And the more Gabe became comfortable, the less he had to clutch the reins, which meant the less his hand throbbed. He let himself look around and take note of the fields and pastures on either side of him. They hadn't changed that much since his childhood. Memories of riding with his brothers along the same path came rushing back to him. They'd take off on their horses as soon as their chores were done on the weekends. Sometimes they'd just talk about the things they wanted to do when they were older, sometimes they'd set an imaginary finish line and race each other there. They were good memories and Gabe had to admit that growing up on Rancho Lindo hadn't been all that bad.

A pang of shame made him drop his head. He'd been taught his whole life to never take nature for granted and to always respect the land. People who didn't see firsthand how food got to their tables might have a harder time understanding what it took to keep the trees green, to keep the livestock healthy, and to keep the soil rich. But what was his excuse? Nature had provided him a pretty good life in so many ways. How could he have gotten so far away from all of this? It was about time he truly appreciated what he had in front of him.

And that included Nora.

Tomás and Peanut arrived on his right. "How does it feel to get back in the saddle again?" his brother asked.

"Good," Gabe said honestly. "You were right about Juno."

Tomás had said that he'd picked Juno for Gabe because of her easy temperament and mentioned she was good for inexperienced riders. At first Gabe had insisted he didn't need a horse with figurative training wheels. Sure, it had been a few years since he'd gotten on a horse, but he was no beginner. But Tomás had told him he just wanted to be sure Gabe didn't overdo it or feel any pain afterward. Juno was the perfect horse for his comeback ride not just because she was gentle, but because she could tell what a rider needed from her.

They stopped when they reached the main fence and parked themselves under the branches of a large oak tree. It wasn't a particularly hot day, yet the shade was a welcome reprieve for both the humans and the animals.

Gabe stretched his legs and felt an unfamiliar burn. He knew though it had nothing to do with his injury and instead had everything to do with certain muscles being out of practice. It would take some time before his body and his mind recalled those kind of memories.

"Are you hurting?" Tomás asked with obvious concern.

"A little," Gabe said, trying not to grimace. The last thing he needed was Tomás worrying about him like Abuelita and his mom. "But I'm fine. Just a few more rides and soon I'll be racing Cruz."

That seemed to relieve Tomás. "It's good to see you back on a horse," he told Gabe. "Honestly, it's good to see you back, period."

"Now don't go and get all mushy on me," Gabe teased.

"Whatever. I'm just making an observation, that's all."

"A mushy observation."

"You're a jerk."

Gabe slapped his brother on the back. "That's more like it."

Despite his teasing, Tomás's words had hit a chord with Gabe. It had been good to get back on a horse and it had been good to go riding with his brother like old times. Part of him even considered asking the others to tag along once he was sure he could keep up.

They walked another several feet until they came upon a cluster of old bunkers.

"Mom told me that Dad and Cruz wanted to tear these down last year. What happened?" Gabe asked.

"They did," his brother answered. "But then they changed their minds."

"They did? Or you helped them change it?"

The bunker was where all of Rancho Lindo's temporary or seasonal workers stayed back when their abuelo was running everything. The permanent ranch hands, if they needed them, got their own cottages over on the other side of the property. The bunkers were basically three buildings. Each building had a small kitchen and bathroom. But the majority of the space used to be taken up with bunk beds—at least that's what their abuelo used to tell them.

"We should fix them up," Gabe mused. "Maybe even rent them out to tourists who come to Santa Ynez and Solvang for wine tasting vacays."

"That's a great idea, actually. In fact, I seem to recall you having that exact same great idea when we were teenagers."

Gabe scoffed. "I don't remember that."

"You even told Dad that he should build three more just like them."

"Okay, now I know you're making things up," Gabe insisted. "That sounds way too industrious for teenage Gabe."

He laughed and walked toward the bigger of the two structures. When they were kids, he and his brothers would hang out on the porch and talk about anything and everything. Sometimes, they'd explore inside even though Chucho had warned them a thousand times to stay out of there. Their mom was always worried that the roof could collapse at any moment. Every time she'd find out that they'd been hanging out there, she'd beg their dad to tear them down once and for all.

Yet, it was all still standing.

Gabe walked back and forth, trying to peek through windows blanketed in dirt and grime. From what he could see, the inside was exactly how he'd remembered it—a disaster.

"Hey, where is everybody today anyway?"

"Mom and Abuelita went to go have brunch with the Sanchez sisters," Tomás shared. "And the rest of the guys wanted to go check out this new leather store over in Santa Ynez."

"And Dad?"

"It's Sunday," Tomás said. "Where do you think he is?"

He didn't have to answer. Santiago Ortega was a man of habit. Sundays were for God and golf. And always in that order. Gabe couldn't remember the last time he'd been on a course. He never understood the point of the sport. Perhaps that's why he wasn't good at it. He was more of a basketball and soccer fan. No, it was usually Nico who accompanied their dad to the Cattleman's Club. Although he always suspected that his brother enjoyed the Bloody Marys, and the cocktail waitresses who served them, more than actually hitting the little white balls.

Gabe couldn't help but think that it was better that his dad wasn't around for his first ride back.

As if Tomás could read his thoughts, he said, "We should all ride together sometime."

Gabe nodded but didn't let on that he'd been thinking the same thing. Tomás kept talking. "We should all do more things together."

"What are you talking about? We do things together every single day," Gabe scoffed.

"Sure, we work around the ranch together," Tomás explained, "but we don't really just, you know, hang out. We eat dinner and then everyone scatters to do their own thing. That's not hanging out."

"Are you saying you want us all to go to a bar together?" Gabe asked incredulously. "You actually think Cruz would do that?"

Tomás shrugged. "He might."

Gabe knew better. "Tell you what. You get Cruz to agree to go out with us and I'll be there."

"Come on. He's not that bad."

"Maybe he's not that bad around you. But me? He might as well be Dad."

"He's just under a lot of pressure right now, Gabe."

"What do you know? We do have something in common after all."

Gabe knew Tomás was right. The truth was he had noticed Cruz had been especially grumpy the past few weeks. And Gabe wasn't the only one on the ranch who got to experience his crappy mood. He'd even asked Cruz one day if everything was all right with him and all he'd gotten for his concern was a scowl and some mumbling about focusing on his job.

Gabe had kept his mouth shut ever since. That was the real reason why he had no desire to hang out with his older brother at a bar.

But Tomás persisted. "Look, I know he's hard on you. It's because he knows you can handle it. And he's been right. You may grumble anytime he gives you something to do, but you do it."

"I do it because I don't need Dad in my other ear telling me the exact same thing."

"Or maybe," he continued, "you do it because you enjoy it."

That made Gabe laugh. "Now you're pushing it. There is nothing around this place that I do because I enjoy it. Well, maybe except for helping with the garden."

In fact, there were quite a few things he liked doing at Rancho Lindo, and they all had to do with Nora. She'd been asking him to help her around the garden more and he was always happy to oblige. They had fallen into an easy friendship, although it was getting harder to deny his attraction to her. Part of him suspected that the feeling was mutual. But he wasn't about to risk being wrong.

Tomás pulled out two pieces of jerky from his bag and handed one to Gabe. His brother knew him so well. "So how are you and Nora getting along these days," Tomás said after swallowing his first bite of jerky. "I can see she at least tolerates you now...kind

of like Princesa. Does that mean she doesn't have—
what did you call it that night?—an *attitude* anymore?"
His brother made air quotes when he said the word
attitude.

"Oh, Nora still gives me an attitude. Only difference
is now I don't mind it so much. I guess I've gotten used
to her," he answered.

"Or maybe you've just come to the realization that
she's never gonna like you like she likes the rest of us?"

"Wrong. In fact, she's even teaching me how to
grow some microgreens. We're friends now," Gabe said
proudly.

He purposely didn't mention the fact he'd been wres-
tling with some very not-friend-like thoughts about
Nora recently. The other day they'd gone into town to
pick up the new trays she was going to use for her first
flax planting. Every single person they'd run into had
smiled so genuinely and brightly at her. It was obvious
the people of Esperanza loved her.

And it was no wonder. She greeted each of them
warmly, some of the lucky ones even got a hug. Though
he and Nora were in a hurry, she made the time to
ask how they were doing, how their kids were doing,
even how their dogs were doing. The best part of the
afternoon was when Deputy Lucas approached them
outside the general store. Nora acted exactly the same
with him as she had with old man Davis. She was
friendly, but not too friendly. That's when Gabe knew
for certain that the poor guy had no chance with her.
And that pleased him way more than it should have.

As she drove them back to the ranch, he'd caught
himself studying her more than once. Her hair was
pulled into a pile on top of her head, exposing the

delicate cut of her jawline and smooth neck. She honest to goodness had made him lose his breath. It was a new feeling for him, thrilling yet also inconvenient. Gabe had become an expert at pushing his emotions to the side. While his dad had a knack for pulling anger out of him, Nora, it seemed, brought out his desire. He had struggled to get a handle on it, but every muscle had already balled itself into a tight bundle of electricity, threatening to combust at any moment. He had ached to undo his seat belt, lean over, release her hair so it tumbled onto her shoulders, and then bury himself there for as long as possible. It was all he could think about the rest of that day and night. His pent-up desire eventually manifested itself into a very vivid dream where he found Nora in the greenhouse and she'd collapsed into his arms for a heated kiss. Then the two of them had ended up on top of a stack of potting soil bags. Needless to say dreamtime Gabe got dirt in all of the wrong places.

He nearly choked at the searing memory and decided to slow down on the jerky.

"Well, if that's the case, I'd better warn you, then," Tomás told him after Gabe stopped coughing.

"Warn me about what?"

"Nora may seem sweet and gentle—and she actually is. But if you do anything to that garden of hers? Ooh boy. Watch out."

Gabe held up a hand. "I know. Trust me."

They both laughed at that. Tomás walked over and patted him on the shoulder. "First you're back on a horse and now you're going to learn how to grow microgreens. Sounds to me like you're finally starting to get used to things around here again."

Gabe considered his brother's observations. It was true that he had fallen into a routine and he didn't hate it. And he hadn't bothered calling any other contacts about job opportunities. In fact, he'd been so busy that he hadn't even had a run-in with their dad or Cruz in weeks.

Did this mean he'd already made his decision about staying at Rancho Lindo for good?

The realization threw him as hard as a bucking bronco. He needed to sit with it for a while. And he couldn't do that with Tomás watching his every move.

Gabe quickly mounted Juno and waved at Tomás. "Ándale, hermano. Hurry your ass up. It's almost time for dinner."

Chapter Eighteen

Whatever you're about to do, I'm in."

Nora turned around to see Gabe entering the stable right behind her. "Careful what you wish for," she said with a laugh.

He stopped just a few inches away from her. "At this point, I don't even care."

"That doesn't sound good. Everything okay?"

He shook his head and then contradicted himself. "Yeah. Yeah. I'm fine. Just trying to remember if I did everything on Cruz's list today. So what have you got going on?"

She shrugged and took another step closer to him. "The usual. I just got back from town and stopped at the house to drop something off to your abuelita."

That seemed to pique his interest. "What did you drop off? A small white paper bag, perhaps? I want to know. Scratch that. I need to know."

"Maybe," she said, definitely trying to not smile. "Maybe not."

Nora bit her lip, and she waited for Gabe to try to get her to spill the beans. He might be her favorite, but Doña Alma and Nora were close, and if she had wanted Gabe to know, then she would've told him by now. "Fine," he said. "You two keep your secrets."

"Oh, we will."

They both laughed, and the feelings that had been stirring in her chest for weeks only seemed stronger. Especially since he was right there in front of her.

"Are you headed to the garden now?" he asked.

"No, actually. I came to get a horse so I can ride out to the orchard. I need some apples," she said, lifting up the empty canvas bags she was holding.

"Really? Want some company?"

She must have had her shock registered all over her face.

"What?"

"I didn't think you rode anymore."

"Well, turns out it's just like riding a bike. Tomás and I have been riding for a few weeks now. I just had to let my brain get caught up with my muscle memory."

"Good for you," she told him earnestly.

Gabe and Nora got their horses ready and set out toward the west side of the property. The mid-October afternoon was beginning to cool down. They were both quiet as they rode. She wasn't quite sure why he wasn't really talking. As for her, she just wanted to take it all in—the nice weather, the landscape, and being with him.

About fifteen minutes later, they arrived at their destination. Rancho Lindo's orchard spanned twenty acres. Besides apples, it was also home to tangerine, tangelo, orange, date, and apricot trees.

"Wow. I haven't been here in years," he said.

They rode down the main path lined with rows and rows of lush trees. It was a majestic view, and Nora could tell that Gabe was impressed.

They stopped about halfway through the orchard and tied up their horses to one of the water posts. Nora unhooked the canvas bags from her horse's saddle and gave one to Gabe.

"There are some pole pickers lying around," she told him. "Just grab one if you need it."

"Oh, I'm picking too? I thought I was just along for the ride."

Nora looked at him with her hands on her hips. "Have you met me? In case you forgot, I absolutely enjoy putting you to work whenever possible."

He laughed and had no choice but to follow her to the trees. "How about we make this a contest?" he said. "Whoever picks the most apples in fifteen minutes, wins."

Nora faced him. "Wins what?"

Gabe considered some options. "Okay, how about the loser has to pick and clean the next batch of eggplants?"

That made her laugh. The ones in the garden had little prickly thorns, and he'd pricked his fingers a few times, even with gloves. He hated the little suckers.

"Fine," she said. "But the apples have to be perfect. So if they have bruises or worm holes, they don't count toward the total."

"Deal," he said. Gabe set a timer on his phone. "Okay. Time starts now!"

Fifteen minutes later, Gabe met Nora under one of the bigger trees. She could tell by his irritated expression that she'd been way more successful.

"Well?" she asked as he dropped his bag in front of her.

"I'll stop by tomorrow to check the eggplants," he said dejectedly.

Nora couldn't contain her giddiness until she looked in his bag. "Really, Gabe? Did you even try?"

"Yes, I tried," Gabe began explaining. "I was moving pretty quickly for the first five minutes. Then it got harder. Most of the apples already on the ground were no good, and the ones hanging on the lower branches weren't ripe. I had to keep jumping from the ground in order to reach some of the higher ones since I couldn't find one of those damn pole pickers anywhere."

"They get buried under the leaves and bad apples. You have to kick things around to find them."

"Well, now you tell me," he said, putting his hands on his hips. "And it's not my fault I'm so bad at this. I haven't been apple picking since I was maybe twelve years old. I'm guessing this isn't enough for what you need. Hand me your pole picker, and I'll get you some more."

"It's probably easier to use a ladder," she said, pointing to the one already set up a few trees down the row. "I'll pick them, and you hold the bag."

"It's okay," he said as they walked the short distance. "I'll get on the ladder. You hold the bag."

Nora shook her head. "Why? Because I'm a girl and you're afraid I'm going to fall on my pretty little head?"

He looked her. "Well...yes. That's exactly why."

She let out a frustrated sigh. "I think our bags have proven that I am the expert apple picker here. So I'm going up that ladder, and that's final."

Gabe opened his mouth and then thought better of it.

When they got to the tree, he moved the ladder under the branch she pointed to and spotted her as she climbed up a few steps. She began plucking one apple at a time and then handed them to him so he could put them inside the bag.

"Okay, I changed my mind," he said below her. "This is so much better than me going up there."

"What?" Nora looked down and then realized that he was staring at her backside. "You really are a brat, you know that?"

His laughing came to a stop when she purposely plucked an apple from a nearby branch and let go of it, barely missing his head. "Oops," Nora said.

"You almost hit me," he said.

"My aim isn't the best. That's why I said *oops*."

"Don't make me come up there, Miss Nora," he half-heartedly threatened.

"No need. I'm done. Coming down now."

He waited until she was only four rungs from the bottom when he scooped her off the ladder.

She yelped in surprise. "What are you doing, Gabe. Put me down."

"You almost fell. I'm saving you…again."

Nora stared at him as if he had three heads. "I did not almost fall. You grabbed me."

He shrugged. "Guess this is what you get for trying to give me a concussion."

She rolled her eyes. "Please. An apple from that height would not have given you a concussion. Can you put me down now?"

His bright eyes told her just how amused he was. "Maybe I should carry you through the orchard, and you can pick apples this way," Gabe told her.

Part of her wouldn't have minded that at all. Not one single bit.

"I don't think so," she protested instead.

"Or I could just put you on my shoulders," he said, lifting her farther up.

"You wouldn't," she dared.

It was an innocent challenge, but it packed so much innuendo that it sent shivers straight down her back. The good kind of shivers. She almost forgot to breathe for several seconds.

"Try me."

Gabe caught her off guard. Heat singed her cheeks, and she wondered if he could feel the warmth coming off her. She didn't argue right away. The inches between them filled with more than her unspoken words. It took every ounce of self-control not to do anything more with her hands than hold on to him. What she wouldn't give to slide her fingers through the strands of hair at the nape of his neck.

"Put me down, Gabe," she whispered.

"Give me a reason to," he challenged. He seemed to really be enjoying this more than he should have.

It was too much.

She sighed and met his eyes. "Put me down, and I'll tell you what's in the little white paper bags."

He seemed to debate the offer for a few seconds. Eventually, he set her down on the ground.

He folded his arms against his chest. "Well?"

"Almond Rocha."

"Almond Rocha?"

Nora raised her hands. "What can I say? It's her one vice."

She'd been sneaking Almond Rocha to Doña Alma for months. It started when they'd both gone into town together, and she'd bought two pieces for herself. Then she swore Nora to secrecy, since Señora Ortega tried to limit the amount of sweets the elderly woman ate. The next time, Doña Alma just gave Nora the cash to buy it for her.

"She gives me two dollars whenever I go into town," Nora continued explaining. "I always bring her back a couple of pieces, and she eats one a day. I know because I do spot checks."

Gabe roared with laughter. "Spot checks?"

The more she thought about it, the more she could admit it was a little funny. But it was the only way she could justify it. "Well, I don't want to be the reason she goes into a diabetic coma. She thinks your mom doesn't know, but she figured it out after the first time I brought her some. Your mom said I could keep bringing it to her, but to let her know if she ever asked for more."

"This is too much." Gabe was laughing so hard that he was doubled over. "But it's my family, so of course it is."

"Okay, okay. You can stop now."

He didn't and continued shaking his head. "Well, now I know what to get her for her birthday," he said, and burst out laughing all over again.

Nora waved her hand in front of his face. "No, you absolutely cannot give her Almond Rocha for her birthday. She'll know that I told you. Please don't. I think she enjoys the secrecy as much as she enjoys the candy."

It took a couple of minutes, but Gabe finally calmed down. He wiped his eyes and caught his breath. "Okay, fine. I won't get her any candy. And I'll keep her secret as long as you do me a favor."

She sighed. "What? You want me to start sneaking candy to you too?"

"Yes, actually," he said with another laugh. "But that's not the favor I was thinking of."

"Then what is it?" she asked.

He looked at her very seriously. "I need you to not hit me when I tell you what I'm about to tell you."

Her heart dropped, and she stilled. "Gabe, what did you do?"

He gave her a sly smile and then moved in front of her. "I found out my friend Ben golfs with the owner of that new organic grocery start-up. You know, the West Coast version of Whole Foods?"

"The Green Grocery Store?"

He pointed at her. "That's the one. Anyway, I sent him some microgreens samples and he shared them with the guy and he loved them. We connected earlier today and the owner is going to visit the ranch next week to tour the garden and greenhouse. He's interested in selling your microgreens in his stores, Nora!"

She couldn't believe what she was hearing. Was Gabe really telling her the truth or was this some sort of sick prank?

"Are you serious right now?"

"I'm dead serious. I swear this is happening."

"Gabe, he has like ten stores."

"And he says next year he's opening at least ten more. He has plans to expand to the East Coast in about five years too."

There were moments in your life when you knew something was about to change it forever. This was it for Nora. She felt it in her gut. She trusted it.

"Oh my God. Oh my God," she yelled, jumping up and down with joy. She grabbed his hands. "This is amazing. You're amazing."

"All I did was ship some samples. This is all you, Nora."

Happy tears gathered at the corners of her eyes and she couldn't contain her gratitude any longer. She threw her arms around his neck and kissed Gabe on the lips. It was a quick and innocent peck. And as soon as she realized what she'd done, she pulled away from him and covered her mouth.

"I'm sorry," she blurted. "I didn't mean to. I'm just so grateful and—"

He grabbed her hands. "It's okay, Nora," he said softly.

"It's not. And you know why."

"I promise you I'm not complaining," he said, holding her hands a little tighter, as if he was worried that she'd disappear. "Please, don't let it make you less happy than you were just a second ago."

"I just don't want to confuse what we are." Even though confused was exactly what she was. Gabe still hadn't decided if he was going to help run Rancho Lindo. How could she get involved with a man who could leave any day now? Not to mention, they'd just eased into a friendship. Was it worth risking all of that?

Based on his actions the past few weeks, and by what he'd done for her today, Nora had to admit that it might be.

He pulled her closer to him and searched her eyes. "I'll be the first to admit that I wasn't sure what was happening between us and maybe that's why I haven't let myself hope that your feelings for me could be anything more than friendship. And if that's what you want, then that's what I'll give you." Gabe let her go and raised one hand to touch the side of her face.

She couldn't breathe or move. This moment between them was almost too much.

Almost.

"Are you saying that you're attracted to me?" Nora wasn't trying to be coy. She honestly couldn't believe that Gabe could want her in that way. "How?" she had to ask. "Why?"

He gave her a sexy smile that almost buckled her knees. "How could I not?" he whispered. "If you only knew what you do to me with those big brown eyes of yours...with those perfect lips." One finger traced the edge of her jawline down to the middle of her chin and then up to the edge of her mouth. She let out a shaky sigh and her heart raced at his revelation.

Too, too much.

Nora watched in slow motion as Gabe pressed his lips to hers. The moment overtook her and she closed her eyes. She didn't trust herself to believe what had just happened. She'd waited for this moment for so long, it didn't seem to be real. And if it was real, what on earth was she supposed to do now?

She felt warmth, softness, and then nothing. She opened her eyes again and looked for him in almost a panic, only to find him exactly where he'd always been. Right in front of her.

"Was that okay, Nora?" he asked softly.

It was more than okay, honestly. Yet she still couldn't find her words. So she only nodded in response. He smiled at her and kissed the tip of her nose. Then he moved back to her lips, kissing her more intently. This time there was no hesitation. His lips were demanding. She felt only heat and desire.

It wasn't enough. Not even close. Something powerful—something she couldn't deny anymore—had ignited between them.

Nora did the only thing she could do in that very big moment between them.

She kissed him back.

Chapter Nineteen

Gabe looked at Nora and wondered what was going through her mind.

She'd been acting like a skittish cat ever since she'd walked through the kitchen's back door and found him and Abuelita drinking their afternoon café con leche.

"Nora, are you okay, Mija?"

The question from Abuelita startled her even more, and she lost control of the three large baskets she'd been carrying. Cherry tomatoes spilled onto the tile floor and scattered in several directions.

Gabe jumped off his stool and dropped to the ground in an attempt to grab as many of the small red balls as he could before they rolled under the refrigerator. Nora joined him after setting the baskets safely onto the floor. As they scooped up the last of the wayward berries back into their containers, their hands briefly touched. Gabe noticed how Nora yanked hers away first—almost as if his touch had burned her.

He knew it hadn't, though. He also knew her new nervousness around him was most likely because of what had happened between them in the orchard the day before.

After their last kiss, they'd ridden back to the ranch in silence. He'd tried to talk to her once they'd put the horses away. But she'd made some excuse about finishing up some work and then was gone.

And now she was here picking up cherry tomatoes, trying to act like nothing had happened at all.

Gabe wasn't going to let her pretend too long. The feel of her lips against his was seared into his memory— a memory he wanted to repeat. He knew he had to get her alone so they could talk.

"Are you okay?" he whispered after helping her to her feet.

Nora gave him a quick smile and nodded. "I hope we got all of them," she said as she picked up the baskets and placed them carefully onto the kitchen island.

"If not, I'm sure the dogs will enjoy finding any stragglers," he said with a laugh. "What are you doing with so many cherry tomatoes in the first place?"

"For the farmer's market," Abuelita answered. "After we wash them, we're going to fill bags by the pound. It's easier to sell that way. You should stay and help us, Mijo."

"No," Nora shouted before he even had a chance to answer.

He turned to face her and squinted in confusion.

"I mean, you don't have to. I'm sure you have lots to do, and we can handle it like we always do every week," she rushed to say.

He actually did have a lot to do. But there was no way he was going to get anything done until he talked to Nora—without Abuelita listening in.

"Well, I guess I'll just finish my coffee so I can get out of your way. But before I head back to the stables, can I show you something in the greenhouse, Nora?"

"Show me what?" She didn't even bother to look at him as she pulled out the bundles of ties and stacks of plastic bags from each of the baskets.

He tried to think of something. "Well, I had an idea about how to expand your shelving for the microgreens and I wanted to get your thoughts on it."

That grabbed her attention and she glanced over her shoulder. "Really?"

"Really. And it will only take a few minutes."

Abuelita pulled a basket toward her. "Go on, Mija. I can get started without you."

Gabe could see the debate going on in her head. In the end, she agreed to follow him to the greenhouse.

"Sorry I made you drop your cherry tomatoes," he told her as they stepped off the back porch.

"You didn't," she replied.

"Okay, then I'm sorry I made you so nervous to see me that you dropped your cherry tomatoes."

"You didn't do that either."

They didn't talk again until they were inside the greenhouse. He really did have an idea about the shelving. But he hadn't really flushed it out, so the conversation was short. Too short.

After less than five minutes, Nora was ready to go back to the house.

"Are we really not going to talk about what happened yesterday," he said before she could leave. Gabe wasn't prepared for the sense of desperation to keep her there talking to him. Now that he knew what could be, he panicked at the thought that they were over before they even had a chance to begin. And, dear God, how could he already miss her when she was just inches away from him?

"What is there to talk about?" she said. "We kissed. And then we stopped."

"And I need to know how you feel about that," Gabe admitted.

She looked down at her shoes. "How do you feel?"

Normally, such a question would've made him run for the hills. But he knew that if he wanted Nora to trust him, then he had to tell her the truth.

"I feel...confused," he said. "But in a good way."

Nora raised her head and met his eyes. "What does that mean?"

It meant that he felt happier than he had in years. She was a bright and warm light in his life and he was drawn to her. He was also terrified. How could he not be? Gabe hadn't been looking for this. But now that he had it, he wasn't ready to let it go just yet.

Gabe took a step closer. "It means that I wasn't expecting it to happen, but I'm glad that it did. I'm just not sure if you are."

She shrugged. "I guess I'm feeling a little confused too."

"Tell me," he said softly.

Nora took a breath. "I wasn't expecting it either, but I didn't mind it."

He couldn't help but laugh. "Wow. Just what a guy wants to hear."

"You know what I mean. But..."

"But what?"

"But I'm not sure if it should happen again."

His heart fell into his stomach. Gabe finally

understood. Nora was afraid that he was going to hurt her like before. "Because you don't trust me."

She shook her head. "I don't trust myself."

Now his heart was on the ground. "Why?"

"I've spent most of my adult life thinking I was invisible to you. When you first got here, I told myself you didn't deserve me or Rancho Lindo. I thought I knew what kind of man you were and that meant I had no business thinking there could ever be anything between us. Yet, even after all of that, if you kissed me again, I don't think I'd want you to stop."

Her admission reawakened his desire. "I don't think I'd want to stop kissing you either."

"But what if, one day, you did want to stop?"

Gabe realized that Nora's doubts were because she was thinking of what would happen down the line. He wanted to tell her to just enjoy what was happening right now.

"Nora, we can't live our lives by what-ifs. I've seen firsthand that nothing is ever guaranteed. You once told me not to be afraid to share what I was feeling. Well, I'm feeling that I want to kiss you again right here, right now."

He took another step until their faces were just a few inches apart. The need reflected in her eyes let him know that this was what she wanted. He was who she wanted.

Gabe wrapped his arm around her waist and pulled her against him. Then he kissed her again. And again. Heat bloomed in his chest and then spread everywhere else. He became lost in the way she tasted.

When she finally pulled away though, he wondered if he had been the only one.

"What's wrong?" he asked.

"I'm scared," she admitted.

He pulled her against him and held her tight. A shudder of relief rippled through his body, as if it had been starved for the feel of her after just one day. "Nora, you have to believe me. I really didn't plan for things to happen the way they did. I know I hurt you a long time ago and it might still be hard for you to trust me. But I swear that I'm telling you the truth when I say I care about you."

She raised her head to meet his eyes. "I care about you too. And that's what I'm scared of the most."

"Look, we don't have to rush things. We can take our time with this. And if you feel like it's too much, then you just tell me. Okay?"

Nora bit her lip and he knew she wanted to tell him something but was debating whether to do it.

"What are you thinking in that beautiful mind of yours?" he said, offering her a smile to let her know she could tell him anything.

"What if...what if we don't, you know, work out? I don't want to be another reason for you to leave Rancho Lindo."

Gabe wanted to reassure her that wouldn't happen. But he had no idea where their relationship could go. All he knew was, in that moment, he had no desire to be anywhere else but in Nora's arms. "I care about you, Nora. You could never do anything or say anything that would make me not want to be around you. I know that in my gut. So I'm all in. No matter what."

He felt her body relax against him. His words had eased her doubts. His too. Because he had believed what he'd said.

Chapter Twenty

It was a bright crisp morning. The kind that held promises that the day ahead was going to be a good one. For Nora, that meant it was the perfect day to get things done.

Because if she was busy, then she wasn't thinking about her conversation with Gabe the day before.

Nora decided to focus first on harvesting as much as she could from the northwest quadrant of the vegetable garden. She was able to fill two bushels of potatoes and five with carrots. After her usual inspection, she ended up with a large handful of good but ugly carrots. That meant she'd take a break from her busy day and go visit an old friend.

"Is he awake?" Nora asked Tomás as she walked into the stable a few minutes later.

Tomás tipped his head and said, "Go see for yourself."

She set down the bushel of carrots she'd brought and pulled out one of the larger ones.

"Hey friend," she said softly as she arrived at the second stall on the right. "I brought you something."

The black-and-white Appaloosa sauntered over to the gate and greeted her with his usual snort. Nora showed him the carrot and he took a big bite. She scratched the top of his head and watched him take another chomp.

"Coco sure loves his carrots," Tomás said as he walked over to her.

"Ever since he was a pony."

Nora could still remember the day she first met Coco. It was a Wednesday morning and she'd been in the garden with Doña Alma. Tomás had come running to find her because he wanted to show her the new pony his dad had just brought to the ranch. She had grabbed one of the carrots she'd just plucked from the ground and took off with Tomás to the stables.

"She's so pretty," she'd said as she held the carrot so the new pony could eat. "What's her name?"

Señor Ortega laughed. "She is a he and he doesn't have a name. Why don't you give him one?"

Nora couldn't believe it. She'd never named a horse before and she took the responsibility very seriously. It was the only thing she thought about for days. Nora carried around a notebook with her and anytime she thought of a name, she'd write it down. When she narrowed it down to three choices, she polled as many people on the ranch that she could.

Then one warm afternoon, when all her research was finally complete, Nora walked into Señor Ortega's office and told him she had finally decided on a name.

"Qué bueno. I've been calling him 'horse' this whole time," he said with a laugh.

And that was the day that Nora got a new best friend named Coco.

"How's his leg?" she asked Tomás.

"Better. I'm going to take him out to the corral later and see how he does putting more pressure on it. Olivia checked it out yesterday and said it would be okay."

Tomás had noticed Coco limping last week and they'd both been watching his leg carefully since. She was so relieved to hear that his leg was healing. And now that the worry had been lifted, Nora couldn't help but dig a little more.

"Olivia seems like a really good vet," she began. "She's also very pretty."

"I guess."

Despite Tomás being seemingly oblivious, Nora pressed on. "You should totally ask her out."

"What? I don't think so."

"Why not? She's super smart, and because she's a vet, she's not going to care if you show up smelling like a horse."

Tomás laughed and shrugged off her suggestion. "I'm too busy right now trying to get this boarding business off the ground. I don't have time to date."

"You're never going to have the time. You have to make the time. At least that's what Doña Alma used to tell me."

Coco finished off his carrot, and Nora gave him one last kiss. Then she headed back inside with Tomás. They walked into the small office next to the stable, and she took the seat behind the tiny desk while he leaned against the doorway.

"You really need to get a bigger office," she said. "If Olivia ever sees this, she's going to stop coming over."

"Like I said. Not interested."

Nora sighed. She thought about what Gabe had said before. Could Tomás still be in love with his ex?

"Can I ask you a question? Like a personal question?"

He folded his arms across his chest and nodded. "Go ahead."

"Have you dated anyone since Mia?"

"Depends on what you mean. I've had a couple of first dates here and there, but I haven't been in another relationship."

"But why?"

"I don't know," he said with a shrug. "I just haven't met anyone that I'd like to go on a second date with."

"Seems to me like you haven't really tried," she said.

He narrowed his eyes at her, and she knew he was debating himself. He definitely wanted her to be wrong, but they both knew she wasn't. Not about that anyway.

To her surprise, Tomás didn't try to convince her. Instead, he asked, "Do you know why it seems like horses are more comfortable around me than my brothers?"

"Because they trust you," she answered.

"Right. But do you know why they trust me?"

Nora shook her head.

"It's because I'm consistent. I'm reliable. When they see me approach, they know what to expect."

"That's good," she offered.

He scoffed. "Good for horses. Bad for relationships."

Nora tilted her head in confusion. "I don't understand."

"That's why Mia and I broke up. She wanted me to do the unexpected and leave Rancho Lindo and go to New York with her. But I couldn't. Because when it comes down to it, I like the fact that my days are all basically the same. Mia didn't want her future to be just a string of the expected. I don't think most women do."

Nora took a moment before responding. She knew Tomás didn't like talking about his feelings. He was an Ortega man after all. And she really didn't want him to think she was just as nosy as Doña Alma. But she also knew what it was like to hide behind your work. Tomás might have been the horse whisperer of Esperanza. It still didn't mean he didn't deserve someone to actually talk back once in a while.

"Tomás, every woman is different," Nora told him. "But you're never going to figure that out if you don't go looking. Or is there a part of you that believes you and Mia are going to get back together someday?"

She surprised herself for actually having the nerve to finally ask the question everyone had wanted to ask. A small part of her worried he'd be hurt or offended. But if he was, he didn't look like it.

"Honestly, I did believe that in the beginning," Tomás admitted. "I thought she'd move to New York, hate it, and come back to Esperanza within a year. When that didn't happen, I realized that maybe I never really knew her. How could I be with someone for so long and not see how different we were?"

Thoughts of Gabe rushed through her mind. "People change sometimes. People grow up," she said.

He let out a long sigh and leaned his head against the door frame. "Maybe. All I know is that dating and relationships aren't exactly things I'm good at and I'm not in a hurry to try them out anytime soon. I guess what I'm saying is that I'm not ready. That's why I don't want to ask out Olivia."

"I don't understand."

"Olivia is awesome. Don't get me wrong. She deserves someone who will appreciate that. She deserves a man who will look at her and say, 'She's what I want.' I can't say that, so I shouldn't ask her out just to waste her time. Besides, she's the only vet within twenty miles. I need her to not hate me."

And that was why she knew Tomás would make someone very happy someday. He deserved happiness too. "Tomás, trust me. No one could ever hate you."

That made him laugh. She figured she'd put him on the spot enough for one day. She stood up and told him she was going to leave so he could get back to work.

But he blocked the doorway so she couldn't leave. "Not so fast. I answered your questions, now you have to answer mine."

"Fine. But I can tell you right now that I don't want to date Olivia either."

"You know that's not what I was going to ask," he said with a chuckle.

Nora's heart began to race with panic. She had an idea of what was coming next, and she didn't want to be there when it did.

"I really should get back to work," she said, trying to ignore the fluttering in her stomach.

"What's going on with you and Gabe?"

She didn't dare look him in the eyes and instead moved out of his line of sight and pretended to look at the pictures hanging on the wall of his office. "He's been helping me at the farmer's markets, and he's interested in learning about the microgreens."

Tomás laughed at her explanation. "My brother

never eats vegetables. I doubt he's interested in learning how to make them grow."

Nora shrugged. "Well, he is. He thinks he can get a grocery store to carry them."

He arched his eyebrows in what seemed like surprise, maybe even appreciation. "That would be great. Still doesn't really answer my question."

She turned around and moved to sit on the corner of his desk. "Fine. We're friends. Maybe even more than that. But we're not calling it anything. We just like hanging out with each other."

And kissing each other.

Tomás walked over to her. His expression was full of concern. "We were talking about it and we think—"

She held up her hand. "Whoa there. Who's *we*?"

"Daniel and Nico," he said as if it was obvious. And it was. "Oh, and one time, Cruz was there."

Nora jumped off the desk as if it had burned her. "You guys are talking about me and Gabe?" she asked incredulously.

"Well, yeah. We love you like a sister, Nora. We don't want to see you get hurt."

"I appreciate that. I do. But I don't like the idea of the Ortega brothers hanging out and drinking beers and talking about how they have to save poor little Nora from Gabe."

"Come on. It's not like that. We just think you guys should take things slow."

Nora was officially mortified. It was bad enough that she was still confused as to what she and Gabe were. But to know that their relationship status was also a topic of conversation among his brothers was beyond embarrassing.

"Thanks for the advice, but go tell the other dating counselors that I don't need it. I'm a big girl. And while I love you all for caring so much, please, please, keep your noses out of this. Okay?"

Tomás raised his hands. "Okay. I'll pass on the message."

"Okay. Thank you."

Nora stomped out of the office but stopped after just a few steps.

Ugh.

She stomped back and found Tomás exactly how she'd left him. "Let me know how Coco does later."

"I will," he said with a soft smile.

Nora wanted to still be mad and make some sort of dramatic exit to prove how mad she was. But she couldn't. So she smiled back.

Why, oh why were these Ortega men so charming?

Chapter Twenty-One

A year ago, Gabe would've punched out any man who caused him as much pain as Lou Jackson had. But the ex-marine and physical therapist was good at his job and that was the only reason why he didn't have a black eye yet.

Even though it was only his third appointment with Lou, Gabe could already feel his hand getting stronger, as well as less stiffness in his shoulder. So he endured the strengthening and stretching exercises. His surgeons had told him he'd never regain one hundred percent mobility.

He was determined then to get ninety-nine percent.

When they were done for the day, Gabe took a seat in Lou's small office next to the gym so they could talk about his progress.

"Are you noticing a difference?" he asked Gabe.

"Yeah. My hand doesn't cramp up as much at the end of the day. And I can grip my tools a little tighter. Before I started therapy, there were a few times when my hammer just flew out of my hand. Luckily, I only hit someone once. But it was my youngest brother, Daniel, so it didn't really count."

Lou bellowed out a hearty laugh. "I guess that means he wasn't hurt too bad."

"Nope. Just his boot."

Gabe answered a few questions about the kind of work he was doing around the ranch to make sure he wasn't risking a setback. Lou seemed satisfied that nothing would be a problem.

"Still having the nightmares?" he asked after writing down some notes.

Gabe nodded. "Yeah, but not as much."

"Is it the same one?"

"More or less," he replied. "And sometimes I can wake myself up before the crash."

"Good," Lou said. "Sounds like you're getting them under control."

"I guess. The other night I actually was able to change the dream a little. Like instead of walking out to the Humvee, I walked into the greenhouse on the ranch."

"Really? And then what did you do?"

"Just looked around," Gabe answered. He didn't add that he'd actually been looking around for Nora.

"And how did you feel being in the greenhouse?"

Gabe thought for a few seconds before answering. "Fine. Calm."

"Safe?"

"Yeah, I guess so."

Lou put down his pen and sat back into his chair. "This is great progress, Gabe. I really think the work you've been doing in the greenhouse has been helping in more ways than one. It's like a different form of therapy for you."

"I never thought about it like that," he told Lou. But it did make sense. Ever since he'd returned to Rancho Lindo, he'd been drawn to the greenhouse. And not just because it was a good place to take a quick cat nap.

And not just because of Nora either.

Although he had to admit she was probably a big part of it. Because holding her and kissing her were the highlights of his days now.

"Speaking of another form of therapy," Lou began.

Gabe already knew what he was going to say. "I don't know if I'm ready for that yet."

The large man shrugged. "Fair enough. I just want you to know what your options are. There's a group that meets at the VA every week, or I can send you some names of a few private therapists in the city."

It was the second time that Lou had brought the suggestion to Gabe of seeking some sort of counseling. He hadn't ever been diagnosed with PTSD, but Lou had told him he wouldn't be surprised if he had some form of it. Especially because of the nightmares. It was true that he wasn't having them as often as before. Still, they happened enough to make for a few sleepless nights and that meant a few afternoon naps here and there.

"I'll think about it," he told Lou.

"That's all I ask, man," he said. "A few of my other clients attend the VA group, so I can vouch for the counselor there. I've seen some great results and I really do think it would help with your recovery."

He'd done the group counseling thing when he was at the rehab center and he wasn't a fan. Growing up, he'd been taught to keep his emotions and feelings to himself. Mainly because there was no time to do anything that didn't involve keeping the ranch running.

He had to admit though that it had been nice talking to Nora that day by the creek. It had felt good to let someone else know what he had been through. Not that he needed anyone to carry the burden for him. But sharing it had definitely made him feel lighter.

Even thinking about that afternoon now untightened his shoulders. He figured it wouldn't hurt to have the option.

"Why don't you give me the names of those private therapists just in case," Gabe said. "I'm not promising that I'm going to call any of them. But I'm not saying I absolutely won't."

Gabe arrived at the main house just after three in the afternoon. The kitchen, like the rest of the rooms, was empty. His mom and abuelita had taken a day trip to downtown Los Angeles to buy supplies for Abuelita's upcoming birthday party. And his brothers still hadn't come back from their trip to deliver a steer to a buyer up north. He figured his dad must have driven himself to town.

He couldn't believe he actually had some time alone.

The first thing he did was go upstairs and change into a pair of basketball shorts and T-shirt. He came back into the kitchen and found last night's leftovers in the fridge.

As he waited for the pot roast to warm up, Gabe studied the paper Lou had given him with the names of the therapists. There were four and all had offices less than thirty minutes away. The more he considered calling one of them, the more ridiculous he felt. Gabe had been a soldier. He was strong and capable. He didn't need to talk things out with anyone. All he needed was time. He could get better on his own.

No, he *would* get better on his own.

The microwave dinged, signaling his food was ready. Gabe tossed the paper onto the kitchen island counter. He decided he didn't need it after all.

He was just about to grab a pot holder from a drawer when he heard some sort of squeak.

Gabe looked around and couldn't make out where the noise had come from. He shrugged it off and reached again for the pot holder.

This time, the sound was more like a whimper.

He walked into the family room and heard it again. That's when he realized it was coming from the corner, behind his mom's recliner. A bad feeling settled in his stomach as he got closer and figured out that the noise belonged to Princesa.

Gabe found the dainty demon dog curled up in a ball on the floor next to a puddle of what he assumed to have once been her kibble.

"Are you sick?" he asked, and squatted down beside her.

She responded to his concerned question with a low growl. That gave him some relief.

"Okay," Gabe told her. "Wait here. I'll be back."

He returned after a few minutes with some paper towels, cleaning spray, and a bowl of fresh water. After wiping away her vomit, he tried to convince her to take a drink. She wouldn't budge.

He told her again that he'd be back and this time he showed up wearing his work gloves.

"I'm going to pick you up now, Princesa," he warned.

Despite the layer of protection, he didn't trust that she wouldn't try to scratch or bite him like always.

To his surprise, she did neither.

And that's when he really began to worry about the grumpy gremlin.

Gabe wasn't sure what to do. He thought about calling his mom but even if they left LA now, they wouldn't get back to the ranch for several hours because of traffic. The guys were already on their way, but he wasn't sure if they would be any help either.

With Princesa still in his arms, Gabe walked over to the guest bathroom and grabbed a clean towel from the cabinet. He wrapped Princesa in it and sat on the couch with her on his chest.

His dad came through the back door only a few minutes later. But he stopped in his tracks when he entered the family room.

"What?" Gabe asked.

"What are you doing to Princesa?" he asked.

"I'm not doing anything. I don't think she feels well."

"She's not attacking you? She must be sick," his dad surmised.

His acrimonious relationship with Princesa was well known around the ranch. Little dog hates the big guy. It was the source of many jokes in his family.

"I guess. Here, you take her," Gabe said, and started to hand Princesa over.

But she was not having it and bared her teeth at his dad.

"I don't think she wants me. She wants you," he said.

Gabe brought her back to his chest, and Princesa laid her head against him. "Well, what do you know," he said in amazement.

"Guess she's your friend today," his dad said.

"Perfect. Now what?"

"I'll take Princesa to the clinic."

"I'll go with you," Gabe said after standing up.

"I can still drive, you know."

"Fine. You drive, and I'll hold her. I'm going to try to put some shoes on, and then I'll meet you outside."

His dad nodded and left him to do what he needed to do.

They made it to the clinic in just a few minutes and right away one of the employees escorted them to a room. And before they could even sit down, Olivia the vet was walking through the door.

"Hey guys," she said softly.

They greeted her.

Olivia asked Gabe to put Princesa on the metal examination table but he hesitated. "She's kind of feisty. I don't know if she'll stay still for you."

"That's okay. I'm used to feisty animals."

He nodded and slowly lowered her onto the table. She let out a few weak yips and growls, but once she was down, she stayed still. Olivia spent a few minutes checking her vitals and examining her stomach and neck. Another employee entered the room and gave Gabe a clipboard with some forms to fill out.

His dad took it from him right away. "I'll take care of this."

"Okay," Olivia finally said. "We're going to take Princesa to the back so we can do some lab work and do a few tests. I'd also like to take some X-rays. Is that okay?"

"Whatever you need to do, please do it. What do you think is wrong?" his dad asked.

Olivia shrugged and stuffed her hands into the pocket of her white coat. "It's hard to say without running those tests. It could be a blockage in her intestine or a virus."

Gabe didn't like either of those options.

"Okay, I'll come talk to you guys as soon we know more. You are welcome to wait here or in our lobby."

Gabe watched as the vet tech picked up Princesa, still wrapped in the towel, and took her away.

"Sit down, Gabe. You're making me nervous," his dad said.

He obeyed and stayed quiet as his dad continued filling out the paperwork. When he was done, he set the clipboard on the small table next to his chair.

"It's probably going to be a while. If you're hungry, I can wait here while you go grab a sandwich from the diner or something?"

"I'm not hungry," Gabe said right away. It was true. Whatever appetite he'd had earlier was gone now.

"Okay. Then we'll just wait."

"I hope she's going to be okay. You know, because Mom loves her," Gabe said, still staring at the door the vet tech had taken Princesa through.

"Did you know that when Mom brought Princesa home that first night that she slept on the floor in the laundry room because Princesa wouldn't stop crying in her kennel?"

Gabe laughed. "I didn't know that."

"That dog means everything to my Margarita. We will do whatever it takes to bring her home."

They stayed quiet for another minute. Then he heard his dad clear his throat.

"So I saw that paper on the kitchen counter. Did

you re-injure yourself? Is that why you're looking for a doctor?"

Gabe took a deep breath and couldn't help but feel like history was repeating itself. He braced himself for his dad's anger. "It's not a list of medical doctors. They're counselors. My physical therapist thinks I should talk to someone about my accident."

"Oh."

"But I don't need to."

"But your physical therapist thinks you do?"

Gabe sighed. "There's nothing shameful about doing something to help your mental health. Therapy is great for the people who need it. I just don't need it. I am your son after all."

They stayed quiet for several minutes, and Gabe was grateful. He wasn't in the mood to talk about the pros and cons of therapy with his dad. To his relief, Olivia walked back into the room.

"Good news. The X-rays are clear. Blood work came back fine. She probably just ate something that upset her stomach. So we're going to send her home with some probiotics. Feed her only chicken and rice for a day or so and then bring her back if she doesn't improve."

"Thank you, Olivia," Gabe said.

"Yes, thank you," his dad said. "Margarita will be very happy to know her baby is going to be okay."

Olivia gave them a few more instructions and then left them alone again to go get Princesa.

His dad let out a long sigh. "Look, I know I say things about doctors not knowing everything. But there are good ones, like Olivia, who do know how to help things be better."

Gabe's mouth dropped open. Was his dad, in his own way, trying to tell him to go to therapy? "Since when do you want people to talk about their feelings?"

His dad shrugged. "I'm just saying if there's a way for you to get better, then you do it. Because maybe if you're healthy again, then you can help your brother run the ranch."

"I can't help run the ranch if you and Cruz don't trust me to make some of the bigger decisions or listen to my ideas. If you want me to do this, then I'm going to do this. All the way."

"Okay then," his dad said. "Let's see what you can do."

Chapter Twenty-Two

Nora leaned closer to the rectangular growing tray on the middle shelf and searched for life.

"Well, do you see it?" Gabe asked from above. He was towering over her as she was bent over trying to get a better look at her first sprout from her newest product, flax microgreens.

She scanned the dark soil one more time before finally spotting a speck of green. "I see it!" she squealed in excitement. "I see it!"

Nora jumped up and down before throwing her arms around Gabe's neck in a celebratory hug. He picked her up and she squealed again. When he set her back down, he didn't let her go right away. His hot breath fanned the loose hairs near her ear as his arms squeezed her tighter against him.

To her surprise, she didn't tense in response. Instead, she relaxed into the hug and inhaled. The familiar scent of whatever fabric softener he used for his laundry tickled her nose. She'd become used to it, along with the smell of his body wash, shampoo, and shaving cream. By now she knew his scent like she knew her own.

He looked down at her, and his eyes blazed with a yearning that she'd never seen before. It made her weak. Not physically. Emotionally.

"Nora," he began.

Like a wizard, he had the ability to alter her reality. A reality where she had no self-control and might attack his mouth with her own if he gave her the smallest sign that he wanted her to do just that.

God help her, he looked like he wanted exactly that.

Suddenly, the racks of microgreens seemed to close in on them and the very oxygenated air grew thinner— if that was even possible. Her lips fell open, and when his eyes dropped to them, Nora shivered in anticipation of a kiss.

His mouth was on hers within seconds. Slowly, she lifted her arms and wrapped them behind his neck. He groaned and dug his fingers into her hips, pulling her tight against him. But as much as she ached to surrender herself to their mutual passion, Nora knew it wasn't the time or the place.

Reluctantly, she broke their kiss.

"Where are you going?" he whispered, and moved his mouth to her neck.

"Nowhere," she managed to reply. "But someone might walk in."

"So what?"

Nora laughed and eventually wriggled out of his grasp. "We need to get back to work, Gabe."

He offered her a frown, but didn't try to pull her back to him.

She focused her attention back on the tray, breaking whatever trance she'd been caught up in. "By my estimation, we'll have full-grown sprouts in about another week. Then we can start selling them at the farmer's market another week or so after that."

He cleared his throat. "Sounds good," he said, his voice thick. "You should probably start letting your regulars know so they can get their orders in now."

"Great idea," she said, and walked back to the table where she had been assembling and filling more trays. She'd been interrupted by his visit a few minutes earlier and then his insistence that he'd spotted the first sprout.

Gabe joined her at the table and began helping. He didn't need any instructions anymore. She watched as he grabbed a handful of soil from a nearby tub and then expertly sprinkled soil onto the trays she'd already filled with water.

"Hey, I've been meaning to ask," she began, "how's your physical therapy going?"

He pressed his lips together and nodded thoughtfully. "Good, I guess. I am noticing my hand doesn't cramp up as much."

She put down the packet of seeds she was about to open. "Gabe, that's so great!"

He gave her a smile so genuine that it was contagious and she had no choice but to grin right back at him.

"I actually think working here with you has been its own kind of physical therapy. Digging in the dirt, pulling out vegetables, and trimming plants are making my fingers and hand work in a way I haven't been able to do before."

Nora nodded. "You're right. I don't think most people understand the physical labor it requires to make things grow."

"Lou, that's my physical therapist, was so impressed

that much about gardening yet, but I definitely know how to lead a team of soldiers."

"Are you sure?"

Gabe grinned from ear to ear and nodded. "I mean, obviously I'd have to do some research and figure out the logistics. But I really like the idea. Of course, it would be up to you. The garden is yours. I'd never push a project on you that you didn't want to do."

Nora didn't know how to respond to the fact that there was an opportunity to do something very meaningful with the garden or how to respond to the fact that Gabe was talking about his future at Rancho Lindo for the very first time.

"You've actually thought about this, haven't you?"

He stopped scooping and looked at her. "I have. It's weird, right? The more I talked to Lou about it, the more it became clear how great a program like that could be." He stopped talking and scrunched his eyebrows together. "Why are you looking at me like that?"

She didn't need a mirror to know that she must have some sort of dopey expression on her face. She couldn't help it. "It's nice to see you so excited about something."

Gabe nodded. "I guess I am kinda excited. And I have you to thank for that. After all, weren't you the one who has been telling me for months to find my purpose here?"

Warmth spread through her. Seeing Gabe so excited about the future made her heart do flips. And she'd never been more attracted to him.

Nora walked over to Gabe, took his face in her hands, and kissed him.

After a few breathless moments, it was Gabe who pulled away this time.

"But somebody might walk in," he told her with a teasing smile.

"So what?" she asked, and found his lips one more time.

Chapter Twenty-Three

Ay, Mijo. Que guapo," Abuelita said as soon as Gabe walked into the kitchen.

Daniel and Nico both looked up from their bowls of ice cream.

"Muy fancy, brother," Daniel said, and whistled at him.

"Are you actually going out? At night?" Nico asked.

"I am," Gabe said, and took a seat at the kitchen island. "Nora and I are going to check out a new mariachi band. They perform at this restaurant over in Buellton, so we're going to have dinner too."

Nora had been searching for a new group ever since the one she'd booked for Abuelita's party emailed her a week ago to tell her they'd decided to break up. Apparently, two of the brothers were in some type of feud and each decided to leave and start their own groups. He never knew there could be such drama in the mariachi circuit. Once he heard there were fighting brothers involved though, then he understood.

Abuelita clapped in delight. "I'm so happy you are going to see them. Señora Ramos says they are very good. She goes to see them perform at the restaurant at least once a month."

"I just hope the food is good. I'm starving," he said, and picked up an apple from the bowl on the island counter.

"You're always starving," Nico said, and went back to eating his ice cream.

"Okay, niños, I'm going to my room to watch my shows. Make sure you put those bowls in the dishwasher when you're done."

"Yes, Abuelita," his brothers said in unison.

"What are you two up to tonight?" Gabe asked after Abuelita left the kitchen.

"Not much," Daniel said. "Hey, maybe I should tag along with you guys?"

Gabe wasn't sure if he was serious. He hoped he wasn't. He'd been looking forward to spending time with Nora away from the ranch for days now. The last thing he wanted was his younger brother playing chaperone.

That's when Daniel started laughing. "Damn. You should see your face right now. I've never seen someone have such a visceral reaction to just an idea. And I spend most of my days with this guy here." Daniel pointed to Nico, who then scowled at him, basically proving Daniel's point.

"Yeah, well, I spend most of my days—and nights— with the both of you and those other two. Can you blame me for wanting one night to myself?"

"But that's the thing, Gabe. You're not going by yourself. You're going with Nora."

He finished off the apple and walked over to throw the core in the trash. "So what?" he said when he was back at the island. "She has to go because she's the one who's going to hire a group for the party."

"So it's not a date?" Nico asked.

The question came out of left field. And he wasn't ready. Was it a date? Was it not a date? They hadn't used that word, but now that his brothers were asking?

Maybe? Still, he wasn't ready to tell them that.

"It's dinner and listening to mariachis. That's all."

They looked at each other. "Are you going to tell him or do I need to do it," Daniel said to Nico.

"You do it."

Daniel nodded and cleared his throat. "Take a seat, Gabe. We want to talk to you."

Annoyance mixed with dread made his eye twitch. He wasn't sure exactly what his brothers needed to tell him. But he knew from a lifetime of experience that it was never good when the two of them ganged up on him.

Gabe checked his watch. "Fine. You have exactly five minutes." He sat back down on the seat he'd had before on the opposite side of the island counter from them.

"What are your intentions with Nora?" Daniel asked.

"Are you serious? Since when did you become her dad?" Gabe had to laugh. Then he saw that Daniel was indeed very serious. "If...if something was going on with Nora, what makes you think it would be any of your business. Or yours." He directed the last part to Nico, who looked like he was getting ready to say something too.

Daniel sat straight up and folded his arms across his chest. "It's our business because we care about her."

"Exactly," Nico finally weighed in. "And we don't want to see her get hurt. If you break her heart, we're the ones who are going to help put it back together."

"Like the last time," Daniel added.

First his mom and now his brothers? Why did his family think he was some asshole who went around breaking women's hearts? He'd had two real romantic relationships in his life. And they didn't end because he did something bad. They ended because relationships were hard when one person lives on the other side of the world for most of your time together. Sure, he didn't have the best track record with staying in one place for long. But one had nothing to do with the other.

Gabe stood up and put his hands on his hips in defiance. "That was a long time ago and I've apologized to Nora and she's accepted my apology. Yes, we've gotten pretty close and yes I'm attracted to her. But whatever is or isn't going on is between us and not the rest of this family."

Daniel shrugged. "Fine. But if something bad does happen, just know that you're going to have to deal with us."

"And Abuelita," Nico added. "Because you may be her mijito, but she will absolutely choose *her* Nora over you."

It was as if a cold front had arrived in the middle of the kitchen. He couldn't even be mad at Nico for saying what he said. He was right. Abuelita would probably never forgive him if he hurt Nora, even unintentionally. What on earth was he thinking getting involved with Nora?

Gabe couldn't shake the chill of his brothers' warnings even after he picked up Nora. Luckily, she was in a chatty mood and did most of the talking during the thirteen-minute drive to Buellton. Comprades Restaurant turned out to be bigger and busier and noisier than he'd expected. They were seated in a booth near the right side of the stage where Mariachi Guadalajara were scheduled to perform at eight p.m. In the meantime, Gabe studied the menu more carefully than needed.

He felt off. And he knew why. The trick was going to be not letting Nora know why.

After they ordered, their mutual silence was a drastic contradiction to the cacophony of voices in the large dining room.

"Are you feeling okay?" she finally asked after a few minutes.

Gabe took a quick swig of his beer before answering. "Yeah, yeah. Of course. I didn't realize it was going to be this loud."

Nora looked around and nodded. "There are a lot of big groups and families. Not exactly the place for an intimate dinner."

"Well, we are here to listen to the mariachis so we're basically here for a concert. Only difference is we get to eat real food before instead of snacks."

"That is true. Can you imagine if some poor couple came here for a date?"

Gabe froze. Was she being sarcastic? Or was she talking about them? Was this her way of asking him what they were? Back in the kitchen with Daniel and Nico, this had been the last thing he wanted to talk about. He knew now that it was a conversation they were going to have to have sooner or later. And what better place to do that than at a Mexican restaurant?

Because depending on how the talk went, at least they had access to chips and salsa. And beer.

He decided it was best to just rip the bandage off.

"So I had an interesting conversation with Daniel and Nico right before I picked you up," he began.

"Really? What was it about?"

Gabe cleared his throat. "You."

Her eyes grew big and she pointed to herself. "Me? Why?"

Just as he was about to answer, a small group of waiters and waitresses began belting out "Las Mañanitas" as they carried some sort of dessert with a candle sticking out of it to the long table next to their booth. Soon, others in the restaurant joined in the serenade of whichever person was celebrating a birthday.

He looked over at Nora and realized she had joined the choir. That made him laugh.

"Why were you singing?" he asked after the waiters and waitresses ended the performance. "You didn't know whose birthday it was."

"So what? There's no better reason to celebrate the fact that someone lived another year on this planet. It doesn't matter if you know them or not."

"That's a nice way to think about it."

"It's the reason why I wanted to help plan Doña Alma's party. I love birthdays. Well, now I do."

He didn't miss the tinge of sadness to her tone at that last part. "When didn't you love birthdays?"

Nora shifted in her seat and he knew he'd hit a sore spot. He was about to tell her that she didn't have to answer. But then she answered.

"When I was younger. A birthday used to be just another day for my dad to disappoint me."

Gabe wasn't sure how to respond to that. He knew that Nora didn't have a relationship with her father, but he had never pressed for the details. Nico and Daniel, and probably Abuelita, might know more. For the first time, he wanted to know too.

"I'm sorry. You never really talked about him, so I figured you didn't know him."

She sighed. "I did. It probably would've been better if I hadn't. He was in and out of my life when I was a little girl. And then one day, he was gone for good. I haven't seen or spoken to him in over twenty years."

Her tone was light but her eyes betrayed the deep emotion in her words. He didn't know the man, but Gabe wanted to knock him out. He'd bet good money that Daniel and Nico would want to take a swing as well. He reached across the table and squeezed Nora's hand.

"I hate that he hurt you," he told her. "No kid should have to go through something like that."

Nora gave him a sad smile. "No, but I like to think of it this way. That experience taught me to value loyalty and, in return, I'm fiercely loyal to those who are there for me."

Slowly, a new picture began to emerge. Gabe finally understood why Nora was so protective of his family and Rancho Lindo. A pang of guilt hit him. She deserved better than what he could give her. She deserved someone who knew what he wanted.

Hadn't she once told him that she didn't do temporary?

And if Gabe wasn't ready to make a long-term decision about Rancho Lindo, didn't that make this thing between them temporary?

He tried to keep up the small talk as they ate. Then he got a reprieve when the performance began. Luckily, the group was very good. He'd always been a fan of mariachi music and recognized some of the songs. When it was over, Nora excused herself to go talk to one of the musicians. On the way back to their table, he noticed a woman stop her. They hugged and chatted for a few minutes. Gabe paid the bill, grabbed Nora's purse and coat, and waited for her to come back.

When she did, he asked, "Who was that?"

"Andrea? Oh, she and Nico dated for a few months earlier this year. I really liked her. I was sad when they broke up."

His curiosity was piqued. "Why did they break up?"

"Why does Nico break up with all of his girlfriends? I guess he got bored."

The drive back to the ranch went way too fast this time. He'd been enjoying himself, despite his earlier doubts. Besides, it wasn't like Nora was asking for a relationship. He hoped she was enjoying being with him too. Even if they weren't giving it a name.

He thought about Nico and that woman. His brother had always been kind of a player and he used to tease Gabe that they were the same. Daniel and Tomás were the ones who did relationships. Not them. Gabe would probably be furious if Nora had decided she'd liked Nico because he knew that his brother didn't like being tied to one woman for very long.

So why was he any better?

When they arrived at Nora's house, she asked him to come in for coffee. He wasn't really thirsty or cold, but he agreed just to be able to spend more time with her. He took a seat at her two-person kitchen table and watched her carefully as she moved from cabinet to counter and then back again.

He should've already told her how fantastic she

looked in that little black dress of hers. It accentuated every curve, making his imagination run wild with thoughts of peeling it off of her. When she finally set a mug in front of him and sat down, Gabe needed an ice bath more than a hot cup of coffee.

"Why are you staring at me like that," she said after taking her first sip.

"Like what?" He asked the question but he knew very well what she was referring to.

"Like I have something you want."

Wow. She was a mind reader. And as much as Gabe yearned to show her exactly what he wanted, he knew he had to take things slow.

"Actually, there is something I want from you," he said carefully.

Her eyes grew big. "What?"

"I want you to answer a question."

Did her face just fall? Or was he seeing things through lust-colored glasses?

"Okay. What's your question?" she replied.

"Did you ever have a crush on Daniel or Nico?"

She nearly spit out the drink she'd just taken. "What? Are you serious?"

"I'm very serious. You know, Nico was actually voted 'Most Likely to Become a Model' in his high school yearbook."

She laughed. "He could've been on the cover of GQ. Same with Daniel. The answer is no. They're like my brothers, you know that. Besides, neither of them are my type."

"And what's your type?" he asked. He'd meant to tease her, but now he was really invested in knowing what kind of man Nora wanted.

"What's yours?"

Gabe raised his eyebrow. "Nope. I'm the one asking questions tonight. Please elaborate on your answer."

"Yes, Nico is good-looking. But he's also a flirt. And Daniel is a Chatty Charlie. I'm more partial to the strong and silent type. There's something to be said about a man who can tell you a thousand words just by the way he looks at you."

He nodded. "Interesting. Can you always tell what I'm thinking by my expression?"

She considered this for a moment. "Not always. Like right now, I have no idea what's going on in that head of yours other than you're probably wondering if I have food."

It was true. Those enchiladas from earlier hadn't filled him up.

Luckily for him, Nora said she had leftover spaghetti and offered to warm some up for him. Of course, he took her up on her offer. She watched him from across the table as he ate and he felt a little guilty for keeping her up. "Are you sleepy?" he asked after he rinsed his bowl and then joined her on the couch.

She gave him a small smile. "I was before. But now I'm okay."

He scooted closer. "Can I ask you another question?"

"So curious tonight," she said with a laugh. "Go ahead."

"Are you going to let me kiss you?"

This time her smile was shy. "Maybe. But, first, you have to answer one of my questions."

He raised his hands. "Go ahead. I'm an open book."

Nora rolled her eyes as if she didn't believe him. "Okay, prove it. What was the first thing that came to your mind when you saw me in the greenhouse that first day? And you have to use your words. No smirks or winks allowed."

He lowered his gaze for a second and then met hers head-on. "I wondered where on earth had this beautiful woman come from. I wondered what it would be like to kiss you."

Gabe could tell that she hadn't expected him to say that. "Even after you knew it was me?"

"Especially after I knew it was you," he whispered. His eyes fell on her mouth and her lips called out to be licked, bitten even. He ached to know what it would be like to have those lips on every single part of his body. It was like every argument he'd had in his head that night about why he should keep his distance was tossed aside. He could think of no good reason why they shouldn't sleep together. They were both consenting adults and perfectly capable of not making it mean more than it needed to.

He watched as she inhaled a sharp breath and that's when he knew. She was thinking the exact same thing.

"You're so beautiful," he said, tucking a strand of her hair behind her ear. He allowed his eyes to travel down her body—as if to clear a path before his lips took over the exploration. But he stopped when he noticed the horseshoe-shaped scar just above her right knee.

"Is that from..." he began, pointing to the small mark.

"When I fell out of the tree," Nora answered his unasked question.

Gabe met her eyes. "I didn't think you remembered."

"I didn't," she admitted. "At least not until a few months ago."

"Sometimes I wish I didn't remember."

He'd been so scared when he'd seen her small body hit the ground. Her scream had brought Luz running out of the cottage and for a few terrifying seconds he wondered if Honora was dead. But as soon as her tía gently rolled her over onto her back, she opened her eyes and began crying. His relief was short-lived, though. Luz had called Chucho so he could drive them to see the doctor. And Chucho had arrived with his dad. Right away, his dad had blamed Gabe for the accident. Chucho had come to his defense, saying he didn't think Gabe had dragged Honora up the tree. But his dad wouldn't hear it. That's when Gabe wondered if his dad was angry because he thought Nora would have never climbed the tree in the first place without Gabe's lead or was he pissed because he'd figured out that Gabe had been playing instead of doing his chores.

Either way, his dad had grounded Gabe for a week. And because he wanted to be mad at somebody too, he had decided it was all Honora's fault. So he'd stayed away from her even when his house arrest was over.

"I'm sorry," he heard her say.

"For what?"

"For whatever I did back then that made you not want to be my friend. It makes me sad because things could've been different between us."

Guilt stung his chest. Gabe reached out and touched her cheek. "Hey. You have nothing to be sorry for. If anyone should be apologizing, it should be me. I was a dumb kid, that's all. You didn't do anything."

He moved his hand from her face and then slowly rubbed his thumb over the scar. Even though the skin was raised, it was still smooth.

"That tickles," she whispered.

The storm of desire that had been brewing all night finally broke through and Gabe had no more willpower left to try to wrangle it. He was done fighting with himself. He bent over and lowered his head just above her knee. "Does this tickle too?" he said before brushing his lips softly over her scar.

Nora's knee jerked and he moved his hand to still her leg. When he kissed it again, he heard a gasp this time.

Gabe sat back up and cupped Nora's face between his hands. Her cheeks were warm and flushed and he noticed how fast she was breathing. But it was the way she was looking at him, her eyes bright with need, that told him she was as desperate as he was.

She was done fighting as well.

Slowly, he moved closer and met her lips in one soft kiss.

It was slow and sweet. And then it wasn't.

"I've been wanting to do this all damn day," he said in between breaths.

Her arms went around his neck as his body pushed her farther into the couch. His hand dug into her hip and then slid down her thigh. After several furious open-mouthed kisses, they finally broke apart.

"How is this happening?" Nora whispered.

He pulled her arms off of him and held her hands with his. "If you're having doubts, it's okay. We don't have to do anything you aren't ready for. I just need to be with you right now. It doesn't matter how."

She shook her head furiously. "No more doubts. I want this. I want you."

And in that moment, Gabe knew it was his turn to fall.

Chapter Twenty-Four

What about this one?"

Nora looked up from the rack she'd been sifting through to see Gabe holding a bright turquoise Hawaiian shirt.

"Sure," she said, slowly nodding her head. "Let's get four matching ones for your brothers too."

He made a face and put the shirt away. "You're joking, but you know Daniel and Nico would love that."

She laughed. "Totally."

They had stopped at a men's boutique in Santa Barbara's La Arcada Plaza to look for something nice for Gabe to wear to Doña Alma's birthday party. It was just a few days away now, and Señora Ortega had pulled Nora aside that morning and begged her to go shopping with Gabe. Judging by the Hawaiian shirt he'd just picked up, his mother had every reason to be concerned about his fashion sense.

"I don't know why I can't just wear my long-sleeved denim shirt," he said after joining her at the same rack.

"Because you already wear that every Sunday to

Mass. It's going to be a special day, so you need to wear something special," she explained. "What about this one?" Nora showed him the dark gray dress shirt she'd just pulled off the fixture.

"That's nice. But is it *special*?" he said mockingly.

Nora lightly slapped his arm and hung the shirt back where she'd found it. They walked around the store for a few minutes and decided to try another shop.

"Just so you know, I'm not wearing a suit," Gabe said as they stepped outside onto the plaza's main courtyard.

Nora turned to him. "Why not?"

"Because I'm not a suit guy?" he said as they started walking. "Besides, I already talked to the others, and everyone's going to wear jeans and a nice shirt. And their dress boots, of course."

She shook her head. "Yet you didn't want to be matching with them? I don't understand you Ortega boys at all."

Gabe laughed. "Because what would be the fun in that? I thought you loved analyzing me?"

Nora was about to reply with a sarcastic comeback when he reached between them to take her hand. The personal contact was a surprise. Of course, by now they'd done way more than hold hands. But the gesture seemed more intimate, more familiar. Because it was in public.

He must have sensed something and leaned over. "Is this okay?" he said, tightening his grip just a little.

"Yes. It's nice," Nora said softly, trying to wrestle the tornado of emotions currently wreaking havoc on her insides. She'd bet a million dollars that her face was as red as her prized raspberries.

As they walked past a few more boutiques, Nora allowed herself to enjoy just being with Gabe. If anyone had told her four months ago that she'd be taking an afternoon stroll with him holding hands, she would've laughed in their face. And then promptly thrown up. Not because the thought would've disgusted her, but because it would've frightened her. Even now, she was a little scared of how wonderful it felt to be with him just doing normal, everyday things. On the ranch, it was easy to get lost in the work and the tasks at hand. Being out here with him like this was different. And now that she had a taste of what their relationship could be, did she dare hope for more?

"Hey, the turtles are still here," Gabe announced, and pulled her in the direction of the plaza's famous fountain.

An amused Nora watched as he bent forward to take a closer look at the two red-eared slider turtles swimming around. The turtle fountain was a popular tourist attraction at La Arcada. The historic plaza was also home to some of the city's best restaurants, art galleries, outdoor sculptures, and Old World–inspired architecture. Nora preferred shopping at La Arcada to the larger more crowded malls in the area just for the charming ambiance. And she too enjoyed watching the turtles.

"I think those are babies," she said, pointing at the two smaller turtles submerged in the water.

"Then those two over there are probably mom and dad."

Nora looked at the pair sunbathing on one of the fountain's sculptures. She had no idea if Gabe's assumption was right, but it was nice to imagine the family spending their days together swimming. "Probably," she agreed.

They watched the turtles for a few more minutes before Gabe proclaimed that he was starving.

"Fine," she told him. "How about this? You let me pick out your shirt, and I'll let you pick where we eat."

"Miss Nora, you have a deal."

Less than thirty minutes later, Nora and Gabe were seated at one of the plaza's sidewalk bistros waiting for their lunch to arrive.

"So do you really like your shirt or did you just agree because you wanted to hurry up and eat?" Nora asked after taking a sip of her iced tea.

"Both," Gabe said.

She shook her head. "I knew it."

"I'm kidding. I really do like the shirt. It's dressy, but it's also comfortable."

Nora laughed, but she was also pretty happy that Gabe was pleased with his purchase. It actually hadn't been that hard to convince him to buy the midnight-blue embroidered guayabera linen shirt.

"My tío Jesus used to wear something just like it." Gabe continued, "I remember always wanting one of my own."

"I wish I could've met your tío," Nora said.

"Me too. He would've loved you because you are amazing." Gabe eyes met hers, and she almost couldn't handle their intensity. He wasn't just looking at her, he was devouring her, and she could almost read the naughty thoughts in his head.

The waitress arrived with their food, and she welcomed the distraction. Brand-new feelings had rushed from her heart to her head, and she was almost dizzy with euphoria. Something was changing between them. Their relationship—their connection—had grown over the past week.

She had never been happier than at this moment sitting across from Gabe as he enjoyed a hamburger. So why was a small part of her worried that it wasn't going to last?

"Oh, hey, I talked to John this morning," Gabe said, cutting through her doubts.

"What did he say? Did he change his mind?" a panicked Nora asked. John Dimas was the CEO of the Green Grocery Store, and he was scheduled to visit Rancho Lindo in a few days to learn all about her microgreens.

Gabe shook his head and laughed. "Why does your mind always jump to the worst possible scenario?"

It was true. It was the way her mind worked. Something good had happened. That meant something bad was about to follow.

Her mom used to say that it was how the universe balanced itself out. She used to picture it like a scale. On one side all of the good and beautiful things about life. And on the other, all the bad and dark stuff. If the scale tipped too far in either direction, the universe would erupt into chaos. Nora had loved her mom. But she hated how she'd taught her to be such a pessimist.

It also didn't help that her mom's skewed way of looking at the world had proven true over and over again. Every good thing that had ever happened to her was always followed by something bad. The first time was when her third-grade science project was picked to represent her elementary school at the district science fair, but then her dad never showed up to the awards ceremony. The last time had been when she'd finally quit the job she hated only to get a phone call a week later that Tío Chucho had passed away.

Nora used to tell herself that wasn't pessimistic as much as it was realistic. She was never one to wear rose-colored glasses. Because if something bad was headed in her direction, she wanted to be able to see it. And prepare herself.

Especially when it had the power to really hurt her.

"I don't *always* think that," she told Gabe anyway. "So if he's not canceling, then what did he say?"

"He just wanted some background information on the ranch. He says that way when he gets here he can just focus his time on the microgreens."

She nodded. "That's a good idea," Nora replied, and took a bite of her club sandwich.

"I think so. Plus it shows his interest. It's a good sign."

"Did you talk to your mom about dinner?" she asked.

"I did, and she's on board. I told her about some of our ideas but basically I said she and Abuelita were in charge of the menu. I'm not going to pretend to know better—or tell them what to make."

Gabe had originally wanted to take John out to dinner after the business part of his visit was over. But Nora had suggested having dinner on the ranch. What better way to show how good her microgreens were than to have John eat them?

"Can I tell you something?" Nora asked after Gabe polished off his last french fry.

He gave her a warm smile. "Always."

She took a deep breath and then confessed, "I'm scared. What if I mess this up for the ranch?"

"Hey," he told her, and reached across the table to grab her hand. "There is no possible way for you to do that. If John decides to pass, then it's going to be because it's something with him or his company that can't make it work. And if that happens, then we go find someone who can."

"Maybe you should do all of the talking, then."

"I'm not the expert. You are. You are more than capable at explaining what you do and how you do it. You taught me, didn't you? And I don't like answering questions—I'm too impatient. Just ask my dad."

Her worries lightened, and she squeezed his hand. "Thank you. That means a lot. I didn't realize you could be so inspirational."

Gabe winked at her. "I have my moments. Besides, you believe in me, and I believe in you. That's how this thing works, right?"

"Right," she said. The butterflies were back and so was the light-headedness.

They were officially a thing.

Chapter Twenty-Five

Nora couldn't help but feel like a guest in her own house.

Correction. Her own greenhouse.

She made sure her smile stayed put even as the uneasiness grew in her stomach. Her eyes scanned the small group of men huddling in the middle of her territory and tried not to be too intimidated. Of course, Gabe, Cruz, and Señor Ortega belonged there as much as she did—but she couldn't remember one time that they were there all together. It was all a little overwhelming. And then there was John.

John had arrived at Rancho Lindo less than thirty minutes ago. Since the first handshake, the Ortegas had kept him busy talking about the ranch.

Nora never had the gift of gab—especially in a group situation. There seemed to always be someone who was louder with more important things to say than her. Instead, she usually found herself listening more than talking. It was no wonder she'd stayed so long at her own job despite not being happy for a while. She had tried to offer her own ideas or explain her findings for with my progress at my last session that I had to break it to him that it wasn't just because of him," he said with a laugh. "He actually wanted me to tell him about the things I've been doing, and I had to show him, like act it out, so he could see which muscles were being used."

"Uh-oh," she said with a grimace. "I hope he didn't have a problem with anything."

Gabe shook his head as he continued to work. "Not at all. In fact, he really believes that being here in the greenhouse surrounded by all of the plants is actually helping me heal. I joked that maybe we should let some of his patients volunteer here as part of their recovery plan."

Nora paused in surprise. "Seriously? What did he say?"

"He thought it was a good idea," he replied.

Nora stopped filling trays altogether and looked at Gabe. "Really?"

"Really," he said, finally meeting her eyes. "I told him it was a possibility down the line. What do you think?"

Nora wasn't sure what to think. Of course, the thought of using her garden to help other wounded soldiers like Gabe sounded amazing. But she had only been at this for a year. She wasn't qualified to lead any type of formal rehab program.

"I think it's a wonderful idea. I'm just not sure if I could take on that extra responsibility and do all the things I already have planned to expand the garden."

"I could do it."

She was taken aback. "You?"

"Yeah," he said, chuckling a little. "I may not know

certain data. But her voice would always get drowned out by a colleague or even her own boss. On the rare occasion when she finally did say something, her nerves or awkwardness would get in the way. So much so that she'd become flustered enough to give up.

And that was why it was hard for her to speak up sometimes.

Like now.

She watched with a mix of admiration and jealousy as Gabe talked about how Rancho Lindo microgreens could become the emerald of the Central Valley. He was confident and convincing. Daniel was right. Gabe was a natural salesman. He could charm the boots off a rodeo clown.

An unsettling realization hit her. Is that what he was doing with her? Had she been so blinded by all that radiating charm and sexiness that she'd forgotten he could disappear one day like before?

Stop. You can't be worried about that now. Focus on this big opportunity instead.

Nora tried to concentrate on what Gabe was saying. It must have been funny, because the other men were laughing. That's when she met his eyes. His eyebrows furrowed in confusion as his own laughter died down. She wondered what he saw on her face for his expression to turn serious.

"You know what, John?" Gabe said. "I think I've been talking your ear off long enough. How about you hear from the expert herself."

Nora's chest tightened with even more anxiety as Gabe pointed to her and everyone else turned in her direction. A rising panic in her chest almost made her run the other way. Why on earth had she thought she could do this? She wasn't a talker or a charmer like Gabe. She didn't have decades of experience like Cruz. She'd only been growing microgreens for barely three years.

Gabe must have noticed her hesitation. Nora met his eyes and he winked at her. It was his way of letting her know that he believed in her. At least that's how she took it. And it did the trick.

She took a deep breath and started her spiel.

As she talked and talked about her growing process, her confidence grew as well. Soon, she didn't feel like she was in the spotlight. The pressure to say the right thing and convince John that he needed to give her a contract fell by the wayside. All she cared about was making sure other people understood what she did and why.

She led the group through each step and showed them all of the equipment she used. John had lots of questions and Nora had all the answers.

After almost an hour later, she finally had run out of things to say. "Our growing process is not just sustainable and eco-friendly, but it's also based in science," she said to wrap up her presentation. "That means we're always on the cutting edge when it comes to finding new varieties and improving upon that growing process."

And with that, Nora asked for any last questions. When no one had any, she thanked John for his visit.

"I'm the one who should be thanking you, Nora," he said. "Gabe has been singing your praises for weeks and now I know why. I've learned so much today."

Nora knew her cheeks must have turned beet red. She wasn't sure how to respond to such a compliment. Gabe gave her a huge grin and then patted John on the shoulder. "See, I told ya," he said, a hint of pride resonating behind the words. "Nora is an expert in showing you what's possible."

Maybe no one else noticed the way Gabe's eyes softened when he said that last part. Or maybe they missed the way he'd slightly nodded in her direction. But she did notice. And she fully believed that she was supposed to. It sent a jolt of warmth and affection through her veins. Her heart swelled with a new stunning realization.

She was falling in love with Gabe Ortega.

Chapter Twenty-Six

Nora may have wowed him in the greenhouse, but his mom and abuelita were the stars in the kitchen.

Gabe's stomach growled at the vegetable feast that welcomed him after he walked inside. It truly was a sight to behold, especially in this kitchen.

"Oh my gosh," Nora whispered beside him.

His family had never been vegetarian. In fact, Daniel's attempt to eat vegan lasted exactly one meal. Not because his heart wasn't in it, but because he couldn't take the stricken looks of disappointment from both their dad and abuelita. Cutting back on red meat was one thing. It was completely different to announce he was no longer going to eat cheese or eggs either.

But judging by some of the delicious-looking vegetable dishes sitting on the kitchen counter, Gabe wouldn't have minded if there was no meat on the dinner table.

Everyone greeted his mom and abuelita before excusing themselves to wash up. Nora, Nico, and Daniel went upstairs, while Cruz directed John to the downstairs guest bathroom.

While his dad used the kitchen sink to wash his hands, Gabe couldn't help but walk over and give his mom a big hug.

"Is it what you wanted, Mijo?" his mom said. "We made a butternut squash soup that's going to be topped with the micro broccoli, a mixed microgreens salad with pomegranate dressing, carrot microgreens risotto, and spicy grilled shrimp tacos with all the toppings, including the cilantro and arugula microgreens. Oh, and flan for dessert."

Gabe still couldn't believe what they'd created. "It all looks amazing," he said.

"Pues, you told us to make things so the grocery man could see how good Nora's vegetables are."

He laughed and shook his head. "I know. But I guess I figured you'd make a salad and a side dish. I never expected all of this."

Abuelita clapped her hands and then linked her arm through his. "We just want to show him how special Nora's garden is."

Pride and affection swelled inside him. That was the first time he'd ever heard Abuelita refer to the garden as Nora's. For as long as he could remember, everyone on the ranch had called it Doña Alma's garden or el huerto de Abuelita.

He patted her hand. "Thank you, Abuelita. This is perfect."

After washing his own hands, Cruz and his dad told Gabe they wanted to talk to him in the home office before dinner. He figured they wanted to ask his opinion about how everything was going so far.

He was wrong.

"Why is he only interested in the microgreens?" his

dad began. "We should be talking to him about getting our beef in his stores too."

Cruz nodded, of course. "That's where the money is going to be, Gabe."

His dad shook his finger at him. "Listen to your brother. He knows how much we get with our other contracts. We should focus on the beef. The microgreens can be part of the deal, or we push that later."

Gabe couldn't believe what he was hearing. Had they not been listening to a word he had told them or what John had told him today? The Green Grocery Store already contracted with one ranch for their beef products and only because that supplier could meet John's specific criteria. Rancho Lindo didn't have the capability or the money to do what Green Grocery required. At least not right now.

Besides, Nora's microgreens were the only reason why John was there in the first place.

"Beef isn't what John is looking for," he explained.

His dad scoffed. "Because you didn't tell him it was."

Familiar frustration made him ball his hands into fists at his sides. "Aye, Dad. He came here to decide if he wants his stores to carry Nora's microgreens. That's it. He didn't come here to find a new beef supplier. And if we change the pitch now, chances are we're going to get zero contracts instead of one."

"You don't know that," his dad accused.

Gabe couldn't hold his anger in any longer. He groaned and then dragged his hand over his face. "Why can't you just trust that I do? Huh? Why can't you just pat me on the back and tell me that I did something good here? Is that so damn hard?"

He didn't give either of them a chance to answer.

Instead, he stormed out of the office, through the kitchen, and back outside.

If John wasn't inside talking to his other brothers, Gabe would've jumped in the truck and taken off. He should've known that his dad and Cruz would question his idea only for the sole reason that it was his. If his dad or Cruz wanted to try to get John to consider their beef, then why didn't they speak up when he told them about the microgreens pitch in the first place? Hell, they could've said something or given him a quick tour after the greenhouse. But Cruz had only answered questions about possible production expansions and their current clients. If anything, he'd been the one to talk about the ranch's other businesses only because he wanted John to know they were a stable supplier. He wanted John to know he could count on them to deliver.

This whole time he'd been trying to convince John that they—that he—knew what they were doing. Who knew he should've been trying to convince his family too?

"Everything okay?"

Nora's tender voice stopped him before he let out the scream he'd been holding.

She came up to him and touched his arm. His first instinct was to hide it. But he didn't have it in him.

He shook his head. "No. But it will be."

Her eyebrows furrowed in worry. "Did John say something?"

Gabe pulled her to him for a much needed hug. "Not John. It's just the usual crap with my dad. Don't worry about it, please."

"Too late."

He moved so he could look down and meet her eyes. "This has nothing to do with you or John. And I'm not about to let the stuff with my dad ruin the amazing dinner my mom and Abuelita worked so hard on. Let's go inside and wrap up this deal."

"But..."

"No buts, Nora. John is interested. I can feel it. I bet we'll have a contract within the week."

"You really think so?"

He didn't want to lie. And he didn't want his dad's doubts to cloud his optimism either. So he offered what he could. "I do. He'd be dumb not to do it. And if for some reason it doesn't happen, I need you to remember that if he passes, it won't be because of something you did or didn't do. You were fantastic today. You said all the right things and had all that science mumbo jumbo to back it up. I'm so proud of you."

That earned him a soft kiss. He took it and, like magic, all of the frustration and anger he'd been feeling just a few minutes earlier evaporated.

"Okay, how about we skip dinner and just go back to your cottage instead," he said after she pulled away.

Playfully, she slapped his arm. "No way. Doña Alma would never forgive us."

"This is true. Okay, fine. We better go inside before I change my mind."

Dinner turned out to be better than he had hoped. It helped that his mom was in a chatty mood and that the food was as delicious as he'd predicted. John ended up staying until almost nine. Gabe offered to follow him back to his hotel in Santa Barbara to make sure he didn't get lost.

"It's really dark on the road leading out of Esperanza.

And some of the intersections can look pretty similar, so it's easy to get turned around or confused."

John waved him off and stepped into his rental SUV. "I'll be fine. Thanks again for having me. I'll be in touch soon."

Gabe and Nora watched as he drove toward Rancho Lindo's main gate and then they got into the truck so he could take her home.

"I'm so tired," she said after buckling her seat belt. "If I closed my eyes, I could fall asleep right here, right now."

"Are you still doing the farmer's market over in Thousand Oaks tomorrow?" he asked.

"Yep. I have to set up by eight. I hope it doesn't rain."

He reached over and grabbed the hand resting on her knee. "I wish I could go with you instead of helping set up for the party."

"I can't believe it's already going to be tomorrow night. Doña Alma is so happy too. She showed me her dress earlier and I swear she was giggling like a little girl."

Gabe laughed at the thought, especially since he knew it had to be true. Every morning, she'd report how many days were left until her party. He'd never seen his abuelita this excited about her birthday before.

They arrived at Nora's cottage a few minutes later. Gabe helped her off the truck and held her hand as they walked to her porch. The night air was cool but he was heating up just thinking of finally getting Nora all to himself.

He decided he couldn't even wait until she opened the door.

Tugging on the hand he'd been holding, Gabe drew

Nora to him. Before he could kiss her though, she reminded him, "I have to get up early."

He reached over to push a wayward strand behind her ear. "I know."

"And it's probably not a good idea for you to come inside."

"Why? I promise I'll behave."

She laughed. "The fact that you even have to say that tells me that you know that you won't."

"Don't we need to, uh, go over everything and discuss?"

"We can do that tomorrow," she said with a soft chuckle.

"Or I could come inside and we could, you know, discuss other important things."

She arched her eyebrow to the starry sky. "Oh, really? Important things like?"

"Like how much I enjoy kissing you here." He tilted his head and brushed his lips just underneath the lobe of her right ear. "Or here," he whispered before kissing the side of her neck.

Her soft gasp was like gasoline on fire. Gabe couldn't contain his desire any longer. He found her mouth and pushed through the barrier of her lips with his tongue. When he finally tasted her, it was his turn to gasp in satisfaction.

But he still wasn't satiated.

Gently, he nudged her backward until she was against one of the wooden pillars of her front porch. He moved his hands to cradle her face and continued his fevered exploration. With every kiss and lick, Gabe became both lost and found again. Nora was unexpected, yet she was also everything he was looking for.

A storm of emotions swirled inside him. He knew something had changed—something wonderful and scary at the same time. Eventually, he'd have to figure it out. But it could wait. Instead, he just wanted to focus on the feel of Nora's body against his. He wanted nothing more than to spend the rest of the night wrapped in her arms. Unfortunately, she had other plans.

"Gabe," she said with a ragged breath in between kisses. "I have to go."

"No, you don't," he whispered.

She pulled her head away to meet his eyes. Her smile was even more pronounced thanks to her swollen and puckered lips. She looked so damn sexy. He had to taste her again.

He moved to kiss her, but she moved so he couldn't. "I really do have to go to bed."

Gabe shrugged. "Fine. Let's go to bed."

"Yeah, like you're going to let me sleep," she said with a laugh.

As much as he wanted to continue teasing her, he knew he had to let her go. She was right. There was no way they would get any sleep if she let him into her bed tonight.

He hung his head in almost exaggerated disappointment. "All right."

Gabe dropped his arms and took a step back. Nora laughed again and moved toward her front door. But before she could reach it, he grabbed her hand.

"Thank you," he told her.

She looked at him quizzically. "For what? You're the one who called John. You made this happen, not me."

"But you let it. You never doubted me or told me

a million reasons why it couldn't happen. You just trusted me and let me run with the idea."

"Or, maybe, you finally trusted yourself?"

He wasn't sure what she meant by that. When he didn't say anything, she began to explain. "I think you don't like expectations because you don't trust that you can meet them. So, instead of just trying, you decide they're not even worth the effort."

"You're definitely worth it," he said, rubbing his fingers across the back of her hand.

She considered his words for a moment. "Thank you for saying that."

"It's the truth. And you're right about me and expectations. Part of me thinks if I can't do something perfectly, then why bother? That's why I stayed in the army so long. I wasn't just good at what I did. I was the best."

"And you weren't here?"

"Nope. Cruz was. Whatever I did, my dad was always there to tell me that I needed to do it like Cruz or have Cruz show me how to do it right. I guess I got tired of trying to be like him. I needed to go do something out of his shadow."

She shrugged and squeezed his hand. "You'll find something of your own again."

"Maybe I already have," he said softly.

Even under the soft haze of the porch light, Gabe could see a new shine in Nora's eyes. Her face became a canvas of unspoken emotion. Yet deep down, his own heart was listening.

They watched each other for a few seconds, neither one of them brave enough to say anything else.

Finally, she pulled her hand out of his grasp and

smiled. "Good night, Gabe," she said before unlocking her door and heading inside.

"Good night, Nora," he called after her.

Gabe knew he was still grinning by the time he parked the truck in front of the house. Despite the confrontation with his dad, it really had been a good day—maybe even one of the best he'd had since moving back to Rancho Lindo. What a difference a few months could make. Although Nora was a big reason for his attitude change, he had to admit that once he stopped fighting the pull of the ranch, it was easier to adjust to his new life. Or was he simply remembering how it used to be—before he started to think of his legacy as a shackle?

The vibration of his phone on the seat next to him interrupted his reflection. He laughed when he saw John's name flashing on the screen.

"You got lost, didn't you?" he said as soon as he answered.

His friend chuckled. "Not even a little bit. I'm already back in my hotel room."

"That's good. So what's up?"

"I had planned to wait a few days and let everything sink in, but I'm too damn excited. I want to contract with Rancho Lindo to be our microgreens supplier."

Maybe if he had been a proper businessman Gabe would've played it cool and contained his excitement. But he had never been proper about anything.

"Woo-hoo!" he yelped into the phone as excitement plowed through him.

They talked a few more minutes about next steps, including getting their lawyers involved and having a few more executives from the company visit within the next month. Details still had to be finalized, but the plan was officially in motion. He couldn't wait to hang up with John and call Nora.

Better yet, he was going to turn right back around and tell her in person.

"I have to be honest. I was really impressed," John said after they agreed to schedule another call next week.

"I knew you would be. Nora knows what she's talking about. She's done a fantastic—"

John interrupted him. "I was talking about you, Gabe. For a soldier, you're also a pretty good salesman."

Gabe couldn't help but laugh. "I guess I was just excited about this opportunity for Rancho Lindo."

"It was more than that. You really know what the market is looking for right now. Organic and sustainable aren't just buzzwords anymore. People don't just want quality produce, they want to make sure they're supporting local and family-owned businesses. Your experience and knowledge that comes from growing up on a working ranch is exactly what I need."

He stilled. "What are you saying, John?"

"How would you like to work for Green Grocery?"

His mouth fell open from shock. "Doing what?" Gabe asked.

"Doing exactly what you did today. Sourcing new and quality products from local ranches that Green Grocery can carry in our stores."

"Seriously? Wow. That sounds great. I can already think of few places around here that have some standout products."

"Fantastic. I definitely want to hear more about

those later. But I'd actually like for you to oversee our region down south. You know, San Diego, Imperial, and Riverside counties."

His amped-up excitement dropped about a million decibels. John was offering him a job that would take him away from Rancho Lindo, the town of Esperanza, and Nora. The irony wasn't lost on him. Just when he'd started to warm up to the idea of staying, someone was finally opening a door that could allow him to leave.

"You still there, Gabe?"

He cleared his throat. "Yeah, sorry. I guess I'm kind of in shock. I definitely wasn't expecting this when I called you last month."

"Me neither. But I know a good opportunity when I see it. And it's my amazing luck that I stumbled across two of them today. So what do you say?"

Hundreds of things ran through Gabe's mind, yet he still wasn't quite sure which ones he should let come out of his mouth. It was too much. He needed to process.

"Is it okay if I take a few days and think about it? Don't get me wrong, I'm definitely interested. But I need some time to talk it over with my family since they were kind of relying on me to help run Rancho Lindo after my dad retires."

"Of course. I understand. Do you think you could give me an answer next week? I want you in this position, but if you're not going to take it, then I do have someone else in mind. So I need to get this finalized soon."

"Gotcha. Yeah, I'll let you know for sure by next week. Uh, I just want to make sure, though. This isn't going to affect Nora's contract?"

"Not at all. Like I said, two opportunities. No matter what you decide, we're still moving forward with the contract for the microgreens."

"Great. I really appreciate that. Thank you so much, John. For everything."

After hanging up, Gabe sat in his truck for a few more minutes. Had John really just offered him a job? Was he actually going to consider taking it? Just from the few details John had shared, it sounded like the position could be perfect for him. Well, except for the hundreds of miles it would put between him and Nora.

Nora.

He had to tell her about the contract for her microgreens. But he decided to call after all.

She answered after the second ring. As soon as he heard her voice, he knew he couldn't tell her about John's offer. He didn't want anything taking away from what she had done. Besides, why mention it when he still wasn't sure it was going to happen.

Gabe pushed the unsettling thoughts out of his mind.

No, he wasn't going to say anything until he knew exactly how to tell her. The most important thing she needed to know tonight was that they were getting the contract.

"You'll never guess who I just talked to," he began.

Chapter Twenty-Seven

Sometimes, Nora really hated how her mind worked.

She should've been thrilled, giddy even. Rancho Lindo had been chosen to be the exclusive microgreens supplier for the Green Grocery Store and instead of celebrating like a normal person, Nora couldn't shake the feeling of dread she'd woken up with that morning.

So, while she was happy and excited about the contract, Nora's pessimistic nature told her there was a proverbial shoe out there that was getting ready to plop right through her bubble of joy.

Maybe that's why she couldn't stop thinking about her conversation last night with Gabe. He'd sounded happy when he'd told her about John offering them the contract for the microgreens. He kept telling her how proud he was of her and how proud she should be of herself. He promised that he was going to take her to celebrate the good news next weekend since Doña Alma's birthday party was today.

There was no reason for her to worry that Gabe hadn't meant any of things he'd said.

No reason at all.

But he was more subdued than she'd expected. She'd wanted more details, but he couldn't answer all of her questions. Finally, Gabe had told her he didn't want to keep her up any later than he'd already had and promised they would talk today when she got back to the ranch after the farmer's market since they'd have a couple of hours before Doña Alma's party started.

"I'll tell you everything then," he'd said.

His tone, though, was more serious than excited. It made her think that there was something he'd held back—something that might upset her. So in between being excited about the contract and also worrying about what Gabe wasn't telling her yet, old doubts and second guesses kept her from a restful night's sleep.

Luckily or unluckily, the Thousand Oaks farmer's market was keeping her busy enough so she couldn't dwell too much.

But during her first break between customers, she texted Gabe to ask how preparations were going for the party.

Nora: How's it going?

Gabe: Okay, I guess. My mom has put on her drill sergeant hat. I'm in charge of tables and chairs.

Nora: LOL.

Gabe: How's it going over there?

Nora: Busy! I'm already sold out of the micro broccoli, arugula, and chives.

Gabe: That's awesome! So glad it didn't rain.

Nora: Me too. So that means I'll be here until the end. I should be on the road by 2:30 at the latest. Did you still want to meet me at my house so we can talk more about what John said last night?

Gabe: Yes. Just text me when you get to the ranch and I'll meet you at the garden instead so I can help you unload. Then we can go to your place to talk.

Nora: OK. Have fun! ☺

Gabe: Ha. Ha.

Nora was about to send another text when two customers walked up to her tables. She slipped her phone into her back pocket. As the man and woman selected some apples and carrots, she convinced herself that she must have been reading too much into Gabe's tone last night. His texts had sounded normal and he still wanted to talk to her before the party. Whatever it was, it couldn't have been too bad. Otherwise, he would've told her last night. She chalked it up to her own unfounded paranoia. She pushed whatever worries she had out of her mind and approached her customers to ask if they had any questions.

At 2:26 p.m., Nora was in the truck ready to leave Thousand Oaks. Her GPS told her she'd arrive at Rancho Lindo in a little over an hour. Since the party started at five, that meant she would have less than two hours to unload, talk to Gabe, shower, and get ready. She pulled her phone out and texted Gabe.

Nora: All done! Leaving now.

Gabe: Me too. Rental company shorted us 3 tables and 18 chairs. I'm going with Cruz to pick some up

from the church. I should be back home by the
time you get here.

Nora: Ok. See you soon.

But only thirty minutes into her drive, Nora's truck
had other ideas.

She struggled to maintain control of the steering
wheel as the vehicle bounced and rocked on the high-
way. Eventually, she managed to safely get the truck to
the side of the road.

"Dammit," Nora said to no one after discover-
ing a flat tire. Her second "Dammit" came after
remembering that she'd removed the spare to make
room for two more crates of apples. She would
have to ask someone from the ranch to bring it to
her. Knowing that Cruz and Gabe were busy with
the additional chairs and tables, Nora called Daniel.
When he didn't answer, she called Nico, who was
happy for an excuse to take a break from party
setup.

Twenty-five minutes later, he pulled his car behind
the truck.

"You okay?" Nico said after walking up to her.

"Yeah, I'm fine. That tire, however, is completely
dead." Nora pointed to the shredded mangled piece of
rubber still attached to the truck.

Nico winced. "Ouch."

"Exactly. So how's it going over at party central?"

"Sheer chaos. But that's the Ortega process, right?
It may not look like we know what we're doing, but it
always works out in the end."

Nora laughed. "That's very true."

Nico threw up his hands. "Oh, hey! I heard the news.

Congrats on landing the contract! This is huge, Nora. You must be so proud."

She couldn't help but blush. "I am. But you know it couldn't have happened without Gabe. He set up the whole thing and really convinced the owner to take a chance on us, I mean the ranch."

"Wow," Nico said, with a huge grin on his face. "Your face just turned as red as those tomatoes over there in the back of the truck. So you two are really a thing, huh?"

"Me giving some credit to Gabe has nothing to do with my relationship with him."

Nico's eyebrows arched in surprise. "Relationship?"

The sting of embarrassment probably reddened her cheeks even more. "That's not what I meant," she rushed to say. The last thing she needed was Nico going back to Rancho Lindo and telling everyone, especially Gabe, that Nora thought she was in a relationship with his brother. They hadn't labeled whatever it was that was happening between them. She didn't want Gabe thinking that she was assuming. Although, truth was, she hadn't allowed herself to wonder what Gabe thought about it all.

"Relax, Nora," Nico said with a chuckle. "I'm just teasing."

Relief washed over the panic and she was able to smile at him. "You're just as bad as Daniel."

"Nope. I'm worse," he said proudly.

That earned him a soft punch on his right arm.

"All right. All right. I'll shut up. But can I just say one more thing?"

She nodded, thinking he wanted to get her riled up

again. But then she noticed that he wasn't smirking or smiling. Nico had his serious face on.

"Don't get me wrong. I love my brother. But, sometimes, I don't love how he goes about things. Especially when it comes to treating people the way they deserve."

A sense of uneasiness crept along Nora's skin. She really didn't want to be having this conversation on the side of the road—or anywhere, for that matter. "Nico, I appreciate your concern. But I'm a big girl. You don't need to worry about me."

"Of course I have to worry about you, Nora. You're practically my sister."

"So you think you need to protect me from your brother?"

"Oh, I don't think. I know. Gabe is a hard nut to crack. I just don't want to see you get hurt trying to get inside that stubborn heart of his."

"I know. And I appreciate you looking out for me. Whatever is happening between me and Gabe, I'm not going into it with my eyes closed. I can handle it. I can handle him."

Nora couldn't believe how confident she sounded. She almost believed herself.

Nico shrugged. "If you say so."

"I do."

"Cool. Now let's get that tire changed so we can go party."

As Nico walked back to his car to get the spare, Nora tried to shake off the unsettling feeling in the pit of her stomach. She didn't want to give him any hint that his words had affected her more than she'd let on. Of course she had some doubts about Gabe. How could she not? But all of them seemed to fade away when she was in his arms. He was not the same man he was a few months ago. And he definitely wasn't the same boy who'd stood her up all those years ago. He had proven that to her in so many different ways. She owed him the benefit of the doubt. And that meant trusting that he wasn't going to hurt her.

"Bad news," Nico yelled from behind his car's open trunk.

Nora walked over to him. "Don't tell me. The spare is flat too?"

"No. It's perfect. But I can't put the perfect tire on the truck without a jack."

"What are we going to do?" she cried. Nora looked at the time on her watch. It was already 3:45.

Nico pulled out his phone. "I'm going to get Daniel's ass to bring us a jack. He was the last one to use the car, so he's probably the one who took it out."

She nodded. "And tell him to get here as fast as he can. But to also be safe!"

He gave her the thumbs-up and began to dial.

By the time the three of them finally arrived at Rancho Lindo, they had less than twenty minutes to get ready for the party. She also found out that Gabe had been recruited to meet the mariachis, so that meant neither of them had time to meet up. They agreed to have their talk after the party instead.

Nora: Sorry I couldn't make it here earlier.

Gabe: Don't be sorry. I'm just glad you're safe.

Nora: Thx. I'll be at the party as soon as I can. I'll unload everything tomorrow instead.

Gabe: Ok. But I have to warn you. If you come too

late, I may just have to sit with Doña Rosa and
Doña Sylvia. They told Abuelita the other day that
they were planning to dance with me all night.

Nora: LOL. I guess have some competition then.

Gabe: I guess you do.

Nora: Well, then, I'll make sure to hurry.

Gabe: Please do. I can't wait to see you.

Nora: ☺

Chapter Twenty-Eight

The smiley face made him laugh.

It was a perfect Nora-esque response. He could even imagine the blush of pink spreading across her cheeks and nose at his admission that he couldn't wait to see her. He thought about texting her something more suggestive to make her blush even more.

Gabe was about to text back when a black SUV pulled up alongside where he had been waiting on the driveway. He greeted the mariachis and briefed them on where to set up and when to start playing. He was in the middle of introducing them to his mom and abuelita when he spotted Nora walking through the backyard gate.

The sight took his breath away.

She wore her hair down in soft curls that framed her beautiful face. Her wine-colored dress fell just below her shoulders, exposing her smooth neck and collarbone. The perfect fit did nothing to hide her curves. But as much as he loved the way it looked on her, Gabe ached with the need to take it off.

He excused himself and headed right for Nora.

♘

Abuelita's party was turning out to be quite the event.
The Ortegas' large backyard was packed with guests,
and everyone kept telling Gabe how much they were
enjoying the food and the music. After most of the
people had finished eating, Daniel escorted Abuelita
to the rented dance floor, and one by one the brothers
took turns being her partner. She looked like she was
having the time of her life. He felt lucky to be a
part of it.

After a few more songs, Gabe and Nora finally were
able to have their own dance.

It felt so good to have her back in his arms. So much
so that all he could do was hold her quietly and just
take in the moment between them.

"I know I've already told you this, but I have to
tell you again. You look absolutely stunning tonight,"
Gabe finally said after a couple of minutes.

"Thank you," she told him. "So do you."

"Thank you. I have good taste," he teased.

She looked up at him. "Excuse me, sir. I'm the one
who picked this out for you, remember?"

"I do remember. And I picked you, so that's why
I have good taste." He laughed at his own joke but
stopped when he noticed that Nora wasn't laughing.

"What's wrong?" he asked, studying her face.

She shook her head and gave him a small smile.
"It's silly."

"I love silly. So now you have to tell me."

Nora looked away and then found his eyes again.
"Sometimes I still can't believe this."

"Us?" he asked.

She nodded shyly, and he couldn't help but kiss the top of her head.

"Me too. Me too," he said.

They continued dancing in silence for another minute. Gabe knew his heart was beating a mile a minute. Deep, new emotions filled him up, and he knew something had changed in him when it came to how he felt about Nora. There was something about the way she talked to him, the way she looked at him even. It was as if she could see into every hidden corner of his soul—the places where he held his true feelings and his greatest fears. Nora got under his skin in ways no other woman ever had. He didn't know whether to despise it or drop to his knees and thank her.

He had to get her alone sooner rather than later and let her know about the job offer.

"I know you wanted to talk," she said, as if she could read his thoughts. "Are you going to come back to my place after the party?"

"We could go now? I don't want to wait. Let's go to my room upstairs."

"Oh, now I get it," she said with a laugh and rolled her eyes. "I am not leaving your abuelita's party just to go make out with you in your bedroom. You're awful."

Gabe met her eyes. "No, no. I really want to talk to you."

"Sure you do."

"Nora, I—"

The song finished, and his mom walked over to them before he could pull Nora away from the party. "We're going to be cutting the cake soon. And then we'll have her open her gifts. Mijo, can you let the mariachis know?"

Dammit. There wouldn't be enough time to talk to Nora after all. The conversation would have to wait until after the party.

"Sure, Mom."

Nora touched his arm. "While you're doing that, I'm going to drive home real quick and grab her gift. I just realized I forgot it on my couch."

"You can give it to her tomorrow."

"No, I can't," Nora chuckled. "She already told me she wants it tonight."

Gabe nodded in understanding. Abuelita had given everyone a very specific list of what they could buy her for her birthday. Her excuse was that she was too old to get gifts she would never use. And he knew full well she expected to receive everything tonight.

Nora gave him a peck on the cheek and told him she would be back soon. He was just about to go talk to the mariachis when Lina approached him.

"I never knew you were such a good dancer, Gabriel," she said after giving him a hug.

"Well, it has been a while since I've had the chance to show off my moves," he joked.

"Or maybe you were just waiting for the right partner?"

Instead of answering, Gabe just smiled.

Lina's eyes grew big. "Madre de Dios. I came over just to tease you but now I can't. Not when I see that huge smile of yours. I'm happy for you, Gabriel. I'm happy for both of you."

Gabe thought about it. He was happy. Probably the happiest he'd ever been. And it was because of Nora.

"Thank you, Lina. That means a lot."

She hugged him again and then said she was going to go find her husband.

He began walking across the patio, but after taking only a few steps, his phone alerted him that a new text had arrived. Thinking it was Nora, he quickly checked the notification. It was from John.

John: About to get on my flight but wanted to send you and Cruz a draft of the contract ASAP. Go over it with Nora and the lawyers. Be in touch soon.

Gabe was impressed by how quickly John was moving things forward. He scrolled over to his inbox and found the unread email. He opened it and read the few sentences from John basically repeating what he'd said in his text. Gabe clicked on the PDF document labeled *Gabe's Contract* and quickly scanned the first page. Panic seized his chest, compressing it to the point where it felt like he couldn't catch his breath.

This was bad. Very, very bad.

John hadn't sent the contract for the microgreens. He'd accidentally sent a draft of the contract for the position he'd offered to Gabe.

And he'd also sent it to Cruz.

"Dammit. Dammit. Dammit," he yelled.

The last thing he needed was Cruz finding out about the job offer before he had the chance to tell Nora. He had to make sure his brother didn't say anything to Nora or anyone else in the family. Not just because he wanted to tell Nora first, but also because he didn't want anything to spoil Abuelita's party.

Gabe didn't find Cruz anywhere outside, so he went into the house. That's when he saw his dad sitting on one of the kitchen stools. He was leaning forward with his head in his hands.

For a second, he considered asking him if Cruz had mentioned the email from John. Except there was no way he could tell their father everything. Not yet. Then he noticed the way his dad's shoulders were slumped.

"What's wrong?" he said, and went over to him.

His dad lifted his head and Gabe didn't like what he saw. "Dad, what's wrong?" he repeated, and put his hand on his left shoulder.

"Just tired. We did a lot today, didn't we?"

They had done a lot. His dad hadn't. In fact, Gabe only saw him briefly in the morning when it was time to spray down the patio with the hose. Then he didn't see him again.

"Maybe your blood sugar is low. I think Abuelita is going to cut her cake soon. Have Mom get you a slice."

His dad nodded and patted the hand still on his shoulder. "Good idea. I'll go find her."

Gabe watched as his dad walked out of the kitchen. A nagging sense of worry almost made him follow. Then he heard footsteps coming down the stairs, and Gabe hoped they belong to Cruz. But it was Nico who appeared in the doorway.

"Is Cruz upstairs?" he asked.

"No. Haven't seen him," Nico said. Then Tomás and Daniel walked in.

"Mom wants us all outside. The mariachis are getting ready to sing 'Las Mañanitas' to Abuelita," Tomás told them.

Gabe nodded and then asked, "Hey, do you know where Cruz is?"

"I'm right here."

The four of them turned to see their oldest brother walking out of the home office.

"We need to talk," Gabe told Cruz.

"Oh, so now you feel like telling me things?" Cruz asked, putting his hands on his hips in a seemingly defensive stance.

He froze as he realized what he meant. The email. The contract. Cruz had to have seen it.

"Can we go into the office?" Gabe said.

"No," Cruz said, and took a step closer to Gabe. "I'm tired of being the one who keeps everyone's secrets around here. They're your brothers too. Whatever you have to say, you're going to say it to them at the same time."

The words knocked the air out of his chest. Dammit.

"What's he talking about, Gabe?" Daniel asked.

"Cruz...don't do this."

"I'm not doing anything, little brother, except telling the truth. Isn't that what you wanted?"

"Seriously, guys? What the hell is going on?" Nico said.

"Gabe here just landed himself a cushy job with the Green Grocery. He's moving to San Diego."

"What? This can't be happening right now," Tomás added.

Gabe took a few deep breaths and tried to calm his accelerated nerves. This wasn't how he wanted his family to find out. Especially since he hadn't accepted the offer from John yet. Cruz had no right to blab. He was furious, and he let Cruz have it once and for all.

"What exactly are you pissed off about? The fact that I might take the job in San Diego or the fact that there's someone who actually thinks I know what I'm doing?"

"Gabe."

He heard Nico, but he was too riled up to stop.

"You know why John offered me that job? Because he's just like me. We're always looking for opportunities. We don't settle with what we have. We always want more."

"Gabe!"

"What, Nico?" he yelled. But his irritation instantly turned into panic when he saw the concern in his brother's eyes. And the fact that he wasn't even looking at Gabe. Nico was looking behind him.

Gabe slowly turned around and saw Nora standing in the kitchen's doorway. She was holding a small, white paper bag.

"Doña Alma told me to put this in her room. She wanted to make sure no one else ate them," she said softly.

"Nora..." he began.

But she didn't let him finish. "Just make sure she gets them, okay? There's an extra piece in there, you know, because it's her birthday."

Then Nora gave the bag to Gabe, turned her back on him, and walked away.

Chapter Twenty-Nine

Gabe was calling out to her, but she didn't care.

Her breaths were coming fast and furious. If she didn't calm down, she'd give herself a full-blown panic attack.

How was this happening?

It didn't matter that this time she'd heard it for herself. It didn't make it easier. It didn't change the fact that Gabe might leave.

Again.

"Can you let me explain?" he yelled.

Nora took a long, deep breath and patted her burning cheeks. Once her heart rate slowed to a non-dangerous rate, she stopped walking and turned to face him. "Explain what? How you forgot to tell me this very important thing?"

"I didn't forget. And I was going to tell you today. I was just waiting for the right time," he said.

"And when was that going to be, Gabe? When you were already working there?"

Nora's heart raced. Part of her didn't want to hear

what he was saying. The other part of her needed to hear more so she could make it make sense.

How was this happening? Again.

"Of course not. You know I was trying to talk to you just before the party. Besides, I haven't even decided that I'm going to take the job in the first place."

"What's the position?"

"Vice president of product development for the southern region."

"So you're going to move to San Diego." It wasn't a question.

"If I take the job, then yes, I'd have to move to San Diego."

She couldn't help but scoff.

"What?" he asked.

"We all know you're going to take it. Isn't this what you've been waiting for this whole time? You really want us all to believe that you're considering not taking it?"

"Yes, because that's the truth."

Nora folded her arms across her chest. "When do you have to let John know by?"

Gabe swallowed down his uneasiness. "Next week," he admitted.

"Well then. I guess you have a lot of thinking to do."

"Nora..."

Her head throbbed with a dull ache and her stomach was tied in a billion knots. It was supposed to have been a beautiful night. Instead, it had been one long nightmare. She knew Gabe wanted that job more than he wanted her. Anger, sadness, and regret washed over her like a bucket of stone-cold, sobering water.

She was done talking.

"Good night Gabe," she said, and left him standing in the driveway before the flood of tears she'd been holding in finally escaped.

♘

Morning came before Nora was ready. And it was bittersweet.

Part of her wanted it to arrive because that meant the awful night would finally be over. But, at the same time, she wanted it to stay away so she didn't have to face the day and everything that it was going to bring with it.

Gabe had texted a few hours earlier to let her know that his dad was going to be admitted into the hospital again. His mom had taken him to the ER in the middle of the night. He added that once his dad had a room, he and his brothers were going to go see him.

Then, he asked a favor.

He had no right, of course. He had no right to ask anything of her. She'd been ready to reject it. Then he'd texted what he wanted. He asked if she could go to the house and pick up Doña Alma and take her to Sunday Mass.

Nora hated that a small part of her had wanted him to text her that there was no way he was going to take that job because he couldn't bear to leave her. Because he loved her.

Fury radiated from every pore. She was so mad at him, but she was even angrier at herself for hoping he would choose her. Nora should've known better.

After all, he'd never said anything about his feelings for her. She'd been a fool waiting for some declaration of love from a man who would probably rather get gored by a bull than admit he had some emotions. Sure, he liked having sex with her. But lust and love were not the same thing. It was her own damn fault for not remembering that.

Despite her rage, she knew Doña Alma shouldn't be alone right now. It was the only reason why she got out of bed when morning arrived. And the anger was a welcome reprieve from the pain. She would cling to it until she could be sure Gabe Ortega no longer held her heart.

When she got to the house an hour later, the elderly woman wasn't ready. In fact, she was still in her pajamas.

"I thought you wanted to go to Mass?" Nora asked when she found Doña Alma sitting in the kitchen eating a piece of cake.

She shrugged. "That's not what I say to Gabriel. I tell him to ask you to come over in case I want to go to Mass."

"And since you're not dressed, I guess that means you don't."

Nora couldn't help but laugh. She set down her keys and phone on the counter and took a seat next to her. Doña Alma cut her a piece of cake, dropped it on a nearby paper plate, and pushed it in front of her. Then she gave her a fork.

"Mmmm. This is good," Nora said after her first bite. "I didn't get a chance to taste it last night."

"The boys said you didn't feel good. Are you okay now, Mija?"

She wasn't. But she decided that telling her the truth wouldn't be a good idea. "A little bit. The cake is making me feel better, though."

The older woman nodded. "There's about half a sheet left. I'll cut you a piece so you can take some home."

"Cut me two pieces," she said. Nora knew she'd need the sugar and carbs later.

They ate in quiet until both of their plates were clean. She almost asked for a second serving. Then she figured she might as well eat a real breakfast.

"How about we go to Lina's?" she asked Doña Alma.

"That's a good idea. Maybe we should wait though until they all come back. That way Gabe can come with us."

Nora's heart fell. She could only hope that Doña Alma couldn't see it on her face when it happened. Nora doubted that she knew Gabe was probably going to leave soon, which meant she obviously didn't know that Nora didn't want to eat breakfast with him or any other meal with him ever.

But there was no way she was going to tell her that.

"Actually, I have a better idea," Nora began. "It's still your birthday weekend and that means we can still celebrate. I'm going to take you to Santa Barbara instead and we'll have lunch at your favorite seafood place."

Doña Alma clapped. "Can I get lobster?"

Nora chuckled. "It's your birthday weekend. You can get anything you want."

As Doña Alma changed in her bedroom, Nora figured she'd better let someone else know their plans. She pulled out her phone and instinctively she went to the text thread with Gabe. She scrolled up to the messages from yesterday before everything happened.

Nora: Well, then, I'll make sure to hurry.
Gabe: Please do. I can't wait to see you.

I can't wait to see you.

Nora closed her eyes and willed herself to not cry. She knew today was going to be hard. So would tomorrow. And the day after that. It was the same when her dad was finally gone for good. She thought she'd never get over that. But she did. And she'd get over Gabe leaving her too.

Nora opened her eyes and looked down at her phone. She closed Gabe's text thread and opened the one with Daniel to tell him that she was taking Doña Alma out for lunch.

She knew she'd have to talk to Gabe eventually. But there was no reason why she couldn't put that off for as long as possible.

Chapter Thirty

I'm sorry."

Gabe knew he had to say those words first before anything else. They were the only ones that mattered at that point.

He had found Nora in the greenhouse. Of course she would be there. It was Monday afternoon and life on the ranch had to go on.

She looked up, shrugged, and went back to spooning more soil into the pot sitting on the table in front of her. "I know."

He took a step closer, and that's when he noticed the dark circles under her eyes. She looked exhausted. It unnerved him.

Still, he had to let her know how he felt. "I hope one day you'll realize that I never meant to hurt you."

Nora turned her back to him and began shoveling soil into another planter. He was just about to leave when he heard her voice. "How's your dad?"

"Better. My mom just brought him home. He just needed some IV fluids again."

"I'm glad he didn't have to stay that long."

"Me too."

She was quiet again and he figured that was all she had left to say to him.

He was wrong.

"So when are you leaving?" she asked, turning around to meet his eyes.

"I'm not going to town today."

"I meant when are you leaving for San Diego?"

Gabe's mouth went dry. "Oh. Uh, I haven't decided yet. There are a lot of reasons to stay."

"And there are a lot of reasons to go too."

"I guess. But maybe I'm needed more here on the ranch than in San Diego?"

"You shouldn't stay because you think you have to. You should stay because you want to."

He couldn't help but laugh. "That's what Cruz told me yesterday."

She considered this for a moment. "Really?"

"Really," he said.

"Then you should listen to him. You need to figure out where you belong, Gabe. No one can figure that out for you."

"It's not that simple."

"Why not?"

"It's complicated."

She shook her head. "If you're talking about us, then let me un-complicate it for you. You don't need to stay for me, Gabe. I'm a big girl. I can manage without you here."

That stung. Hard.

"I never thought you couldn't. But..."

"But what? I knew what I was getting myself into

with you. I'm not that naïve. And I'm not that stupid to let you hurt me a second time."

Her voice cracked on the last word but she quickly recovered. Still, he knew she was lying. He had hurt her. Again. Maybe it was better for him to leave. Better for his family and better for Nora.

"I didn't mean for this to happen," he said.

She laughed, but there was no joy in her voice. Only regret. "I'm sorry," he repeated.

"You already said that."

Her cool, dismissive tone cut him. This wasn't her. This wasn't the Nora he had come to know and care for. It was like that first day all over again with the tomatoes.

He ached to reach for her and pull her into his arms. What he wouldn't give to go back to when Nora didn't look at him like...that. It was too late. She had already slipped away from him.

Gabe didn't think he could face Nora every day knowing that things between them were so different. He was starting to think that him moving to San Diego was exactly what everyone needed.

"Well, I guess I'll let you get back to work. I'll see you around," he said quietly, and left her.

When he walked inside the house, an icy silence hit him. What he hadn't told Nora was that his parents had called a family meeting. He knew his dad's hospital visit hadn't been as simple as his mom had told them. It could only mean that the news wasn't good.

"Mijo."

His mom's soft voice made him turn around. God, he hated how tired and sad she looked.

"Where is everyone?" he asked, only because he was afraid to ask anything else. "I thought you wanted to talk to all of us."

"In their rooms. Your dad wants to talk to you first. Alone."

Well, that didn't sound good.

"Okay. Is he upstairs?"

"No. He's in the office." She rolled her eyes when she told him that.

He gave her a curt nod and then headed down the hallway to see him.

His dad was behind his desk looking through a stack of papers. He looked more pale. More fragile. Yet there he was doing what he always did. Working.

"Shouldn't you be taking it easy?" Gabe asked as he walked through the doors.

His dad threw up one arm. "I'm not dead yet."

"Okay, but you also need to rest. Somehow I don't think your doctor sent you home to catch up on paperwork."

"Pinche doctors. They don't know anything."

Gabe rolled his eyes. No wonder his mom had done the same.

He plopped down on the leather chair on the opposite side of the desk. "Mom said you wanted to talk to me."

His dad put down the paper he'd been holding and then took off his reading glasses.

"I know you're still mad that we didn't tell you about the cancer, but the truth is we really didn't know how bad it is. Now we do."

A searing panic burned his chest, squeezing the air out of his lungs. He couldn't say anything. He could only sit there and listen. Gabe nodded to let his dad know he was ready to hear the words.

His dad cleared his throat and then opened his mouth. Nothing came out at first. He coughed and tried again. "The cancer is spreading. I'm going to start radiation next week."

Gabe's heart sunk. "And what do the doctors say?"

"They say lots of things. But it doesn't matter because they don't know. I do the radiation, and then they figure it out."

"And then what?"

"Maybe surgery. Maybe chemo. Like I said, they won't know until after the radiation is done."

Gabe didn't know what to say, so he stood up and started to pace.

"So what's going on with this job? Are you going to take it?"

He stopped walking and put his hands on his hips. "I don't know," he admitted. "I thought about it, but I know you need me here."

"I needed you here before I got sick. What's changed?"

Gabe's usual frustration began to boil. He thought carefully about what to say next. The last thing he wanted to do was fight with his dad on the day everything for his family was about to change.

"It's not just you who needs me, then. I want to be here for Mom, and Abuelita and my brothers." He almost added Nora, but that could've spurred on a different conversation he wasn't ready to have. "Plus, I know the ranch is suffering."

"We'll find a way. We always do."

"Dad, you can't just pretend this isn't serious."

"Who said I'm pretending? Rancho Lindo didn't survive this long because our family pretended. I still know how to run this place." His dad sat back in his chair and met Gabe's stare. "I think you should take the job with John."

What? After months of telling Gabe he should stay at Rancho Lindo, now his dad tells him to go? It didn't make any sense. The frustration finally boiled over.

"I think I need to stay."

"Para qué? Para quien? Nora?"

"What about her?" His defenses immediately went up.

"Maybe your newfound appreciation for Rancho Lindo is because you've gotten close? Maybe what you really want is to stay to help her, not us?"

The accusation made him freeze. A million thoughts ran through his head. Did he really want to help Cruz run Rancho Lindo or did he just get caught up in the thought of helping Nora realize her dreams? He thought about their conversation earlier. Regret iced his veins. It killed him to see the hurt in her eyes and know he put it there.

"This doesn't have anything to do with Nora."

"Then why?"

"Why are you questioning me? Isn't this what you've always wanted?"

"Not like this."

"Too bad."

His dad unloaded a litany of curses in Spanish. He waved his hand at Gabe. "This is just like you. I'm giving you an out but you won't take it. It's like, whatever I tell you to do, you have to do the opposite."

"That's not true, actually."

"Otra vez! See, there you go again. You always have

to argue. You've been arguing with me since you were eight years old. Remember when I signed you up to play flag football and then you tell me you wanted to play soccer instead. So I sign you up for soccer and then you never want to go to practice!"

"I wanted to play soccer because you used to play soccer. But then every game, you would be there on the sidelines yelling at me. Run faster, Gabriel! Get the ball, Gabriel! And then on the way home, I'd have to sit there and listen to everything I did wrong in the game."

"Qué? I don't remember that."

Gabe stepped closer to the desk. He was determined now to tell his dad the real reason why he never wanted to take over Rancho Lindo. "My whole childhood was spent trying to do exactly what you told me. But when I could never do anything right, I just gave up."

His dad waved his finger at him. "You gave up because you wanted to give up. And then when that wasn't enough, you left."

He'd had enough. Gabe slapped his hand on the desk. "You told me to leave! And I did because I was tired of being compared to Cruz! I needed to go do something on my own."

His dad flinched at his outburst. That probably made him more angry at Gabe. "So then you go to school! You don't join the pinche army!"

Gabe looked at the floor. "See, even now you can't be proud of me for everything I did over there."

"What? I should be proud that you chose the army over Rancho Lindo, over your own familia? I should be happy that you almost died being a good soldier? The army took you away from us for years. All that time that we will never get back. Para qué?"

"I'm here now, Dad," he said, trying to calm his anger.

"Maybe your body, but not your mind. Not your heart. That's why you should take the job with John."

"And what about the ranch?"

"What about it?" his dad asked.

"Are you planning on selling it? Is that why you and Cruz met with Sandra a few weeks ago?"

Gabe could see the shock register on his dad's face. "How?"

"Nora told me that Sandra has a client who has been wanting to buy Rancho Lindo for a while, but you never wanted to meet with her. Then you did."

"Yes, we met with the woman. But only to tell her once and for all that Rancho Lindo is not for sale. And it never will be."

Gabe shook his head. "Just because you say it, doesn't make it true."

"Of course it does! This ranch has been in my family for generations. I will die before I let anyone else buy it."

As soon as he said it, Gabe's dad's face crumpled. It was as if he was realizing for the first time that those were no longer just words. They were a possibility.

A voice cleared behind him. He turned and saw Cruz standing in the doorway.

"Everything okay in here?" he asked.

Gabe didn't answer. Neither did his dad.

"Okay then. Well, everyone is in the family room waiting."

"We'll be right there," Gabe finally said.

He watched as his dad stood up and collected his glasses and phone. "We can finish talking about this later," he told his dad as he walked by him on his way to the office's door.

"I don't have anything else to say," his dad said without even turning around.

Gabe didn't follow him right away. He needed a minute to cool down and let everything his dad had said sink in. He was finally starting to realize there was only one choice to make. He hadn't expected to make a decision about San Diego so soon. But after the conversations he'd had that day, he realized that a few more weeks wasn't going to change the fact that his dad wanted him to go and Nora hated his guts.

What was left, then?

It was time to say goodbye to Rancho Lindo.

Chapter Thirty-One

Congratulations, Nora."

Cruz offered her a smile and curt nod. Despite his tepid tone, Nora knew he was genuinely happy for her and for Rancho Lindo.

"Congratulations to you too," she told him.

They'd just finished signing the contract with the Green Grocery Store. For some reason, she'd expected the whole process to be more complicated. But the lawyers were able to finalize everything after just a few weeks and had sent over the contract that morning. She didn't even need a pen. Everything was done digitally.

"How do you feel?" he asked.

"Nervous. Scared."

Cruz laughed. "Geeze, Nora. You could've lied and said you felt great."

"Well, I do feel great. But I mainly feel those other things too. This is a big deal for Rancho Lindo and I don't want to screw it up."

"You won't. You know how I know that?"

She shook her head. What on earth made Cruz believe that she wasn't going to fail?

"Because you care. You care about every piece of vegetable and every piece of fruit in that garden. And you care about the ranch. That's how I know."

Emotion tightened her throat. It was true. She did care and she was going to do everything in her power to make sure this deal was a success.

"Thank you, Cruz, for believing in me," she said, blinking back her foolish tears.

"You're welcome. But we both know I can't take all of the credit. He believed in you first."

Gabe was the invisible and silent elephant in the room. He should've been there, sitting beside her. Instead, he was miles away. They hadn't spoken since he'd left. She occasionally overheard updates from Nico and Daniel. And it had sounded like he was doing well in his new job. Nora tried not to care how he was doing at all. Not just because she was still angry, but because she missed him. A fact she made sure to hide from everyone or else they'd never stop apologizing for him or feeling sorry for her.

Nora hated that he was the cloud hovering over what should've been a pretty fantastic day. She was done letting the actions, or non-actions, of others prevent her from enjoying the good things. Same with always waiting for something bad to happen. From here on out, she was going to allow herself to savor the times when things went right. That meant not letting Gabe taint this for her or for Cruz.

"That's true," she said. "But he left and you finished what he started. Without you, we wouldn't have signed the contract so quickly. I'm very grateful for everything you've done."

"Well then, you're welcome," Cruz said, sitting farther back into his chair.

She clasped her hands together and set them on her lap. "So now what?"

"I'm not sure exactly. John said he'd be in touch next week. I think he had mentioned something before about setting up an introductory meeting with the rest of his team. He probably wants to bring them here for a tour."

"Sounds good to me. I already have some ideas on how to rearrange the current setup to make room for more shelving. I guess I'll get started on that so it will be done before the group comes for their official visit." The ideas had actually been Gabe's, but she figured it didn't matter at that point.

Cruz nodded his approval. "Just let me know. Dad says to give you whatever you want."

"He told me to come to him if you tell me no," she said with a little chuckle. "He looked good yesterday."

"He did. I expected the radiation to take some kind of toll and prepared for the days he just wouldn't feel good. But that man is as stubborn as a bull. He's determined to not let the treatments get to him."

"That's how my tío Chucho was at the beginning. Tía Luz would get so mad when he refused to take it slow. Even now, I can hear her voice over the phone complaining about him not taking his medicines or not eating the healthy meal she cooked for him. She always had some new story about what he did or didn't do."

"Oh, trust me, I remember," Cruz said with a thoughtful nod. "I wonder though if maybe that was her way of dealing with his illness? By focusing on what she could control, she wouldn't be consumed by what she couldn't. My mom wants me and Tomás to start renovating their master bathroom this weekend. She says the doorway is too small for a walker."

Based on how he looked yesterday, Señor Ortega could probably still run laps around the main corral. He definitely wouldn't be needing a walker anytime soon. But what Cruz said made sense to her. Just like her tía, the renovation was Cruz's mom's way of coping. Nora couldn't even imagine seeing someone you love suffer like that. She had hated it for her tía and now she hated it for the Ortegas.

"Doña Alma and I have been looking up articles about herbs and spices that can boost your immune system. I already grow most of them, but we found a few new ones that I'm going to order. Like you said, we focus on what we can control," she said softly.

"You really are a blessing. I'm so glad that... that what happened with Gabe didn't change what you think of the rest of us."

"Never. You're my family."

"We are," he agreed.

Emotions she'd been holding at bay came roaring back and it took everything she had to not burst into tears right then and there. She'd been a little worried that things would be different after Gabe left. They were, but not in the ways that mattered. Rancho Lindo was still her home and she belonged there just like the rest of them.

They talked for a few minutes about other things related to the garden. When they were done, Cruz got up and walked over to her. She stood up and smiled at him.

"I don't know if we should shake hands or hug," he admitted.

Nora opened her arms wide. "Something tells me we both could use a hug right about now."

When they parted, Cruz met her eyes. "Are you sure you're okay?"

It was a familiar question, and even though Cruz hadn't used his name, it was understood that he was asking because of Gabe. After he'd left, every Ortega in the house had asked Nora the same question every day for weeks. She hadn't been okay, obviously. But she knew they weren't okay either. And rather than remind everyone how sad she was, how sad they all were, she put up a front and acted like her heart didn't die every time she thought about him. She hated being a mentirosa. But today was important to Cruz, to both of them. She wasn't about to ruin it.

So she forced herself to give Cruz a smile and an answer.

"I'm okay," she said. "I'm definitely okay."

Chapter Thirty-Two

Gabe walked out onto his balcony and inhaled one long breath.

The ocean air tickled his nostrils, reminding him once again just how far away he was from Rancho Lindo.

He'd moved to San Diego three weeks ago and was living out of his suitcase at a beachfront hotel courtesy of the Green Grocery. John had told Gabe he could stay there until he found an apartment. But Gabe wasn't at all ready to start looking. If someone asked, he'd blame his busy schedule. He'd dove headfirst into his new job and had no spare time to do anything but eat and sleep.

Because if he did have the time, he'd have to admit how much he missed Nora.

As if on cue, Gabe's phone rang, and he couldn't believe who was calling. After the way they had left things, he hadn't expected to hear from his brother so soon.

"Cruz?" he asked, even though the caller ID told him that's exactly who it was.

"Hey, little brother."

"Is everything okay? Did something happen with Dad?"

"Nothing happened. Dad is fine. I was calling you about Thanksgiving."

Gabe's panicked heartbeat began to slow down. "What about it?"

"Well, Mom said you were going to be here but she didn't know if you were coming on Wednesday or Thursday."

"Oh. I guess I can be there Wednesday night. Why? Do you need me to do something or bring something?"

"No. But I've been using your room to work out in, and she wants me to clear out all my stuff before you get here."

Gabe shook his head in disbelief. "You turned my bedroom into a gym?"

"Not really. Well, not yet anyway. Once I find a good bench press, then I'll move out your bed and really start fixing it up."

His usual irritation began to bubble up until Gabe realized he had no right to be mad. He was about to look for an apartment that would have his new bedroom. He could no longer claim the one at Rancho Lindo.

"A home gym is actually a really good idea," he told Cruz. "I'm sure all of you are going to like that."

"I think so too."

"So how's Dad doing? Mom told me he already started radiation treatments."

"He's doing okay. Still being stubborn though about making his daily rides around the property."

"How are the guys?"

"Good. Tomás has a lead on another new boarder, and the other two are talking about planning an onsite steer auction in the spring."

"That's great. I'm glad."

They were both quiet for a few seconds before Cruz said, "Go ahead and ask."

"Ask what?"

"How Nora's doing."

Gabe's heart sped up just at the mention of her name. He did want to ask. Desperately. But part of him thought Cruz would tell him he didn't deserve to know.

And he'd be right.

"How is Nora?" he asked. Turned out his need to know outweighed any hesitation.

He heard Cruz sigh on the other end of the phone. "She says she's okay, but I don't think she is."

Of all the words Gabe had thought his brother would say, those weren't even close. Cruz had never been one to talk about feelings—his or anyone else's.

"What do you mean?" Gabe asked.

"I mean exactly what I said. We all ask her how she is, and she tells us she's okay. But Daniel and Tomás say they've noticed a difference. I have too."

Guilt permeated every nerve in his body, eliciting a pain far worse than any physical injury. When Gabe didn't say anything right away, Cruz cleared his throat and added, "She's still planning to visit her tía in January, so I think that will help. Plus, we signed the contract."

"Yeah. John told me. I'm really happy for her. And for all of you. This is going to help put Rancho Lindo on the map again. I just know it."

"You might be right. And I'm sorry I never gave you credit for making this happen. You did a good thing, Gabe."

Compliments from Cruz were few and far between. So when he did get them, Gabe always wondered if he had an ulterior motive. Except this time. His words sounded genuine. Hell, he even sounded proud.

What on earth had happened to Cruz since he'd left? Taking advantage of this more open side of his brother, Gabe asked what he'd been wondering for weeks. "Does she hate me?"

"Far from it. If you ask me, that's her problem."

"What do you mean?"

"If you don't know by now, then I can't help you, brother. But you better figure it out soon or else you're going to be making the biggest mistake of your life."

Chapter Thirty-Three

Having a routine turned out to be Nora's greatest distraction.

Now that she was occupied with plans to increase her production of microgreens, she was almost too busy to dwell on things that were better left forgotten.

Her mornings were dedicated to her usual garden tasks and she spent her afternoons in the greenhouse. The first week after Gabe left, there was more than one occasion when she'd walked inside expecting to find him napping in his favorite spot. She hated the fact that one of her most favorite places on the ranch now made her sad. Nora hoped that wouldn't always be the case. Luckily, she and Cruz were going to add a second structure in the spring and that one would be dedicated to the growing of microgreens. She couldn't miss Gabe in a place he had never been.

Nora had just finished her watering rounds when she got a text from Daniel asking her to come up to the house because Doña Alma needed help. She put away her hose and spray and headed over.

She found Doña Alma sitting in her bedroom rocker

listening to the radio. She had a shoe box filled with photos on her lap.

"Oh good, you are here now," the elderly woman said when Nora walked through the door.

"Daniel said you needed my help with something?"

"Yes, please. Señora Gomez gave me this beautiful photo album for my birthday but I don't understand how to put my pictures on the pages."

Nora walked over to pick up the square-shaped album from the bed and then sat down next to Doña Alma. After thumbing through a few pages, she understood her confusion.

"Where's the box it came in?"

Doña Alma handed it to her and Nora found what she was looking for.

"You use these to put on each corner of the photo and then stick it on the blank page," she explained, and demonstrated with one of the pictures from the box.

She nodded as if she understood. But when Doña Alma tried to do it herself, the corners kept falling off.

"It's hard for me to hold the little stickers," she said. "I like the other kind of albums better."

"How about I help you fill this album and then I can look online later for the other kind?"

Doña Alma gave her a huge smile in appreciation. And just like that, Nora's routine took a detour.

It took about an hour for them to go through the four shoe boxes of pictures and arrange her favorites in the album. It probably took longer than necessary since Nora had at least five questions for each photo. She always loved hearing Doña Alma's stories and learning more about the family's history.

"Is this your wedding photo?" Nora asked and

picked up the black-and-white picture of a young couple in front of a small church.

"Sí," she answered. "That's me and that's my Raphael."

"How old were you?"

"Almost nineteen. And he was twenty."

At nineteen, Nora was still in college not really sure what she wanted to do with the rest of her life. She couldn't imagine also having a husband at that age. "And was this your town's church in Jalisco?" Nora asked.

She nodded and let out a long sigh. "I was also baptized there—all my family was. But the church is gone now. It was damaged in an earthquake and they decided it was cheaper to tear it down than to fix it."

"That's too bad. It looks like it was a beautiful building."

Doña Alma smiled and closed her eyes. "It was. Everything—from the pews to the candle holders that hung from the ceiling—were hand made by the people in my town."

They looked through the boxes to find more pictures from her wedding day so they could add them to the album. They were only able to find one more of her husband posing by himself. Nora was about to put the adhesive corners on it, when Doña Alma stopped her.

"I think I want to keep that one out. I'm going to look for a frame for it."

"That's a good idea. Your husband was so hand-some, Doña Alma."

"He was," she said, taking the photo from Nora.

She could hear the pain in Doña Alma's voice. Nora knew that her husband had died in an accident when he was only in his thirties. That's why when Gabe's parents married, Señor Ortega had insisted that his suegra also live with them on Rancho Lindo. Doña Alma might have been his mother-in-law, but he had always loved and treated her as if she was his own mother.

"I can tell you still miss him," Nora said. "I'm so sorry. It doesn't seem fair to find love like that only to have it taken away from you so early."

"Yes, it was hard. But now I choose to be grateful for the life we made together. I try to remember the good. Then I don't get so sad. Maybe you can do that too for Gabriel."

Nora's mouth fell open. She didn't trust she understood what Doña Alma had just said. "What do you mean? He's not dead, Doña Alma."

"Y qué? You still have to grieve the loss of what you had with him."

Nora winced at her explanation. Not because it was harsh, but because there was some truth in her words. She didn't just miss Gabe. She missed what they could've been.

"I'm not as strong as you, Doña Alma," Nora admitted, and blinked back her unexpected tears.

"That's not true, Mija. You are strong. I see it in you every day."

"Maybe when it comes to my work. But this is . . . this was different."

Doña Alma reached out and grabbed Nora's hand. "Because you loved him."

Nora hesitated. She had never admitted her true feelings to herself, let alone anyone else. But as soon as Doña Alma said the word, she couldn't deny that was exactly what she felt for Gabe. She didn't even try to fight back the tears this time.

"I still love him," Nora said, her voice breaking.

Doña Alma didn't say a word. Instead, she took Nora into her arms and just let her be.

Chapter Thirty-Four

The property was beautiful.

It was the first thought that came to Gabe's mind as he drove up the long dirt road leading him to the main house of Sweeney Ranch.

Located in the heart of the San Diego County mountains, Sweeney Ranch boasted 820 acres of lush land and was home to cattle grazing, orchards, gardens, and even five ponds. Vast rolling meadows were dotted with oak and pine trees.

Gabe and John were visiting that Tuesday morning to learn more about its vineyard and whether their wines would be a good fit with the Green Grocery Store.

They were met outside the main house by Arnold Sweeney, the ranch's owner.

After introductions were made, he asked if they'd like a tour before heading over to the vineyard.

"Definitely," John said.

"Let's do it," Gabe added.

They walked over to the four-person UTV parked in the driveway and got inside. Arnold drove them to the highest point of the property so they could get a bird's-eye view of the ranch.

It was breathtaking.

"Arnold, this is spectacular," John gushed.

Gabe had to agree. Still, there was a part of him that insisted it didn't compare to Rancho Lindo. A pang of nostalgia came out of nowhere. He quickly dismissed it because it wasn't the time or place to be thinking of what, and who, he'd left behind weeks ago.

"You know, Gabe's family own a ranch up north, around the Central Valley region," John stated.

Arnold was intrigued. "Really? Which one?"

"Rancho Lindo. It's in Esperanza."

Recognition swept over Arnold's face. "Oh yeah? Hey, does that mean you're Cruz's brother?"

It turned out the ranching world was just as small as Esperanza.

"I am," Gabe admitted.

"He's a good guy. We met a few years ago at a cattle auction. We were trying for the same heifer. He won her, but then he bought me dinner after as a consolation prize. He's a real joker."

That made Gabe's eyebrows raise to the cloudless blue sky. He was?

"Yep. That's Cruz," he said, even though he still wasn't sure if they were talking about the same guy.

"So Arnold, do you run the ranch on your own?" John asked.

"Heck no. I couldn't do this by myself. I run the ranch with my wife, our two sons, and our two daughters-in-law. Even the grandkids are put to work. Everyone has a job to do. But it's about more than just keeping the business going. Sweeney Ranch is a legacy ranch. It belongs to everyone in my family, so we all have personal interest in expanding it."

"Legacy ranch?" John asked.

"A ranch that's been run by one family for generations. Like Rancho Lindo," Gabe explained.

Arnold nodded. "Sweeney Ranch's history dates back to the late 1800s when the US government signed ownership of the property into private ownership by way of a land grant. The complete property is actually made up of seven legal parcels. It changed hands a few times, but my family has owned the ranch for nearly a hundred years now. We respect the history of this place and have even kept many of the original structures. In fact, the original 1894 Adobe homestead still sits in that lower meadow over there, along with a hundred-year-old barn."

"My family's ranch up in Esperanza also has some original buildings still standing. My dad always threatens to tear them down, but he never does," Gabe said.

"Because it would be like tearing off a branch of your family's tree," Arnold explained. "At least that's how I would feel."

Gabe's interest was piqued. "Have you always lived here on the ranch? Or did you ever leave and then come back?"

"When I was in my twenties, I definitely thought about leaving. Then I met my wife. She was adamant that we stay and raise our kids here. She wanted them to have the childhood I had."

"You never regretted it? Or maybe wished you had a different kind of life?"

"Never," Arnold insisted. "I have many fond memories of growing up here. I mean, just have a look around us. It may have been a simpler kind of life, but it was still beautiful and meaningful. We were taught to appreciate our natural surroundings and understand the importance of honest hard work. Why would I regret that?"

"What about your sons? I guess they must feel the same way if they're still here working alongside you."

"They do. All of us consider it a privilege and a blessing to still have Sweeney Ranch as our home. You know, there aren't too many original legacy ranches left in California anymore. A lot of them are being sold off piece by piece. And these new owners don't understand the history behind these places because they're not connected to them by blood, like we are. I would never want my family's history to be handed over to a stranger who isn't going to respect it."

Gabe could only nod. The thought of Rancho Lindo being broken up and sold off to people he didn't know made him go cold.

"And now you've added a vineyard to that legacy?" John asked.

"We sure did. My dad always thought the soil was good for growing grapes. But it wasn't something he ever had the time to really investigate. After he passed, my sons decided they wanted to find out if my dad was right. And turns out, he was. We've been making our wine for six years now. But we've only ever given bottles to family and friends. Then my daughter-in-law Amelia started selling them at some of the local food and wine festivals. I guess that's how you guys must have heard about us?"

John nodded in excitement. "It is."

"Well, then I guess it's time we go look at the

vineyard. The rest of the family are going to meet us there. I hope you don't mind. That's just how we do things here on Sweeney Ranch."

"I don't mind at all," John answered. "And I'm sure Gabe doesn't either. After all, that's what a family business is, right?"

On the drive back to the city, Gabe's mind kept thinking about Arnold Sweeney and his legacy ranch. And none of those thoughts had anything to do with wine.

He'd never really let himself think of all the Ortega men and women who'd lived their lives on Rancho Lindo. Arnold was right. Everything on the ranch was a part of his family's history. It had survived all these years because his ancestors had protected it with their blood, sweat, and tears. And now, his dad, Cruz, and his brothers were doing the same thing for the next generation.

And what had he done to keep his family's legacy alive? Walked away.

An unexpected pang of regret shot straight to his heart.

Immediately, his thoughts turned to Nora. She wasn't even an Ortega, but she was connected to Rancho Lindo as much as his family was. All these months she was trying to make him understand what he had, what he could lose. Why hadn't he listened?

And why hadn't he been brave enough to stay and fight for Nora and for Rancho Lindo?

He couldn't stop his emotions from rushing in. He'd been a fool to think his feelings—his legacy—could be pushed to the side like they didn't mean anything anymore.

They did mean a lot. She meant a lot.

Gabe finally realized that he'd made the biggest mistake of his life. The only question now was could he fix it or would the universe continually find ways to rub it in his face?

Chapter Thirty-Five

It turned out that even a sugar high couldn't lift her spirits.

How disappointing indeed.

Nora walked out of Lina's Diner with a tummy full of cherry pie and vanilla bean ice cream. But she still couldn't shake the emptiness she'd been feeling for weeks now. Even Nico and Daniel had noticed it. That's probably why they'd shown up at her door at seven o'clock on a Saturday night and asked for her to join them for dessert at the diner. She'd already taken a shower and was in her pajamas getting ready for bed and was in no mood to go out. But they'd begged and pleaded until they'd finally convinced her it was too early to go to sleep.

And although she had enjoyed the pie and the conversation, it didn't make her forget.

"Feeling any better?" Nico asked as soon as they got back into his SUV.

She was seated next to him on the passenger side and forced a smile. "The pie was amazing."

"That's not what he asked," Daniel said from the back seat.

She allowed her smile to dissolve. "I'm sorry. I know you both were just trying to cheer me up. And a good dessert usually does the trick. But I don't know what's wrong with me. I really am sorry."

Daniel scooched forward and touched her arm. "Hey, no need to apologize. You don't have to pretend to feel something you don't. Your heart is hurting and it's going to take some time to heal. You don't have to rush it on our account."

"Thanks," she told him.

"You're welcome. And for what's it worth, I tell off my brother every single time he calls."

"Okay, okay, that's enough," Nico announced, and turned on the car. "Put your seat belt on, Daniel."

As he pulled away from the curb, she looked out the window and let out a small sigh. It did mean a lot to her that Daniel and the rest of the family seemed to be empathetic about the situation. Even Doña Alma had told her how sorry she was that her grandson was an "idiota."

"Hey, I thought we were going home?"

Daniel's question got her attention and she realized that Nico's SUV had just pulled into the parking lot of the community center.

"We are. But first we have to pick up some tables and chairs for Mom's luncheon tomorrow."

Nico opened his door and looked over at her. "Can you go inside first and turn on the lights? I'm going to grab the dolly from the back. Daniel, you help me."

The younger Ortega groaned, but unbuckled his seat belt anyway. Nico handed Nora the keys.

"I didn't realize you had a set of keys to the community center," she told him.

He shrugged. "I picked them up earlier. Go on ahead of us and we'll be there in a minute."

Nora nodded and headed toward the community center's double doors. It took her two tries with the wrong keys to finally find the right one. She pulled open one of the doors and walked into almost complete blackness. The cast of moonlight coming through a nearby window helped her find the row of light switches on a nearby wall. Nora flipped them all upward and immediately the large space was invaded by bright fluorescent lights.

It took a few seconds for her eyes to adjust. And when they did, she gasped.

The community center had been transformed into a dance hall. White twinkle lights wrapped around every pillar and balloon bouquets sprouted from each corner. A strobe light projected a rainbow of colors onto the rest of the space.

And that's when she saw him.

Nora watched as Gabe emerged from a curtain of silver shimmery streamers that had been hung over the entrance to the center's kitchen. Her heart accelerated as though she'd already been dancing all night. He was dressed in a dark blue long-sleeve shirt and jeans. His black boots matched the black felt hat on his head.

Gabe looked like a cowboy.

Seeing him again took her breath away. He made her nervous, even giddy. And her heart responded by beating faster with every step he took.

"Hi, Nora," he said when he was finally standing in front of her.

"Hello, Gabe," she managed to say.

He held out a clear plastic box that contained a red rose surrounded by some baby's breath stems. "This is for you," he said.

She took it but continued staring at him in disbelief. "What are you doing here, Gabe?"

He gave her a small smile and then he gave her a thumbs-up. At least, she thought the gesture was for her until music filled the hall. Someone else must have been there with them.

"What is going on?" she asked.

Gabe stepped even closer. "I'm here to take you to the dance."

Her head spun with confusion. Nora still couldn't quite understand what was happening. What dance?

"I, I'm not sure what is happening right now."

Gabe took the plastic box from her and opened it. He pulled out the small flower arrangement and that's when she noticed it was attached to an elastic bracelet. It was a corsage.

"Honora Torres, will you please go with me to the annual Founder's Day, but not really Founder's Day, summer, but not really summer, dance?"

Because she didn't know what else to say, she nodded. He took her left hand and guided it through the wristlet. Then he led her toward the middle of the hall and took her into his arms.

"I'm nervous," she admitted, not really knowing why.

"We're just going to dance," he said.

She nodded and tentatively reached around his neck. They swayed together and eventually her body relaxed. "I like this song," she said after a few seconds.

"Of course you do. It's a pop song."

She let out a small laugh. "Okay, don't even go there. I definitely remember catching you singing along to a boy band hit a few times."

He smiled and moved his hands to her lower back. She arched into him and it gave him better access to her neck. "You're a good dancer," he murmured against the warm skin there.

She trembled and instantly scolded her body for its betrayal. The truth was, all of the hurt Nora had been feeling and all of the anger slipped away the moment he touched her. Her brain kept shouting that she should've walked out as soon as she saw him. But her heart wouldn't let her listen. She was in love with Gabe Ortega and if she had the chance to be with him, even if it was just for one night, she was going to take it. Maybe she was a fool. Maybe this was like her sitting on the couch all those wasted Saturdays ago, waiting for a man who would never come. Either way, she'd deal with the aftermath later. In that moment, the only thing she wanted to focus on was the fact that Gabe was holding her again.

Nora looked up and smiled at him. "Nice hat," she said.

"Why, thank you," he said, tipping his head down in appreciation.

"It looks just like your dad's."

He smiled. "My mom gave it to me on my first night back."

"Really? So why have I never seen you wear it?"

"I guess because I didn't think I deserved to," Gabe said with shrug.

"Does that mean things between you and your dad are better?"

He nodded. "I called him last night and it wasn't awkward or even that hard. So that's good. It's going to take some time to fix things between us, but I know he'll come around eventually."

Nora took a long breath and finally asked the question she feared the most. "When do you have to go back to San Diego?"

"Tomorrow."

"Oh," she managed to say despite her heart breaking into a million pieces.

Gabe let go of her hip and reached to tilt her chin up with his index finger. "But I'll be back on Wednesday for Thanksgiving and stay through the weekend. Then my plan is to come back to Rancho Lindo every weekend for the next month. I figure that's enough time to train my replacement."

Nora stopped moving. "What?"

He let out a soft chuckle. "I'm coming home. For good this time," Gabe said, and started dancing with her again.

So many questions and thoughts filled her head that she needed a few seconds to sort them all out. Then she asked, "Does that mean you're going to help run Rancho Lindo?"

"Eventually. That's the plan. However, Cruz tells me that I'm going to be on probation for at least six weeks and nothing will be official until then."

"I'm surprised he didn't make it six months," she said with a laugh.

"Me too."

"Can I ask what made you change your mind?"

"I'm not sure. I just know that somehow over these past few months, I guess I finally figured out what I can do at the ranch. Plus, I actually missed my brothers and, of course, my parents and abuelita. And, it turns out, I really missed taking naps in a greenhouse."

She playfully punched him in the arm. They both laughed for a few seconds.

"I missed you," he said quietly.

"I missed you too," she admitted.

"I think I should warn you, though."

Nora braced for what he was about say. "Warn me about what?"

"I'm trying to let others know how I feel. So watch out. Because I have lots and lots of feelings about you."

"Does this mean what I think it means?" she asked.

"I've been seeing a therapist. I'm still not sure if it's for me, but I'm willing to try it out."

"I'm proud of you, Gabe," she said.

They swayed together in rhythm with the music, neither of them speaking for a minute or so. Nora pressed the side of her face against his hard chest. That's when she heard it. Gabe's heart was beating just as fast as hers, if not faster.

"Are you nervous?" she asked softly.

"Yes."

"Why?"

"Because I'm afraid," he admitted.

She lifted her head to meet his eyes. "What are you afraid of?"

He swallowed before answering. "I'm afraid that you're going to say no."

"To what?"

"To more than just this dance." His voice was low as his gaze narrowed on her lips. Her heart immediately sped up and she was sure he could hear it even with the music still playing. She still wasn't sure what he meant. And, if she was being truthful to herself, she wasn't ready to figure it out just yet. She wanted to just enjoy being back in his arms again. The room closed in around them as his fingers curled tighter around her hip.

She lowered her head back onto his chest.

"How on earth did you pull this off?" Nora asked, moving the conversation in a safer direction.

"Nico. And Cruz."

That made her look up at him again. "Really?"

Gabe nodded and smiled. "Well, I couldn't ask Daniel because he has a big mouth and would've definitely spilled the beans. So I asked Nico and then he told Cruz about my plan. Cruz was the one who talked to Mayor Walker about letting us use the community center. And both of them helped me set up everything this afternoon."

"Wait a minute. Is Cruz the one who turned on the music?"

"Yep."

"So where are Nico and Daniel?"

"I told Nico to keep Daniel outside. I'm sure he knows now and is pretty pissed that we didn't tell him."

They both laughed.

"I'm still not sure what's happening here. But it's nice."

"Well, I was hoping for more than just nice," Gabe said with a chuckle.

Nora took a breath. "It's nice dancing with you, Gabe. But I'm a little afraid too."

"Why?"

"Because I'm not sure what this means."

"I'm asking for a second chance. Not just for the dance, but for everything. I know I don't deserve one because of how much I hurt you. But I'm still asking. I belong at Rancho Lindo. I belong with you."

"You do?"

He nodded and gave her one of his slow, lazy smiles. "I do. Do you know why?"

Her voice caught her in throat. She didn't dare utter the inconceivable thought floating through her head. So she shook her head instead.

Gabe stopped moving. He cradled her face with both of his hands and met her eyes. "I've done a lot of stupid things in my life, and leaving the ranch was definitely one of them. But my biggest mistake was thinking that I could live without you. Perdóname."

"I'm sorry too," she whispered. "For everything."

He lowered his head, but hesitated less than an inch away from her lips. "Can I kiss you?"

Gabe searched her eyes, and she knew he was waiting for permission. It took only her slight nod for him to push his mouth against hers for one searing kiss. His scent and taste were like a favorite sweater. They warmed her and comforted her and she wanted to wrap her entire body around them.

Gabe's hands moved from her face to the back of her head, tangling his fingers in her hair. She gasped at the familiarity and he took that opportunity to plunge his tongue inside her mouth. He continued kissing her, devouring her.

That's when she stopped thinking. She was tired of pretending that she didn't still love this man. And just like that, she let all the hurt and anger go, once and for all. She inhaled a sharp breath to keep the tears at bay.

Seconds or minutes later—she couldn't tell—but when they both had their fill of each other for the moment, Nora broke from Gabe's lips to rest her head against his shoulder. He snaked his arm behind her back and held her close. "I love you, Nora," he whispered.

Tears immediately flooded her eyes again. And when she finally blinked, they escaped. "You do?" She repeated the question and looked up to see what his eyes told her.

He didn't answer her with words. Instead, Gabe lowered his head and softly brushed her lips with his one more time. When they broke apart, Nora couldn't contain her feelings any longer. Emotions like she'd never felt before filled her soul. And it made her brave. "I love you too," she told him.

That made him grin and he hugged her hard. "I'm going to prove to you every day that I deserve you."

"I don't need you to do anything. You're enough for me, Gabe. Just the way you are."

"Who would've thought that horticulturist Honora Torres would fall in love with ex-soldier Gabe Ortega. The gossip mill of Esperanza is going to have a field day," he said with a laugh.

"Let them," she said with a smile. "And I didn't fall in love with Gabe Ortega the ex-soldier. I fell in love with Gabe Ortega, a Rancho Lindo honest-to-goodness cowboy."

Acknowledgments

Thank you for reading *Second Chance at Rancho Lindo*. I hope you enjoyed meeting the Ortegas. Like all families, they are far from perfect. But their love for each other and Rancho Lindo is what matters the most.

It's always fun and exciting to create a new series. However, I must admit this was the first one that required me to also do some historical research. I spent weeks reading about the ranchos of California and the Mexican land grants of the 1800s, along with the Bracero labor program of the 1940s. As a Mexican American, some things were hard to digest. At the end of the day though, I was proud to write about a family with such a deep connection to their Mexican heritage and to this country.

And although they are my words, this book would not exist without some very important people.

First, I must thank my agent, Sarah Younger. She was the one who brought me this opportunity and I'll never forget her words: "How do you feel about writing cowboys?" Although I'd never penned a small-town romance before, Sarah had every confidence in the world that I was the right author for this project. I'm so grateful to be a part of her team.

Next, I want to thank my editor Alex Logan. She was the one who planted the seeds of a story featuring Mexican American brothers running their family ranch together in California. I'm grateful to Alex for trusting me to turn her idea into an actual book and for her guidance along the way. And special thanks to everyone at Forever for their hard work and efforts to get this book out into the world.

I dedicated this book to my #LatinxRom author friends because not only are they huge supporters, they are also great role models. They prove to me every day that there's a place in publishing for our stories and that there will always be readers who crave to see themselves and their communities reflected in the pages of our books. Thank you, Alexis, Natalie, Adriana, Zoraida, Liana, Angelina, Diana, Priscilla, and Mia, for your support and friendship.

Thank you as always to my own personal cheerleaders and best friends, Marie and Nikki. The pandemic might have kept us from seeing each other in person, but our group texts got me through some of the toughest days of the past two years.

Finally, I couldn't do what I do without the love and support of my family. They celebrate every success, talk me through every disappointment and, most importantly, just be there when I need them. I love you all.

About the Author

Sabrina Sol is the chica who loves love. She writes sexy romance stories featuring strong and smart Latina heroines in search of their Happily Ever Afters. Sabrina and her books have been featured in *Entertainment Weekly*, Book Riot's "100 Must-Read Romantic Comedies," PopSugar's list of "8 Up-and-Coming Latinx Romance Writers Who Should Be on Your Radar," and her Delicious Desires series has made the Latina Book Club site's annual Books of the Year lists. Sabrina's common themes of food, family, and love are weaved into intricate plots that all connect for a powerful read that lingers in the hearts of readers. She is proud of her Mexican American heritage, culture, and traditions—all of which can be found within the pages of her books. Sabrina is a native of Southern California, where she currently lives with her husband, three children, and four dogs.

You can learn more at:

Website: SabrinaSol.com
Twitter @TheRomanceChica
Facebook.com/TheRomanceChica
Instagram @Sabrina_TheRomanceChica

*Enjoy the best of the West
with these handsome, rugged cowboys!*

WISHING ON A CHRISTMAS COWBOY
by Sara Richardson

Pediatric nurse Kyra Fowler finally has her dream job at a prestigious hospital in London. But first she must fix up—then sell—the Wyoming house her estranged father just left her. But ex–navy SEAL Aiden Steele isn't letting some outsider sell his sister's home to a ruthless developer. Operation Save Star Valley is foolproof: Show Kyra the sights, work a little Christmas magic, and bam! She won't sell. Except that as Kyra falls for the town, Aiden starts falling for her...

*Connect with us at
Facebook.com/ReadForeverPub*

TEXAS HOMECOMING
by Carolyn Brown

Dr. Cody Ryan is back in Honey Grove, Texas, much to the delight of everyone at Sunflower Ranch—everyone except the veterinarian, Dr. Stephanie O'Dell. So he can't believe his fate when a sudden blizzard forces them both to take shelter together in an old barn. Cody's barely seen his childhood crush since he left, so why is she being so cold? As they confront the feelings between them, it's clear the fire keeping them warm isn't the only source of sparks. But once the storm passes, will Stevie and Cody finally give love a chance?

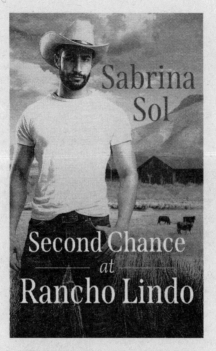

SECOND CHANCE AT RANCHO LINDO
by Sabrina Sol

After being injured in the military, Gabe Ortega has returned home to Rancho Lindo. But despite his family's wishes, he plans to leave as soon as possible—until he runs into a childhood friend. The beautiful Nora Torres is now a horticulturist in charge of the ranch's greenhouse. She's usually a ray of sunshine, so why has she been giving him the cold shoulder? As they work together and he breaks down her walls, he starts to wonder if everything he'd been looking for had been here all along.

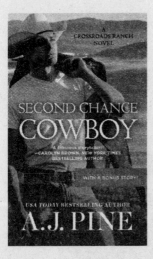

SECOND CHANCE COWBOY
by A. J. Pine

Ten years ago, Jack Everett left his family's ranch without a backward glance. Now what was supposed to be a quick trip home for his father's funeral has suddenly become more complicated. The ranch Jack can handle—he might be a lawyer, but he still remembers how to work with his hands. But turning around the failing vineyard he's also inherited? That requires working with the one woman he never expected to see again. Includes a bonus story by Sara Richardson!

Montana Hearts (2-in-1 Edition)
by R. C. Ryan

Fall in love with two heart-pounding Western romances in the Malloys of Montana series. In *Matt,* a raging storm traps together a rugged cowboy and a big-city lawyer who can't stop butting heads. When one steamy kiss leads to another, will differences keep them from the love of a lifetime? In *Luke,* a stubborn rancher thrown from his horse is forced to accept the help of a beautiful stranger. But as they begin to feel sparks, will secrets from the past threaten their newfound feelings?